HAVE A HIGHLAND FLING WITH M. C. BEATON'S HAMISH MACBETH MYSTERIES

"Reading Beaton is an experience akin to discovering buried treasure. . . . An outstanding read from one of the real masters of mystery."

—*Booklist* (starred review)

"Hamish is at his charming, exasperating best."

—*Kirkus Reviews*

"An engrossing, cozy mystery . . . with residents and a constable so authentic it won't be long before tourists will be seeking Lochdubh and believing in the reality of Hamish Macbeth as surely as they believed in Sherlock Holmes."

—*Rocky Mountain News*

"Befuddled, earnest, and utterly endearing, Hamish makes his triumphs sweetly satisfying."

—*Publishers Weekly*

"Macbeth's charm continues to grow. . . . Fun, silly, and as light as a well-made scone—I wouldn't miss a single book."

—*Christian Science Monitor*

"Another winner."

"A very enjoyable romp with old friends and a good dose of suspense."

—*I Love a Mystery*

"Beaton's plot and characters are as splendidly cast as the scenic backdrop she has chosen for Lochdubh."

—*Des Moines Sunday Register* (IL)

"Lighthearted fun in an interesting and different setting."

—*Deadly Pleasures*

"This series is pure bliss."

—*Atlanta Journal & Constitution*

"On a scale of one to ten, M. C. Beaton's Constable Hamish Macbeth merits a ten-plus."

—*Buffalo News*

"The detective novels of M. C. Beaton, a master of outrageous black comedy . . . have reached cult status in the United States."

—*The Times Magazine* (London)

"Macbeth is the sort of character who slyly grows on you . . . as you realize that beneath his unassuming exterior, he's a whiz at cutting through all the hokum."

—*Chicago Sun-Times*

"Longing for escape? Tired of waiting for Brigadoon to materialize? Time for a trip to Lochdubh, the scenic, if somnolent, village in the Scottish Highlands where M. C. Beaton sets her beguiling whodunits featuring Constable Hamish Macbeth."

—*New York Times Book Review*

DEATH OF A MACHO MAN

PREVIOUS MYSTERIES BY M. C. BEATON

HAMISH MACBETH

AGATHA RAISIN

M.C. BEATON

DEATH OF A MACHO MAN

THE MYSTERIOUS PRESS

Published by Warner Books

A Time Warner Company

MYSTERIOUS PRESS EDITION

Cover design by Tony Russo
Cover illustration by Neal McPheeters

The Mysterious Press name and logo are registered trademarks of Warner Books, Inc.

 Mysterious Press Books are published by
Warner Books, Inc.
1271 Avenue of the Americas
New York, NY 10020

Visit our Web site at
www.warnerbooks.com

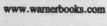 A Time Warner Company

Printed in the United States of America

Originally published in hardcover by The Mysterious Press.
First Printed in Paperback: August 1997
10 9 8 7 6 5 4 3

To Domenico "Pico" Giannarelli
With love.

Chapter 1

> . . . When two strong men stand face to
> face,
> Though they come from the ends of the
> earth.

> —*Rudyard Kipling*

Randy Duggan was called the Macho Man in the village of Lochdubh in the Scottish Highlands and he seemed to live up to his nickname. He was a huge man, over six feet tall, with powerful shoulders, tattoos, and a low forehead. His legs were disproportionally short for his body and his hair was greasy and worn long and curly on his collar. He wore leather jackets with long fringes. He sported odd glasses with slats like venetian blinds, and brightly coloured hats. The locals gathered in the Lochdubh bar just to see him crush beer cans in one of his great fists. His voice had an American twang. He said he had been a wrestler in America.

In fact, to the admiring locals, it seemed as if Randy had been everywhere, seen everything, done everything. He had been attacked by muggers in Florida, shot them dead, and had been commended by the police for his bravery. He had been a lumberjack in Canada and he had shot bear in Alaska. He was the most well-travelled man Lochdubh had ever seen.

It was all too easy to create a sensation in Lochdubh. It was a sleepy Highland village in Sutherland, which is as far north as you can go on the mainland of the British Isles. Tourists came and went in the summer season, but not many, most of them only getting as far north as Inverness.

Perhaps, in the easygoing way of the Highlanders, they would have accepted Randy at face value, and being prime liars and tall story-tellers themselves, were not given to picking holes in anyone's anecdotes, least of all their own. And if Randy had never been faced with any criticism or competition, things might have gone on the way they were and not turned nasty.

Of course, the weather contributed to the edginess that was created in the Lochdubh bar one day when Randy, as usual, was holding forth. The other reason for his admiring audience was that Randy was free with his money, and fisherman Archie Maclean, one of Randy's best listeners, had been barely sober since the big man had arrived in the village, such was Randy's generosity to this, his best admirer.

It was another day of irritating rain and drizzle. Long trails of rain dragged in from the Atlantic and up the sea loch outside the bar. Midges, those maddening Highland mosquitoes, were out in black clouds, no rain seeming to deter them. The atmosphere was muggy and close. It was the tenth day of rain and the damp permeated everything and clothes stuck to the body, and where the clothes did not stick, the midges stung with savage fury. Patel's, the general store, had run out of midge repellent only that day.

Randy had geographically moved to the Middle East in his tales. Little Geordie Mackenzie, a retired schoolteacher, brightened up. He was normally shy and retiring. He had recently moved to Lochdubh and had not yet made any friends. When Randy paused in an account of dining in a Bedouin tent to take another swig of beer, Geordie piped up in a reedy voice, "I was out in Libya during my National Service, and a very odd thing happened to me when we were out in manoeuvres in the desert . . ."

But no one was destined to hear what had happened to Geordie in the desert, for the Macho Man glared at the school-teacher and raised his voice. No one could tell *him* anything about adventures in the Middle East. He had eaten sheep's eyes and run an illegal still in Saudi Arabia and had been thrown in prison in Riyadh, escaping his jailers the day before his hand was due to get chopped off.

Geordie looked crushed and put down. Archie Maclean began to feel irritated with Randy. The big man could have let wee Geordie have his say. The air of the bar was stuffy with cigarette smoke, his wife was a mighty washer and cleaner and the collar of his starched shirt was rubbing against the mosquito bites on his neck. He saw Geordie creeping out of the bar and followed him.

"Don't pay him nae heed," said Archie, catching up with Geordie. "He likes his crack."

"He's a braggart and a liar," said Geordie primly. "I don't believe any of his stories."

"I'm getting pretty tired o' him mysel'," said Archie. "We used to all sit around and have a wee bit o' a gossip. Now we all hae tae listen tae that big tumshie, blethering on and on and on. Damn thae midges. They've got the teeth of them like razors this year. Oh, here's our local bobby. D'ye ken Macbeth?"

"I have seen the constable about the village but have not yet spoken to him," said Geordie.

"Hey, Macbeth!" called Archie. "Come and meet the latest incomer."

They had reached the harbour, where fishing boats rose and fell at anchor on an oily swell. It was Sunday, the Lord's day, which meant the bar might be open but taking a fishing boat out was flying in the face of Providence.

Hamish Macbeth, Lochdubh's police constable, was ambling along the waterfront towards them. He was a tall, lanky Highlander with flaming red hair, a thin, sensitive face, and hazel eyes. Geordie judged him to be in his mid-thirties.

"This here is Geordie Mackenzie," said Archie. "He's just moved in tae Lochdubh."

"Aye, I know," said Hamish. His voice had a Highland lilt. "You've taken thon cottage up the hill a bit behind the Curries. Where did you come from?"

"Inverness, Mr. Macbeth."

"Hamish," said the policeman. "I'm called Hamish."

He gave a gentle smile and the lonely Geordie felt warmed by it. "Hamish, it is. I've just left the bar over there, Hamish, because I cannot stand the lies and bragging of that Randy Duggan any more."

"No harm in a few lies," said Hamish easily. He told quite a lot himself. "You don't have to listen."

"Oh, but I do!" said Geordie, burning with resentment all over again. "His voice fair dominates the bar."

"Aye, I suppose it does. But so long as he's paying for the drinks," said Hamish, "there'll always be folk to listen. Isn't that right, Archie?"

"Och, weel." Archie shuffled his feet. "It was a wee bit o' fun at first, but now it's too much, but ye can hardly tell a fellow o' that size tae shut up."

"Now that's where you're wrong," said Geordie eagerly. He was emboldened by this friendly conversation. "He hasn't often come up against an educated man before, of that I am certain."

Hamish looked amused. "We are not all village peasants, Geordie."

"I'm sorry," said Geordie quickly, "I didn't mean to be rude. But someone should stand up to him."

"Och, be careful, man," cautioned Hamish. "The further away a man gets from his last fight, the braver he gets. I have a feeling in my bones that thon Randy could be a nasty customer."

"I think he's all wind and bluster," said Geordie.

Hamish studied the little man thoughtfully. Geordie, he thought, must be in his late sixties and had probably never been in a fight since he was a schoolboy. Hamish was lazy. He smelt trouble coming but was reluctant to make any effort to stop it. Randy Duggan had appeared out of the blue a few weeks ago. He had tried to book into the Tommel Castle Hotel, but Colonel Halburton-Smythe, the owner, had taken one horrified look at him and said there were no vacancies. Randy had rented a holiday cottage up on the hill near Geordie's. The colonel had reported various spiteful attacks of vandalism, fences cut, the back wall of the hotel spray-painted with a large four-letter word, and the windows of the gift shop broken. Hamish wondered whether Duggan, the Macho Man, was taking his spite out on the colonel but, as yet, he had no proof. Hamish was beginning to think that the big man was a phoney. In his cups, his accent slipped and became more Scottish than American. But until he found something to drive Duggan out of Lochdubh or some proof so that he could arrest him for vandalism, all he could think to do was to try to defuse what he was rapidly beginning to see as an explosive situation.

"It would maybe be the best thing to take Randy Duggan's audience away from him," said Hamish.

"Drink somewhere else?" Archie looked at the policeman in surprise. "There isnae anywhere else to drink."

"There's that bar at the Tommel Castle Hotel," said Hamish. "That's open to non-residents."

"That's posh," said Archie. "Come on, Hamish. Ye cannae see a bunch o' fisherman and forestry workers up there. The colonel would be spittin' blood."

"Think about it," said Hamish. "It would only be for a wee bit."

"I'm game," said Geordie eagerly.

Hamish pushed his cap back on his fiery hair. "It's a quiet season. The colonel should be right glad o' the trade."

Priscilla Halburton-Smythe, the cool and stately blonde, daughter of Colonel Halburton-Smythe, had recently returned from London and was once more running the gift shop. She had at one time been briefly and unofficially engaged to Hamish Macbeth, and since the end of their romance had kept out of his way. She therefore found it irritating when her father summoned her and suggested she call on Hamish to ask for help.

"More vandalism?" asked Priscilla. "You can deal with that yourself, Daddy."

"I have tried to deal with this, but Macbeth won't listen to me. Have you been in the hotel bar in the evenings?"

"No, what's going on?"

"The place is full every night with all the low life from Lochdubh."

"Lochdubh doesn't have any low life."

"Don't be deliberately obtuse. I'm talking about the men off the fishing boats and the forestry people."

"What's up with them? You're a snob."

"I'm a more practical businessman than I was when I started this venture," said the colonel wearily. When he had run into debt, Hamish had suggested that he turn his family home into a hotel. The colonel had done this and the venture was successful, although he never gave Hamish any credit for having had the good idea in the first place. "I'm not a snob," said the colonel, "but most of our guests are, and that you must admit. They come here to fish and shoot and play lords of the manor. They get dressed up to the nines in the evening. They go into the bar for a drink before dinner. The last thing they want is a lot of the local peasantry blocking off the heat from the fire. They even come in wearing wet clothes and steam in front of it like dogs. Have a word with Hamish Macbeth. He'll think of something."

Priscilla decided to have a look at what the bar was like that evening before consulting Hamish. Most of the guests were English and not only did not smoke but, because they were middle-aged, had given up smoking at one time and had all the virulence of the reformed smoker. They were clustered at the bar, pointedly coughing and choking and waving their hands while the locals, grouped in front of the log fire, rolled cigarettes and lit them up, filling the air with pungent smoke. Priscilla realized her father was right. It was no use offending paying guests. They had a business to run.

On her way down to Lochdubh, she felt a little apprehensive at seeing Hamish again. They had been very close. It had been Hamish who had ended their relationship, becoming tired of Priscilla's ambitions to move him up to the CID in Strathbane and make him successful. Also she had never seemed to have any time for love-making. Why this was the case, Hamish had never been able to find out, and as for Priscilla, her mind clamped down tight shut on the subject.

She parked at the side of the police station and went round to the kitchen door. Hamish answered it and stood looking at her in surprise and then said, "Come in, Priscilla. I heard you were back from London."

Priscilla followed him into the narrow kitchen. Despite the warmth of the evening, Hamish had the wood-burning stove lit, a horrible old thing which Priscilla had once unsuccessfully tried to replace with a new electric cooker. There was an old-fashioned oil-lamp in the middle of the table. "What's that for?" asked Priscilla. "Has the electricity been cut off?"

"I like oil-lamps," said Hamish. "It saves on electricity and it gives a bonny light. Coffee? Or do you want a drink? I've got some whisky."

"I don't want anything." Priscilla sat down at the kitchen table and shrugged off her tweed jacket. Raindrops glistened in her fair hair. She looked as smooth, contained and elegant as ever. "What I do want," said Priscilla, "is a bit of help, or rather, my father needs help."

"Must be bad for the auld scunner to send you."

"He's got a point, for once. The locals have given up the Lochdubh bar and are frequenting the hotel bar, smoking like chimneys, chattering away and hogging the fire. The guests are getting restless. We offer them elegant country house accommodation."

"You'd think they would enjoy a bit of local colour."

"Hamish, the fumes from their nasty cigarettes are so strong that they can hardly see anything, let alone local colour. What's the reason for it?"

"Have you been hearing about the Macho Man?"

"I've heard some great ape is enthralling the village with his adventures."

"His name is Randy Duggan. He says he is American but becomes Scottish when he's drunk. He holds forth in the Lochdubh bar and the locals are beginning to find out that although he buys them a lot of drinks, they can't really get a chance to say much themselves. I merely suggested that if they moved up to the hotel bar for a wee bit, he might move on. That sort of person needs an audience."

"Oh, Hamish, I might have guessed you were behind it. So why didn't this Randy just follow them to the hotel?"

"You've been away. Your father wouldnae let him stay at the hotel. So he took one of the holiday cottages up the back. Then there came these acts of vandalism. You heard of those?"

"Yes, and you suspect him?"

"Aye, but I havenae the proof."

"So the problem remains. How do we get the locals out of the hotel?"

"I'll think o' something."

The next day, Hamish made his way to the Lochdubh bar. It was empty of customers, not even Randy was there. The barman, a newcomer from Inverness, Pete Queen, was moodily polishing glasses.

"Quiet the day," said Hamish.

"It'll be even mair quiet if the boss closes this place doon. Whit did I do wrong? The drinks here are cheaper than up at the castle."

"Maybe they wanted a wee change," said Hamish soothingly. "It'll be easy enough to get them back."

"How?"

"It's a good bit out o' the village, the hotel is, and they have to take their cars. I'll start checking them for drunk driving. Then if you were to have a happy hour, just for the one week, drinks at half price, they'd soon come back."

Pete's narrow face brightened. "I'll try anything. It's very good of you, Hamish. Have one on the house."

"Too early for me," said Hamish. "Don't worry. Have you seen Duggan?"

"The big man? He was in here last night saying as how he was getting bored and he was thinking of moving on."

"Let's hope he does." Hamish sauntered out.

Hamish was no longer a favourite with the locals in the next two days. They found they were being breathalysed in the hotel car-park, their car keys taken away from them, and so they had to walk home and then were faced with the same long walk the next day to collect their cars. And outside the Lochdubh bar was a new sign advertising the happy hour. And so they were lured back.

But so was Randy Duggan, the Macho Man.

It was unfortunate for Geordie Mackenzie that while they had all been at the hotel, he had found new friends among the locals and an audience for *his* stories. He could not bear to sink back to obscurity. His resentment against Randy had been building up. The second evening after the locals had returned to the Lochdubh bar was a stormy one. Gales lashed rain against the steamed-up windows of the bar. The fishing boats would not be going out and so the bar was full.

Randy was bragging about how he had been a champion wrestler, when Geordie, who had drunk more than he was used to, piped up, "I don't believe a word you say."

His voice, although reedy, was perfectly clear and precise. Randy stopped in mid-sentence and glared at the retired schoolteacher. "What did you say?" he roared. He was wearing a Stetson, pushed to the back of his head, and he flipped open the slats of his ridiculous glasses.

"I think you're a phoney," said Geordie. "That daft story about eating sheep's eyes. Every phoney who's been to the

Middle East, or who pretends to have been in the Middle East, tells that story. It's a myth. It was a folk story which got around after a British army prank when some chap was told he had to eat sheep's eyes. No Arab actually eats them."

Randy strutted over to Geordie. "Are you calling me a liar?"

"Yes," said Geordie, frightened but defiant.

"Then," said Duggan with a nasty grin, "it's time you cooled your head."

He picked up Geordie by the scruff of the neck and carried him outside. Geordie kicked and wriggled and shouted for help. Everyone crowded outside the bar as Randy walked to the edge of the harbour and held the shrieking Geordie out over the water.

Hamish Macbeth came running up. "Stop it. Stop it now!" he shouted.

Randy dropped Geordie contemptuously onto the quay and faced Hamish.

"You're a brave enough man when you're in uniform," he sneered. "You wouldn't dare stand up to me if you weren't a copper."

Hamish looked at him with sudden hate. He loathed bullies. He knew how humiliated little Geordie was. He flared up. "The day after tomorrow's my day off. I won't be in uniform then."

"Then I'll meet you here after closing time at half past eleven at night," said Randy, and sticking his thumbs in his belt, he strolled back into the bar. Hamish was cursing himself before he even reached the police station. Randy would make mincemeat of him. If word of it got back to Strathbane, he might lose his job, lose his cosy billet in the village. But he knew there was no way of getting out of the fight now.

* * *

The next day, the village was alive with gossip about the great fight to come and the gossip spread over the surrounding moorland and mountains to other towns and villages. Bets were being laid, and most of them in favour of Duggan.

On the morning of the day of the fight, gloomy Hamish was beginning to wonder if he would still be alive at the end of it. Although he knew he had no feeling left for Priscilla, or so he told himself, he wanted to talk to someone about what a fool he had been, and Priscilla was the only person he could think of.

He found Priscilla in the gift shop. She was looking quite animated as she talked to a customer, a distinguished-looking middle-aged man. "Morning, Hamish," she said when she saw him. "Let me introduce Mr. John Glover to you. He's a banker from Glasgow who's staying at the hotel. Mr. Glover, this is our local bobby."

The two men shook hands. John Glover was tanned and handsome with thick black hair, greying a little at the sides. He was of medium height, impeccably groomed and tailored, making Hamish conscious that his uniform trousers were shiny and that his hair needed cutting. And to Hamish's dismay, he felt a stab of jealousy. "I want to talk to you about something serious," said Hamish.

But Priscilla looked reluctant to break off her conversation with John. "Go to my rooms in the castle," she said, "and wait for me. I won't be long."

Hamish slouched out moodily. In Priscilla's apartment at the top of the castle, he paced nervously up and down, and then, to take his mind off his troubles, he switched on the television set. Priscilla had satellite television. Hamish flicked the buttons on the remote control through pop singers and quiz shows, and then stopped and stared at the set in amazement, thinking he was looking at Duggan. It was a wrestling programme. There was the same figure, the same slatted glasses, the same fringed leather clothes and colourful hat. But the announcer was saying, "And here is Randy Savage, the Macho Man, heavyweight wrestling champion."

Hamish leaned forward. Could it be the same man? But no, this one was better shaped, finer built, the only similarity was in the dress. Who, now, thought Hamish, had given Randy Duggan the nickname of the Macho Man? Surely Randy himself. He had said he had been a wrestler in America. Therefore it followed that he had taken the nickname and adopted the dress of one of America's wrestling heroes. But had he been a wrestler? Was anything he said true? Look how he claimed to be American and yet in his cups his accent thickened into a Scottish one, and a Lowland Scottish one at that.

His thoughts were interrupted by the arrival of Priscilla. He switched off the set. "Well, Hamish," she demanded briskly, "what can I do for you?"

She was wearing a black wool dress with a white collar. Her hair was smooth and turned in at the ends. A shaft of sunlight shone on it.

"I've done something silly," said Hamish. "You know that fellow Randy Duggan we were talking about the other night?"

"The Macho Man. Yes, what about him?"

"Well, I've said I'll fight him tonight and I don't know if I'll come out of it alive." He told her about the humiliation of Geordie, finishing with, "It's a wonder you haven't heard about the fight. I'm sure everyone from here to Strathbane is laying bets on it."

Priscilla's beautiful face hardened. "Hamish, what *is* this? Policemen don't hold vulgar brawls with members of the public. Cancel it immediately!"

"I cannae. He would swagger about the village telling everyone what a coward I was."

"Then on your own head be it. I'm sure that Highland brain of yours will find a way out of it. Fight dirty."

"I haff my pride."

"Your pride didn't stop you from going to bed with an elderly spinster, and a murderess at that!"

Priscilla was referring to a case where a Miss Gunnery had claimed to be in bed with Hamish in order to give him an alibi when he was a number-one suspect.

"She was only fifty and I didn't go to bed with her. I told you that."

"Amazing how you went along with it."

"I wasted my time coming here," said Hamish crossly. "I should have known better than to expect a bit o' womanly sympathy from you." They glared at each other.

Then Hamish gave a reluctant laugh. "It's a bit like old times, us quarrelling. Let's have dinner before the fight and talk about things."

"I have a dinner date with John Glover."

"That auld man!"

"Don't be silly. You're no spring chicken yourself. He's very charming."

"Oh, suit yourself," shouted Hamish, his face flaming as red as his hair. He strode out and crashed the door behind him.

He spent a miserable day, dreading the night to come. He had been in a few fights but never up against such a brute as Randy. He could already feel the big man's fists thudding into his face, bone cracking and blood spurting.

The gale had died down, but the rain fell steadily, fat drops running down the windows of the police station. Hamish sat by the stove in the kitchen, arms wrapped across his thin body for comfort, wishing, one way or another, it were all over.

But the clock on the kitchen wall ticked away the minutes and the hours and he could not think of any way of avoiding the fight.

Chapter 2

But I hae dreamed a dreary dream,
Beyond the Isle of Skye;
I saw a dead man win a fight,
And I think that man was I.

The Battle of Otterbourne
—Anon.

Hamish noticed with a sort of gloomy surprise that the rain had actually stopped falling and the pale twilight sky of a Highland summer where it hardly ever gets dark stretched above his head.

He was miserably afraid. Because of his silly pride, he would have to stand there and fight Randy Duggan in a clean and decent manner. If he had come up against such a thug in the line of police duty, he would have used every dirty trick in the book to protect himself. As he approached the harbour, he saw with dismay that the whole village had turned out to watch, even the children, even the minister and his wife. Had they no sense of decency? Going on like a lot of damned Romans waiting to see another Christian thrown to the lions, that's what they were doing.

The crowd parted to let him through, cheering and slapping him on the back and saying things like, "My money's on you, Hamish." He thought that no one in his right mind would have placed a bet on him to win. Then the thought came to him that he owed this bloodthirsty lot nothing in the way of entertainment. If he got a chance, he would tip Randy into the loch. He would not fight fair. He looked at the luminous dial of his watch, a present from Priscilla. It was nearly eleven-thirty, almost the witching hour, the approaching moment when one Hamish Macbeth would get his teeth rammed down his throat.

"You're looking a bit pale, Hamish," called someone, and Hamish smiled and waved and tried to look as if he didn't give a damn about anything. But Priscilla might at least have come. What was she doing? Romancing around with that Glasgow banker when she should be standing by to hold his hand and nurse him back to health after Randy had finished with him.

"Thank you for a lovely evening," Priscilla was saying to John Glover. They were standing in the entrance hall of Tommel Castle.

"Care for a drink before you go to bed?" asked John. "I've got a good bottle of malt whisky in my room."

"No, thank you," said Priscilla quickly. "Maybe another time." Her eyes dropped to her watch. Eleven-thirty! She had resolved to keep away from the fight. She wanted to know nothing about it. But what if poor Hamish got mangled by that brute? John Glover had been pleasant company, but she did not think she wanted to take the friendship any further.

"Will I see you tomorrow?" John asked, wondering why the cool Priscilla was suddenly nervous and distracted. Maybe he should not have suggested a drink in his room. "I did mean just a drink, you know," he said, smiling into her eyes.

"Of course. I mean, I didn't think . . . Oh, could you excuse me. There's something I have to do. Good night!"

Priscilla rushed out to the car-park, got in her car and drove off at speed, scattering the gravel in the drive. There might still be time to stop Hamish Macbeth from being massacred!

Hamish looked at his watch. Eleven thirty-five. Come on, Randy. Let's get it over with. He resented the festive air of the crowd. Patel, the Indian shopkeeper, had brought out his accordion and was playing Scottish reels. The children ran about, shouting and yelling, delighted at being allowed to stay up so late.

And then Hamish began to feel calm. He had been in nasty fights before. He had allowed himself to be intimidated by Randy's bragging. The man had probably never been a wrestler. Priscilla appeared at his side. "What's happening?" she asked.

"Nothing yet," said Hamish. "The fool's probably going to make a grand entrance. I'm surprised to see you here. How wass your date?" Hamish's Highland accent always became more sibilant when he was upset.

"All right. He's an interesting man, very cosmopolitan for a Scottish banker."

"Humph. You're getting a taste for older men."

"Hamish, how you can stand there and pick a quarrel over something trivial when you are about to fight that brute is beyond me. Can't you just do the sensible thing and walk away?"

Hamish did not reply and they fell silent. The crowd had parted to leave a passageway for the expected arrival of Randy. Patel stopped playing. Heads twisted round until everyone was staring up the hill towards where Randy lived.

He drove a showy jeep painted in camouflage colours. It had a distinctively noisy engine, but as the great crowd fell completely silent, there was only the sound of the waves lapping against the wooden piles of the harbour.

By midnight, Hamish was beginning to feel cheerful. Perhaps the incredible had happened. Perhaps the Macho Man had chickened out.

Then Geordie broke the silence. "The man's just a big Jessie," he said in high delight. "I could have taken him on myself." And he squared his thin shoulders and fired off punches into the night air to the cackles of the crowd.

Archie Maclean, the fisherman, piped up. "I'll just go up the hill tae his cottage and see what's keeping him."

He went off and they all waited.

Archie strolled up the hill with his hands in his pockets, whistling. He hoped he'd find the big man cowering at home. That would stop his bragging. It had been fun at first and the free drinks had been grand but Archie, like the rest, was bored with Randy.

The holiday cottage which Randy rented had been built to the orders of an English family who hardly ever used it. It was a square box of a house, built of breeze blocks with a scrubby garden in front where little grew except heather. Archie saw that all the lights were on in the house and he could hear the stereo blasting out. He began to feel nervous and all his old fear of Randy returned. He had been feeling bold until he heard the music, saw the lights, for he had secretly expected to find the place in darkness and the big man gone. He was now nervous of confronting him and hoped he wouldn't be too drunk.

The front door was open and music was pouring out. The stereo was playing rap, one of those vicious hate-the-world numbers.

Archie rang the bell and waited. No answer. "Randy?" he called tentatively, and then louder, "*Randy!*"

Probably passed out, he thought, feeling bolder. He walked inside and stood for a moment in the small hallway. Perhaps Randy was with some woman. He had never shown any liking for any of the village women. But you never could tell. Archie turned the door handle on the living-room door and opened it a little and then peeped round it. The brightly lit room appeared to be empty. He then looked round the bedroom door and into the kitchen. No Randy.

Feeling cocky now, he strolled back to the living-room, thinking he might find out something from photographs or papers about Randy, for, like the rest, he was curious about the Macho Man's real background.

And then he let out a squawk of fright.

He had been walking towards the back window to see if the jeep was still parked where it usually was before he started snooping. For if the jeep was there, Randy might be out in the garden, somewhere close at hand. Archie had walked round the sofa and headed for the window and that was when he nearly fell over Randy Duggan.

He was lying in a heap on the floor, looking smaller and crumpled in death. Most of the back of his head had been shot away, and it could not have been an accident, for his hands were tied behind his back. All this Archie took in with one terrified glance. He never thought to use the phone, or to turn off that horrible music. He simply took to his heels and ran.

He stumbled down the hill, falling on his face from time to time as heather roots caught at his ankles.

As he approached the harbour, he began to shout, "Come quickly. It iss horrible, awful. Oh, my God. Someone help me."

Hamish pushed through the crowd and hurried to meet him. Archie was white and shaking. "He's deid," he said. "Hamish, Hamish. This iss the black day for Lochdubh. Someone's shot the bugger's head off."

Fright and shame set in at the same time among the villagers. This was no longer a spree, a bit of fun. This was real. This was real blood and gore. Somehow they had expected none from the fight. Hamish Macbeth could wangle his way out of anything. Mothers ordered their children home while Hamish hustled Archie along to the police station. "I'll phone Strathbane first, Archie, and then I'd best get up there and see nothing is touched. There's a bottle of Scotch in that bottom drawer. Help yourself."

While Archie gulped whisky straight out of the bottle, Hamish phoned Strathbane, and when that was over he took Archie, who was still holding the bottle of whisky in a fierce grip, out to the police Land Rover and ordered him in.

They drove up the hill to Randy's cottage, up the winding, rutted track. The lights still blazed, the rap music still polluted the quiet Highland air with its violence.

Hamish went into the house and switched off the stereo. The silence of death fell on the room. He stood looking down at Randy, not touching anything, noting the bound hands, noticing the blasted head. It could only have been done by a shotgun. He felt the body; it was still warm. Then he noticed the heat of the room. The cottage had central heating and it was turned up high. Not only that, but a two-bar electric heater in front of the blocked-up fireplace was switched on.

"You'd best give me some sort of statement, Archie," said Hamish.

Archie babbled out how he had found the body. Hamish took notes and then began to prowl around the room. There were no photographs. The furniture was inexpensive and serviceable, the English family having put their own in storage and furnished the place for a holiday rental. There was a bad oil painting of Highland cows over the fireplace. The stereo, an expensive job, was probably Randy's own. Hamish went carefully through the house. The bedroom was as sterile as the rest of the place, apart from a wardrobe full of Randy's colourful clothes and a pile of pornographic magazines on a table beside the bed. The kitchen was bare and functional. There was very little food. He remembered that Randy ate most of his meals in the bar. He returned to the body and, kneeling down, began to go through the pockets. There was nothing there. He remembered that Randy had flashed an alligator-skin wallet in the pub, always crammed full of notes. No wallet. No papers. Not even a driving license or keys to the jeep.

Hamish sat back on his heels, puzzled. He could well imagine someone wanting to kill Randy. He had humiliated quite a lot of the men, apart from Geordie, with his jeers and threats. Someone blasting his head off in a rage was understandable. But to tie the man up and then kill him! And take every little bit of money and identification from the body!

Hamish at last sent Archie home and waited for the police from Strathbane to arrive. And it was as he waited that he realized that he was in serious trouble. The police would hear about the fight that never took place and his superiors would be furious that a constable should even think about indulging in a public brawl. If he kept his job after this, he would be lucky.

He hoped the bane of his life, Detective Chief Inspector Blair, was on holiday. Blair loathed Hamish and would be delighted to make trouble for him.

The arrival of Dr. Brodie interrupted his gloomy thoughts. "I may as well have a look before the police from Strathbane get here," said Dr. Brodie. "I assume he *is* dead? Oh, my," he said, catching sight of the body. "There's no doubt about that. Very dead. Who would have done this, Hamish?"

"I don't know," said Hamish. "I'll need to start asking around. I didnae go to the bar much. In fact, I think I wass chust there the once when Randy was there. That was about the beginning of his stay in Lochdubh and he wass buying the drinks all round which made him no end popular. Hear any gossip? Messing with any of the local women?"

"No, but he was beginning to rile people, or so Angela heard." Angela was his wife.

"You mean, like wee Geordie Mackenzie?"

"I didn't hear about him. But there was a nasty fight with Andy MacTavish, the forestry worker."

"Well, if that doesn't beat all," said Hamish wrathfully. "I neffer heard about that. I am to have a fight with Duggan and the whole village turns out to watch, and yet he has a fight with Andy and nobody hears about it! What happened?"

"You know Andy always fancied himself as a bit of a strong man. He started needling Randy and Randy fixed to meet him in the churchyard. Beat the living daylights out of Andy, by all accounts."

"Is there anything else I ought to know?" asked Hamish crossly as Brodie knelt down by the body.

"Hasn't been dead long," murmured Dr. Brodie.

"That could be because the room was like a furnace. Any other gossip?"

"There was a bit about Archie Maclean."

"There cannae be!"

"Mrs. Wellington, the minister's wife, heard them shouting at each other down at the harbour late last night. Archie was saying that you would whip Randy and Randy was saying. . . ."

"Oh, go on, man. I can take it."

"Randy was saying he could eat chaps like you for break-fast. You were a long drip of nothing. Archie said you were, like Alan Breck, a bonnie fighter, and Randy said what would a little shrimp like him who was henpecked by his wife know about it. Archie was drunk and said, 'You'll live to regret them words . . . if you live.' "

"Lord! Anything else?"

"Later. I think the great and the good have arrived from Strathbane."

Hamish pictured Blair and saw the piggy gleam in Blair's small eyes. He knew he was in bad trouble. He would try to get Blair to keep quiet about the fight that never took place, but he hadn't much hope of being able to do that.

The slow machinery of a murder investigation crawled for-ward. A mobile unit was set up outside the cottage. Forensic men in white boiler suits crawled over every bit of furniture and carpet. The rope binding Randy's hands was studied and pronounced, disappointingly, as being of a kind available in hundreds of stores throughout Scotland.

The long night dragged on. Hamish returned to the police station to type up his report. He waited for the axe to fall.

When Blair arrived with his usual sidekicks, detectives Anderson and MacNab, Hamish took one look at the detective chief inspector's grinning face and knew trouble had arrived.

"Well, Macbeth," jeered Blair, "as frae this moment; you're our number-one suspect."

"Do you mind if I have a word with you in private?"

"Sure, laddie, but it willnae do you any good." Blair jerked his head at MacNab and Anderson. "Wait outside."

When the detectives had left, Hamish said flatly, "You've heard about the fight."

Blair rubbed his fat hands. "Aye, I have that. The whole o' Strathbane'll hear about it tomorrow. You're in deep shit, man."

"Look," said Hamish desperately, "couldn't you hush it up? I've solved cases for you before and let you take the credit. I could . . ." His voice trailed off as he realized he had said the wrong thing.

Blair's face was dark with anger. "I've already phoned Superintendent Peter Daviot, and the other reason I'm here is to tell you, you pillock, that you're to report to him first thing in the morning. Bang goes your cushy job in Lochdubh. He'll never keep you in the force after this."

"So I'm not even on this investigation?"

"Ach, man, ye're aff the force and aff the case." Blair's heavy accent grew more Glaswegian when he was truculent. He turned on his heel and strode out.

Hamish was left to his gloomy thoughts. Why, oh why, had he accepted Randy's stupid challenge? He could hardly think about the case at all. Randy had been a brag and a bully. No one would mourn. But despite his distress over his own circumstances, another terrible nagging thought about his own behaviour struck him. What kind of policeman was he? Randy had come out of nowhere and he had never bothered to make one inquiry about him. And yet, wasn't he being too hard on himself? There had been no reason for the law to investigate Randy. Bragging was hardly a crime. Anyway, it didn't matter any more. He had better think about packing up. Because by the morning, after that interview in Strathbane, he would no longer be in the police force.

Priscilla Halburton-Smythe heard the news of Hamish's impending dismissal at breakfast the following morning from one of the maids. Jimmy Anderson, in the course of an interview with Archie Maclean during which Archie had said he would rather talk to Hamish, had let fall that Hamish Macbeth was being summoned to Strathbane and would be dismissed. She, more than anyone, knew what that would mean to Hamish. Some of the villagers might think of Hamish as an unorthodox sort of policeman and a bit of a layabout, but Priscilla knew that despite his laziness and mooching and occasional poaching, he was deeply committed to law and order and that he loved Lochdubh; but if he was dismissed, he would not be able to stay, and despite all their past differences and hurts and upsets, Priscilla knew that Lochdubh would not be the same without him.

She went into the hotel office and phoned Mrs. Daviot, the Chief Superintendent's wife.

After the hallos and how-are-yous had been dispensed with, Priscilla said, "I am deeply shocked to learn that Hamish might be dismissed."

Mrs. Daviot's voice was cautious. "Well, Priscilla, I did hear something about thet. A policeman prepared to engage in a highly public brawl is herdly the sort of man to keep on the force."

The superintendent's wife's genteel tones grated, as usual, on Priscilla's ears, but snobbery had its uses.

"Such a pity if he goes," she said. "We've always considered him one of us. Lord Farthers was saying to Daddy just the other day, 'Hamish is one of us.' "

There was a slight quaver in Mrs. Daviot's voice as she asked, "You mean the *Earl* of Farthers."

"Don't know of any other," said Priscilla in a cheerful voice, although she was beginning to feel slightly grubby.

"We all know our Hamish is a wee bit eccentric," ventured Mrs. Daviot.

"But with a tremendous knack of solving murders."

"I thought . . . well, how do I put this . . . thet you and Hamish were no longer an item."

"Oh, we're still very close friends."

There was a little silence and then Mrs. Daviot said, "I might be over your way this afternoon."

"And Hamish has an interview with your husband this morning." Priscilla let that hang in the air. If this tiresome woman wasn't going to do anything to help Hamish, then she was not going to waste any more time on her.

"I could maybe just have a wee word with Peter and then drop over and see you."

"How very kind of you," said Priscilla, and with a little smile, she put down the phone.

Hamish sat outside Chief Superintendent Peter Daviot's office, sunk in gloom. The efficient secretary, Helen, clattered away at the keys of the typewriter and threw him an occasional unsympathetic glance. She did not like Hamish, never had. Police headquarters were buzzing with the news that Hamish Macbeth was finished in the force.

Hamish was mentally turning over in his mind what he should do after his dismissal. He could not think of anything he would rather do than be Lochdubh's policeman. At last a buzzer sounded on the secretary's desk. She peered at him over her glasses. "You can go in now," she said.

Slowly Hamish uncoiled his lanky length and stood up. Peaked cap under his arm, he took a deep breath and opened the door of Mr. Daviot's office.

"Sit down, Macbeth," said Mr. Daviot without looking up. Mr. Daviot was annoyed. He had been all geared up to firing Hamish and then his wife of all people had phoned in a panic and gabbled something about her social life being ruined if

Hamish went. More to the point, she had reminded her husband of all the crimes which Hamish had solved.

At last he looked up. "Do you know why you are here, Macbeth?"

"Yes," said Hamish bleakly.

"Yes what?"

"Yes, sir."

"And what have you to say for yourself?"

"It iss not as bad as it looks," said Hamish. "I wass not going to fight the man. Not at all. I said I would meet him but so that I could give him a very public dressing down and also caution him against harming anyone in Lochdubh."

"But according to Blair, the whole village had turned out and they were even laying bets on the outcome of the fight."

"They would hardly have turned out if I had said I was only going to give him a lecture. I wanted as big an audience as possible. You see, sir . . ." Hamish leaned forward with the intense and honest look his face always assumed when he was lying. "Duggan had been bragging and threatening. Now the one thing a man like that cannot bear is a public telling off. Now, sir, haff you ever known me to fight with anyone?"

Mr. Daviot looked at Hamish thoughtfully while Hamish prayed that Mr. Daviot had never got to hear of any of the times he had been involved in a fight. "No-o" he conceded. "But you must see that by ostensibly engaging in a public fight, you have made yourself prime suspect in a murder inquiry."

"Hardly. I was at the police station right up until the time I was due to meet Duggan. I was in my office with the blinds up and the lights on. I am sure you already have the reports that I was seen there by any villager who happened to be walking past. I mean, just because I am a policeman does not mean that there should not be evidence gathered to support my innocence."

Mr. Daviot scowled. Blair had submitted no evidence, merely put in a report about the fight.

"I don't think there has been time," he said.

"But bringing a charge against me which would mean my dismissal is so serious that no policeman would do that without the correct evidence—unless, of course, he had a personal spite against me."

"That's enough of that," snapped Mr. Daviot. Blair's hatred of Hamish was well known. He was now as angry with Blair as he had been with Hamish. He felt that if Blair had wanted to get rid of Hamish, he might at least have tried to do a proper job of it.

"In fact," said Hamish gently, "I feel so strongly about it, that if I were dismissed, och, well, there'd be nothing for it but to put in an official complaint. It would mean coping with the press in the middle of a murder inquiry, but I never wass the one to put up with injustice," he added piously.

Mr. Daviot began to sweat. Hamish looked calm and determined. He did not know that Hamish privately thought he would never get away with this load of rubbish but was determined to go down in flames.

The superintendent could see the police inquiry into Hamish's dismissal, the questions the press would ask. And Hamish would drum up about twenty villagers to swear blind that he spoke the truth, that all he had really meant was to lecture Duggan. Then Mrs. Daviot would go on and on, never forgiving him if the visits to Tommel Castle to see Priscilla Halburton-Smythe were cut off.

He took a deep breath. "I will accept your version of events this time, Macbeth. But never, ever let such a thing happen again. Do I make myself clear?"

Hamish felt relief sweeping over him. He could hardly believe he had got away with it. "Yes, sir. Thank you, sir."

"So be off with you. And when you get to Lochdubh, tell Blair to report to me immediately."

"Certainly, sir."

"Very good. You're dismissed."

Hamish stared at him in alarm.

"I mean, just go and get back to your job!"

Hamish moved hurriedly to the door. Policemen were lurking in the corridors as he made his way out. He quickly assumed a hangdog expression. He suddenly wanted Blair over in Lochdubh to get the news he was fired so that the carpeting he was due to get from Daviot would be even more bitter.

Once clear of Strathbane, he sang cheerfully the whole way home. It was still raining, with wreaths of mist moving up and down the purple heather-covered flanks of the mountains. It was as he was driving the last long winding stretch down towards Lochdubh that he found his mind turning to the case of Duggan's murder. For he *had* been murdered. It would be difficult to ascertain the exact time of death. The murderer had been clever enough to turn up the thermostat on the central heating. But they should be able to get a fair idea from the contents of his stomach. Then there was Duggan's background to be gone into. He found himself praying that it was someone from Duggan's past, rather than one of the villagers. But tempers had been frayed in the village because of the constant rain. What about Geordie Mackenzie? Perhaps a little squirt of a man like that could be burning up with rage and resentment . . .

He found himself hoping against hope that it would not turn out to be one of the villagers.

As he drove along the waterfront, he saw villagers standing around, talking. Up at Duggan's cottage there were two mobile police vans, and the blue-and-white police tape to cordon off the area fluttered in the rising wind. He unlocked the door of the police station and went in. He felt a little pang that there was no longer the scrabble of paws, no dog any more to welcome him. Towser was dead, buried on the hill above the police station. Hamish was just making himself a cup of coffee when the kitchen door opened and Blair came in, an unlovely smile on his fat face. "When do you begin packing up, laddie?" he jeered.

"Soon, I suppose," said Hamish. "Och, I nearly forgot. You're to report to Strathbane right away. Daviot wants a wee word with you."

"What about?"

Hamish shrugged. "How can I read the minds of the great? But frae the look on his face, I would suggest you get there fast."

Blair drove as quickly as he could towards Strathbane. He sensed he was in trouble but could not think why. It couldn't be anything to do with Macbeth. The man was at fault and would have to go and he had reported Hamish's crime like any responsible senior officer should do. Occasionally he craned his head to see his face in the rear-view mirror and practised suitable expressions. Jovial: How's the lady wife, sir? Serious: I have been dragged off an important case. Puzzled and bewildered: What's all this, sir? He decided, after having nearly run over a stray sheep that the bewildered look would be best and kept it firmly in place all the way up the stairs to Mr. Daviot's office.

Peter Daviot was writing busily when Blair entered. Blair stood awkwardly, wishing the super would look up so that he would not lose the appropriate expression. The wind had risen again outside and howled dismally round the square modern block of concrete that was police headquarters. A seagull perched on the ledge outside and regarded Blair with a cynical eye. Blair coughed and shuffled his feet. He felt himself becoming angry. Bugger all suitable expressions. He pulled forward a chair on the other side of the desk and sat down and folded his thick arms, his heavy features now as sulky as those of a spoilt child.

"Ah, Blair," said Mr. Daviot at last. "This is a bad business."

"Duggan's murder, sir?"

Mr. Daviot threw down his gold-plated pen, a birthday present from his wife. "No, I do not mean Duggan's murder. I mean Macbeth."

"It's straightforward enough, sir. He challenged a member of the public to a fight to which the whole village o' Lochdubh turned out to watch, which makes him prime suspect in Duggan's murder, so he has to go."

"Yes, I have your report. A few thin paragraphs. Now Macbeth's story is that he meant to give Duggan a verbal dressing down before the whole village."

"Havers!"

"Probably. But you have produced no evidence to the contrary. You say Macbeth is a suspect. He says that before the fight was due to take place, he was in the police office, in the station, and in full view of anyone going past. Did you check this?"

"There wisnae any reason to," howled Blair, exasperated. "Never tell me you're going to believe that tripe about giving Duggan a talking to."

"Listen, Blair, and listen well. I dismiss Macbeth and he demands an inquiry. In fact, I cannot dismiss him from the force, as you should well know, without a full inquiry. He will put his version of events and the villagers will be asked for their version. Who do you think they will back? Us or Macbeth? Even a Highland policeman suspended from duty pending a full inquiry gets in the press, and the press will start digging up the cases he has solved. His popularity is very high. Good God, man, do you know what Lord Farthers said about him the other day? I'm speaking about the Earl of Farthers, who is a member of our lodge. He said Macbeth was 'one of us.' So not only will we have the press on our backs but one of the most powerful of the Freemasons. Had you put in a proper report, got statements about Macbeth's intention to fight before the villagers heard that he was to be dismissed, we would have had a fairly easy time getting rid of him. But I don't know if getting rid of him anyway is such a good idea. He keeps order. He's lazy and unorthodox, but he gets results. So we'll just have to swallow this. Get back to Lochdubh. I do not want any clash of personalities. You and your men deal with the murder and confine Macbeth to his usual beat. But I want no more reports about him."

"What if he murdered Duggan hisself?"

"Don't be silly. Has the time of death been established?"

"Not yet."

"Would you say this is a gangland killing? Tying the hands behind the back like that?"

"If it had been done in Glasgow or even here, I might have thought so," said Blair heavily. "I'm waiting for the results o' the autopsy. He was a big man, a powerful man. He could ha' been drugged first and then tied up before being shot."

"Well, we're working on Duggan's background. Maybe we'll turn up something there. If the man was a known criminal, then it could have been a revenge murder. That will be all, Blair, but in future do not let your obvious dislike of Macbeth get in the way of a police investigation."

Blair went out, went slowly down the stairs and into the men's room, where he banged his head against the glass. He wished that someone would murder Hamish Macbeth.

Chapter 3

Murder Considered as One of the
Fine Arts

—*Thomas de Quincey*

Blair was more determined than he had ever been before to keep Hamish Macbeth off the case. But Hamish was part of the village and people gossiped to Hamish, and so villagers who had been interviewed by Blair in the DCT's usual bruising manner retreated afterwards to the comfort of Hamish's kitchen. The first to call was Archie Maclean.

"It iss the terrible thing, Hamish," he said crossly, "when the man who does his civic duty and reports the finding off the body should be suspected of murdering him."

Hamish put a mug of coffee generously laced with whisky in front of the fisherman and sat down beside him at the kitchen table. "There is one thing, Archie," said Hamish cautiously. "I have heard that you were down at the harbour with Randy the night before the murder and you were heard threatening him."

"Och, ye'll no' be paying attention to a thing like that. He riled me up and it wass just the words. Hot air. Everyone says they'll kill someone when they're angry with that someone."

"But that someone doesn't usually end up dead!"

"I'm not the only one who threatened the big man." Archie buried his nose in his mug.

"I heard about the fight with Andy MacTavish."

Archie raised his head. He smoothed his sparse grey hairs over his bald patch and twisted his neck in his starched collar. "I wass thinking o' a certain lady."

"Come on, man. Out with it. I'll find out soon enough."

"I should not be blackening the lady's name."

"I'm getting more fascinated by the minute. Why this uncharacteristic gallantry?"

"Whit?"

"I mean it's not like you to bother protecting a lady's name."

"How do ye know that?" demanded Archie wrathfully.

"Let's not quarrel," said Hamish patiently. "You are a suspect, Archie. A lot of people will be suspects. Honest people have nothing to fear."

"They've got everything to fear when a chiel like Blair is barging around accusing everyone."

"Come on, Archie. Out with it. Who's the lady?"

Archie drained his mug and wiped his sleeve across his mouth. "Rosie Draly," he mumbled.

Hamish looked at him in surprise. "The writer!"

"Herself."

Rosie Draly had recently bought a cottage out on the Crask road. Hamish had made a call on her when she arrived. She had not been particularly welcoming. She said she did not have much time for the police. Her car had been stolen in Glasgow and the police had not only done nothing, they had been rude.

Hamish knew that she wrote historical romances, mostly set in the Regency period. She did not take part in any of the village activities. She travelled to London quite often to see her agent. She was in her forties, small and trim with fair hair and a small, closed face. He had almost forgotten about her.

"I didn't know she had anything to do with the villagers," he said. "How did you get to know her?"

"I wass up her way to see Andy, who lives a wee bittie further on. Andy wasnae home and she wass in her garden and I said, 'Fine day,' the way you do and she offered me a cup o' tea. She wanted to know all about the fishing 'cos she was putting a bit about a fishing boat in one o' her books. She gave me one called *His Lordship's Passion*. I couldnae read it but the wife said it was rare, all about them lords and ladies."

"So what's this about Randy?"

"It wass two weeks ago and it wass blowing up something dreadful and we were all stuck in the harbour. I thought I'd take a wee dauner up there I hae a bit o' a crack. I liked talking tae her. I heard the shouting when I got outside. A window wass open and I could see as plain as day, herself and Randy. She wass crying and shouting, 'I'll kill you, you moron, you bastard.' And Randy, he laughs and says, 'Chust you try, you faded auld bitch.' I got myself out o' the way, me already getting fed up wi' Randy and his daft stories. But it couldnae hae been her what did the murder."

"Why not?"

"Think, Hamish. A big man like that, and ladies don't use shotguns. You won't be telling Blair about her?"

Hamish smiled. "I'll try not to."

His next visitor was the forestry worker, Andy MacTavish. He was a big man with a flat-topped head and a thick neck. He looked like an Easter Island statue. "It's a bad business, Hamish," he said wearily. "You'll have to find out who did it or that man Blair will drive me mad."

"I'm not officially on the case."

Andy sat down on a kitchen chair which creaked under his bulk. "You can use your brains, which is more than Blair can. I had a fight with Randy. Was you hearing about that?"

"Aye, what brought that about?"

"He was insulting a lady."

Hamish eyed him narrowly. "That lady wouldn't be a Miss Rosie Draly, by any chance?"

To his amazement, the big forestry worker actually blushed. "Och, Rosie was in the way of talking to me. She wanted to write a story about the Highlands and I was giving her some background. Randy caught me leaving there one day and he sneers that I was getting my leg over. I told him I would knock his silly head off, but he damn near knocked mine off."

Hamish was all at once thankful that Randy was dead, for he had privately believed that all his bragging about his wrestling and fighting was simply a bluff.

"Did you want to kill him?" asked Hamish.

"Aye, I did that, and I told him so. I didn't think anyone was around, for we kept the fight private, like, but you know what it's like here. Someone asked me next day about the fight."

Andy's face was still bruised. "They probably took one look at you and knew you'd been in a fight," said Hamish.

"I could have sworn I could have beaten him," said Andy half to himself. "He had fists like iron."

Hamish looked at him. "Did he wear gloves?"

"Boxing gloves?"

"No, any kind of gloves."

"Aye, he had a pair of leather gloves on."

Hamish was suddenly impatient to talk to Rosie Draly before Blair got to her, *if* he got to her, for the locals would not talk willingly to him. He decided to call at Tommel Castle first and see Priscilla. He wanted to find out a little more about Rosie before he called. It was not often Hamish had to ask Priscilla for gossip, but of late, he had to admit, he had contented himself with his own affairs and had not been much interested in who was doing what in and around the village.

When Andy left, Hamish went out to the police Land Rover, noticing gloomily that it was still raining, heavy rain driven in on an Atlantic gale. He drove up to Tommel Castle, the windscreen wipers working furiously to compete with the slashing downpour.

Priscilla was not in the gift shop. He found her in the hotel reception, coping with an angry French tourist, a small squat woman who was complaining noisily that all the brochures for Tommel Castle Hotel depicted sunshine and blue skies and Priscilla was explaining in very British-accented French that they were not responsible for the Highland weather.

Hamish waited patiently until the row was over and then approached the desk. "Wanted to ask your advice, Priscilla."

Priscilla looked at him impatiently. She was not feeling very warm towards Hamish Macbeth. Because of him, she had endured a boring afternoon on his behalf entertaining Mrs. Daviot to tea. But then, Hamish was not supposed to know about that. "All right," she said ungraciously, "I suppose you want a coffee." She walked off out of the hotel in the direction of the gift shop without waiting to see whether he was following her. She was wearing a well-cut trouser suit with a yellow silk blouse. Her hair was blown about by the wind as she crossed to the gift shop, but a ruffled Priscilla never lasted for very long. As soon as she was inside, she ran a comb through her blond hair, which promptly fell into its usually smooth, well-groomed shape.

She poured two mugs of coffee from the coffee percolator in the corner. "So what's this about, Hamish? How's murder?"

"Murder's not supposed to be my concern. You know, Blair. He's managed to get the official word to keep me off this case."

"And you're not staying off it?"

"Just asking about. Tell me about Rosie Draly?"

"The writer?"

"That one."

"I put her down as one of the many people who rush up to the Highlands to find the quality of life and then the rain and the midges drive them back down south. I shouldn't think she'll last up here much longer. You know how it is, Hamish. We get dreamers and writers and artists, but the Highlands soon defeat them. They think they're running away to the quiet life, but they forget to leave their characters behind and find it's the same old thing up here, but just a bit more boring."

"You're a cynic."

"I don't like seeing people disappointed. Most of the incomers are nice."

"But not Rosie Draly?"

"What makes you say that?"

"Just a feeling."

"I didn't think I had any strong feelings about her at all. She came in here once or twice for a drink. She asked for whisky without ice, and the new barman, Gregor Davies, gave her whisky with ice. He apologized, but she went on and on about it. He called me in. I could not believe she was complaining so much about something so trivial, but it was as if this little mistake had made her want to vent her frustration at having actually bought a house in Sutherland on me."

"Have you read any of her books?"

"No. But I believe there are some you can get from the mobile library. It's due in the village tomorrow."

"What about this John Glover?" asked Hamish.

"Nice chap. Well-travelled. Here he comes," said Priscilla, looking out of the window.

The door opened and John Glover walked in. "Another policeman!" he said. "The place is fair crawling with them."

"That does happen after there has been murder done," said Priscilla. "Coffee?"

"No, thank you, I'm going down to Strathbane to see an old friend."

"Which bank do you work for?" asked Hamish.

"Scottish and General in Renfrew Street." John turned to Priscilla. "I wondered whether you might like to have dinner with me tonight?"

Priscilla did not particularly want to have dinner with John, but the venomous look Hamish cast at the banker made her cross. Hamish did not own her. In fact, Hamish had rejected her. "I would like that," she said with a smile. "Say about eight?"

"See you then," said John. "'Bye, copper."

"You know," said Hamish thoughtfully, "I could swear his clothes were tailored in London. I didnae think that bank managers these days earned enough to wear expensive suits and holiday at posh hotels in the Highlands."

"Scottish and General is an important bank, Hamish. What don't you like about him?"

"I didnae say I didn't like him. I chust think there's something odd about him."

"Could you be a little bit jealous?"

Hamish's face and temper flamed. "Fancy yourself, don't you?" he said nastily and walked out.

He stood outside on one leg like a stork and wondered what had come over him. He put his head round the gift-shop door and said, "Sorry," and then walked off towards the Land Rover. He forgot quickly about John Glover because he was suddenly very curious to talk to Rosie Draly.

When he parked outside, he could see her working at a word processor by the window of the living-room, her face lit by the green light from the screen. He went up the short path and knocked at the door. From inside, she swore loudly and clearly, "Shit!" Then he heard the sound of high heels clattering across the floor.

She swung the door open and looked him up and down, from his red hair gleaming under his peaked cap to his large regulation boots.

"I suppose it's this murder," she said. "Come in."

He followed her into the living-room and looked covertly around. The stone-flagged floor was uncarpeted, and despite a peat-fire smouldering in the grate, the room was stuffy and cold. There were makeshift bookshelves, planks resting on bricks all along one wall, crammed with hardbacks and paperbacks. There were a battered sofa and two chairs, and a dining table on which the writer had been working. Hamish was surprised. He had somehow expected a writer of romances to have a more cosy life-style.

"Well, what do you want to know?"

"May I sit down?" asked Hamish, removing his cap.

"Suit yourself."

He sat in one of the chairs and surveyed her. She was wearing black trousers and one of those striped French sailor's tops which middle-aged women seem to go in for. Her high-heeled shoes were scarlet and strapped, almost old-fashioned, the kind a French prostitute wore when leaning against a lamp-post in a fifties movie. Her fair hair was neat and curled to frame her neat, closed face. Her mouth was thin and small, hardly the mouth of a passionate woman, hardly the mouth of a woman who knew anything about romance at all.

Hamish's first question surprised her. "Why romances?"

"Why not?"

"I just wondered."

"I write historical romances set in the Regency period," she said patiently. "That's eighteen eleven to eighteen twenty. It's a period in history I know a great deal about." Hamish wanted to ask her if she knew a great deal about romance but some-how guessed that the question would irritate her and he did not want to make her angry before finding out what she had had to do with Randy Duggan.

"I won't keep you long," he said. "I gather you had a row with Randy Duggan, the man that's been murdered."

"Oh, him. He was one of the locals I talked to. I'm tired of writing historicals. I wanted to try my hand at a detective story. I became interested in using real people. He seemed an ideal character for a villain."

"So what was the row about?"

"I can't remember any row." She lit a cigarette.

"You were overheard."

"Damn this place! You get more privacy in the city. It was all tiresome. He came on to me and I told him to get lost and we exchanged a few insults."

Despite the tarty shoes, Hamish could not imagine any man making a pass at Rosie, but then, Archie Maclean and Andy MacTavish had both seemed somewhat smitten. He was not getting very far and Blair might soon send someone or come himself to interview her and find out he had already been there. Bugger Blair! This was his beat.

"I would really like to read one of your books," he said.

"Then I suggest you buy one," snapped Rosie. "I only get a certain amount free from the publisher and I like to keep them. Why do you want to read one? To find if there are dark recesses in my character which make me a possible murderess?"

"Something like that," said Hamish and smiled at her.

"You're honest, I'll admit that," she said returning his smile.

"Why did you come here . . . to Sutherland?"

"I thought I would write a historical based on Bonnie Prince Charlie and would soak up the atmosphere." She looked at the rain streaming down the window. "Instead, you could say, the atmosphere soaked me."

"So do you plan to stay on?"

"For a bit. I paid too much for this cottage and I have found out it will be difficult to sell unless I can find some other sucker sold on the Highland dream."

"Och, the place is just fine if you would stop looking for what isn't here," said Hamish.

"I'll tell you what isn't here." She ground out her cigarette and lit another. Bands of cigarette smoke now lay in layers across the stuffy room. "Help. If I need a repair to the roof or someone to dig the garden or a tap fixed, I get the same old story . . . I'll be round tomorrow, but tomorrow never comes up here. There's been a leaking tap in the bathroom since I arrived and I don't know how to fix a new washer on it."

"Have you got the new washer?"

"Yes, why?"

"I'll fix it for you. I'll get the tool-box from the Rover."

"Thank you," she said, surprised. He went out into the driving rain and soon returned bearing his tool-box. She showed him where the bathroom was. After what seemed to her only a few moments, he returned and said, "That's it, fixed."

"Marvellous. Look, I'm sorry I was so rude. Here's one of my books." She picked one off the table. "It just arrived yesterday." Hamish looked at a hardback called *The Viscount's Secret*. "Thank you," he said.

"Don't you want me to sign it for you?"

"Of course," said Hamish quickly. "The name's Hamish Macbeth. Tell me, Miss Draly, how far have you got with this detective story?"

"Not far at all. It was just an idea."

"And how was the murder to be done? Insulin? Rare South American poison known only to a tribe up the Amazon?"

"Nothing like that." Her face, which had softened after the tap repair, had become closed and tight again. "I must get on with my work."

"Just one more thing. What did you think of Randy Duggan? Did you believe his stories?"

"He bragged so much about himself, it was hard to tell what was true and what wasn't. But I've travelled in the States, and yes, I would say he had been there."

"Why did you want to cast him as the villain?"

"Because he was such an old-fashioned sort of bully."

"And Archie Maclean and Andy MacTavish? How were they to feature in the story?"

She got to her feet and clacked on her high heels over to the living-room door. "They weren't," she said. "I just wanted some local colour. Now, if you've finished . . . ?"

He left, feeling baffled. He felt he still knew nothing about her. He decided to go back to the police station and read the book she had given him to see if that would give a clue to her character.

But he found Blair waiting for him, an angry Blair. "I hope you havenae been poking your nose into this case, Macbeth," he growled.

"Wouldn't dream of it," said Hamish, lying with all the true ease of the Highlander. "I am just going through to my office to check the sheep-dip papers. Then there's that break-in over at Cnothan."

Blair's piggy eyes glared at him. The detective chief inspector was impatient to solve this case and prove he had done so without any help from Hamish Macbeth. "I'm surprised you're still on the force," said Blair. "But then, you've got friends like the Earl of Farthers to speak up for you. Ach, it makes me sick. And you not even a Freemason either."

Hamish had never met Lord Farthers. He opened his mouth to say so and then shut it again. Priscilla. Priscilla must have interfered. Peter Daviot's wife would do anything for Priscilla, and Priscilla must have lied about his friendship with the earl. Then he thought of Priscilla and John Glover. "If ye're looking for a suspect," he said, "you might try checking up on thon John Glover."

"We did," sneered Blair. "He's just who he says he is. And at the time of the murder, he was wining and dining with your sweetie-pie."

"So you know exactly when Duggan was killed?"

Blair scowled horribly. The results of the autopsy were not through yet, or if they were, he hadn't heard. Nor had he checked on John Glover, but he wasn't going to tell Hamish that.

When he had left without answering, Hamish went through to the office and picked up the phone. He was sure Blair hadn't checked on John Glover. Why should he?

He asked directory inquiries for the number of the Scottish and General Bank in Renfrew Street, wrote it down and then dialled it. He asked to speak to John Glover, the manager, and was told he was on holiday. Because of Blair, Hamish did not want to say he was the police. He said he was a friend. Where was Mr. Glover holidaying? Somewhere in the Highlands, came the secretary's reply. Mr. Glover never left an address. He said he did not like to be bothered when he was on holiday. So that was that, thought Hamish, replacing the receiver. He decided to settle down and read Rosie Draly's book, but then he wondered if the report of the autopsy had reached Strathbane. After some hesitation, he got through to the pathologist and, imitating Blair's heavy Glaswegian accent, asked if there was any result yet. "I've just sent a report to Mr. Daviot," said the pathologist crossly.

"I happen tae be the officer in charge o' this case," said Hamish in Blair's heavy, brutal tones. "So will you *kindly* just gie me the facts."

"Oh, very well. Roughly it's this. Because of the heat in the cottage, we're not sure of the exact time of death." Then followed a boring lecture on rigor mortis. Hamish stared at the wall until it was over. He straightened up as the pathologist said, "He was drugged before he was shot. That much we can establish."

"Drugged with what?" demanded Hamish.

"Is that Mr. Blair?" The pathologist's voice was suddenly sharp with suspicion.

Hamish cursed himself. "Aye, who else?" he demanded truculently, adopting Blair's voice again.

"We must be careful," came the pathologist's prim voice. "Duggan was drugged with chloral hydrate, then tied up and shot."

"And any idea at all about the time o' death?"

"Between, say, seven in the evening and ten o'clock."

"Thanks," said Hamish and rang off.

He picked up Rosie Draly's book and looked at it thoughtfully. A woman could have killed Duggan. A woman could have drugged him, tied him up, and shot him at her leisure.

But he reminded himself sternly that he had better type out his report on the burglary at Cnothan.

He had just about finished it when John Glover came back into his head. Suppose, just suppose, a man had known that Glover was going on holiday and was pretending to be the banker. He phoned the gift shop and got Priscilla.

"How did Glover pay his bill?" he asked.

"Mr. Glover to you, copper, and he hasn't paid his bill yet because he's still here."

"But when people make a hotel booking, they aye give a credit-card number."

"Hamish! You should be looking for a *murderer*, not harassing a perfectly respectable banker."

"Just checking. When he took you out for dinner, how did he pay?"

"By credit card."

"You went to the Italian restaurant?"

"Yes, and Willie Lamont served us." Willie, in the heady days when Hamish had actually been promoted to sergeant, had been his constable. But Willie had married Lucia, the beautiful Italian relative of the owner, and had settled happily into the restaurant business.

"Right," said Hamish. "Oh, and by the way, thanks for putting a word in for me with Daviot."

"All part of the service, Hamish."

Hamish made his way along to the Italian restaurant, which was not only popular because of its good food but had a reputation for being the cleanest restaurant in the British Isles, thanks to the efforts of Willie, who was a compulsive cleaner. He was down on his hands and knees as Hamish approached, scrubbing the restaurant steps.

"You're overdoing it as usual," commented Hamish. "That's never pipe clay you're going to use. No one whitens the steps these days. Man, your customers'll be leaving their footprints all over it in no time at all."

"Not if I tell them to jump," said Willie and Hamish thought he surely must be joking, but then Willie never joked about cleaning.

"I need your help in a quiet way," said Hamish.

"And what would that be?"

"Thon John Glover paid by credit card the night o' the murder, the night he was here with Priscilla. Any chance of finding out what card it was, what name, what number?"

"Of course. But if it's to do with this murder, then it isn't your case, Hamish."

"Come on, Willie. Don't be starchy."

"I don't want to purvey the course of justice."

"Pervert," corrected Hamish. "And you willnae be. Or can I put it this way. You find out those details or I'll jump in that muddy puddle over there and then jump all over your nice clean steps."

"You wouldnae!"

"Try me."

"Oh, all right. But if I get in trouble with Blair, I'll tell him you blackmailed me."

"Some blackmail, Willie. It's pissing down wi' rain and the pipe clay will get washed away in no time at all."

"That it won't. We have the new canopy."

Hamish looked up and, sure enough, there, waiting to be unfurled over the doorway, was a red-and-white striped awning. "Anyway," he said, "get me what I want, Willie." He made to walk up the steps and into the restaurant, but Willie howled at him, "Jump!" And Hamish did, marvelling again at the madness of Willie's cleaning. Once inside the restaurant, Willie went through to the back where the office was. In a short time he returned and said that John Glover had paid with his Scottish and General gold card; he gave Hamish the number and confirmed that the card had been in the name of John Glover, so that was that. Hamish admitted ruefully to himself that he had only been hoping to find out something suspicious about John Glover in order to pour cold water over Priscilla's growing interest in the man. How odd, he thought, that jealousy should remain when love had gone.

Priscilla felt relaxed over dinner that evening. She began to wonder if a much older man would, after all, make a suitable husband. And then John smiled at her in the candle-light and said, "Perhaps it's just as well I didn't get anywhere with you, Priscilla."

She raised her eyebrows in query. He gave a self-conscious laugh. "As a matter of fact, I shouldn't even be having dinner with you. My fiancée arrives this evening. I told Mr. Johnson, the manager, and booked a room for her."

Priscilla suddenly felt a bit lost. It was not as if she were particularly attracted to John. But she did not want to remain a spinster and she did not like any of the "suitable" young men her parents found for her. She had just been thinking that a comfortable older man might make a sort of undemanding husband. "Do you mean undemanding in bed?" jeered the voice of Hamish Macbeth in her head, for Hamish had accused her of being cold, and that was something she would not admit, even to herself.

"Shouldn't we be getting back then?" she asked brightly. "It would be terrible if she arrived to find you out with some-one else."

He looked at the heavy gold watch on his wrist. "She won't be arriving until about eleven. She's getting a cab from Inverness."

"Were you ever married?"

"Just the once," said John. "It didn't work out. We divorced some years ago. My fiancée, Betty, works in the bank as well."

Hamish would enjoy this situation, thought Priscilla.

Chapter 4

Our murder has been done three days
ago,
The frost is over and done, the south wind
laughs.

—*Robert Browning*

After they had jumped over Willie's gleaming white steps and driven back to Tommel Castle Hotel, Priscilla wanted to go to her own quarters and leave John to greet Betty on her arrival. But John was most insistent that she stay to meet her. Guilty conscience, thought Priscilla, feeling sour. They sat in the bar and made desultory conversation. He certainly is getting very keyed up about her arrival, mused Priscilla, noticing the way the normally calm John started every time he heard a sound outside.

At last there was the crunch of car wheels on the gravel outside. "That should be her," said John. He jumped up and straightened his tie at the bar-room mirror, smoothed his hair and turned and said to Priscilla, "Come along. You two should get on famously."

Priscilla followed him into the reception hall. Mr. Johnson had gone to open the door. Betty arrived in a gust of damp wind and rain. She was small and dark and plump and aged about forty.

John kissed her on the cheek. "Good journey?"

"Rotten," she said.

"Priscilla, my fiancée, Betty John. Betty, Priscilla Halburton-Smythe. Her father owns this place."

"Any hope of a drink?" asked Betty, as the porter struggled in with five pieces of matching luggage.

"Of course," said Priscilla. "The bar is still open to residents."

Betty, like John, had a Glasgow accent, quite light, not as broad as Blair's, say. She had black hair and large black eyes and quite a swarthy complexion. She was wearing a well-cut tweed suit and silk blouse. She exuded strong vitality and sexiness. Although she could not be described as beautiful or even pretty, she made Priscilla feel colourless.

"If you'll both excuse me," said Priscilla after Betty had been served with a large whisky, "I really must go to bed now. I have an early start in the morning."

But Betty had begun to tell John about the iniquities of British Rail and neither seemed aware of her going.

Hamish stretched his long legs and put down Rosie's book with a sigh. The plot had been simple. Viscount finds girl, viscount loses girl, viscount finds girl. There was nothing in it to betray anything about Rosie's character. It was written in a mannered style, competent, literate and strangely lifeless. Hamish, on the occasions when he had been trapped in Highland hotels and boarding-houses, had, during the course of reading anything to hand, read several romances. Some were badly written but they had all been *romances*, in that the scenes of passion had conveyed something of the author's personality and energy. Rosie's love scenes, even allowing for the fact that the genre hardly called for bodice-ripping and lust, were strangely flat. Perhaps she hid her personality in her books as effectively as she hid it in real life. He decided to have a further talk with Archie in the morning.

The small population of Lochdubh awoke in amazement to a sunny day with a fresh, drying breeze. The forensic men still combing Duggan's cottage whistled as they worked and even Blair was seen to smile.

Hamish Macbeth dressed and washed and went outside to enjoy the glory of the day. There were cheerful cries and shouts from the harbour, where the fishing boats were unloading their catch. The twin mountains behind Lochdubh showed their peaks against a clear blue sky for the first time in weeks. Heather blazed on the hillsides, and the rowan trees were already beginning to show scarlet berries. Gorse grew in clumps on the lower slopes of the mountains, acid yellow, adding colour to what had been for too long a dreary rain-washed scene.

And then Hamish saw the tall figure of Detective Jimmy Anderson strolling along. He hailed him. "Too early in the day for a dram?" called Hamish, knowing that whisky could draw information from this sidekick of Blair's.

"Never too early," said Jimmy cheerfully. "Lead me to it."

Hamish went into the police office and took a bottle of Scotch from the bottom drawer of his desk and poured a good measure into a tumbler.

"Cheers," said Jimmy. "Did you hear that Duggan was drugged before he died?"

"I did hear something like that."

"Blair's furious wi' the pathologist. The man kept saying to Blair, 'I told you the other day.' Blair swears he didn't. You were lucky not to fight Duggan."

"Why?"

"Found a nasty pair of brass-knuckle dusters in his cottage."

"I thought that might be the case," said Hamish, remembering how Andy had told him that Duggan had worn gloves. "It is the great pity we have to find the murderer of such a man."

"Aye. Man, this whisky's the grand stuff. Blair's going mad wi' all the suspects."

Hamish's hazel eyes sharpened. "Who, for instance?"

"Well, wee Archie Maclean was heard threatening him, and then Duggan had a fight with some forestry worker called MacTavish."

Blair had been busy, thought Hamish.

"Anyone else?"

"A woman."

"Which one?" Hamish waited for the name "Rosie Draly," but Anderson's next words surprised him.

"A widow. Mrs. Annie Ferguson."

"Oh, come on! Our Annie?"

"He'd been getting his leg over there."

"Who says?"

"She says."

"Neffer!"

"Fact. She went to Blair and said he would find out soon enough."

"I'm slipping," said Hamish ruefully. "I havenae been paying a bit o' attention to the gossip in this village and forgetting that it should be part of my job." He thought rapidly. Annie Ferguson, trim, respectable, late forties, church-goer—*and Randy*!

"Okay, she had a fling with him," said Hamish, "but why did she think she had to tell Blair about it? You would think a respectable body like her would want to keep quiet. I mean, no one would have gossiped to Blair about it."

"She didn't exactly say she had an affair with him, come to think of it. Blair's nasty mind jaloused that. She said she chased Duggan out of her cottage a week ago and threw several pots and pans after him. She shouted that she would kill him."

"She said he asked her to do something nasty, something that no man should ask a woman to do."

"The mind boggles. What was it?"

"That she willnae say. She just sobs and cries and says she cannae utter the dirty words."

Hamish's Highland curiosity was rampant. He suddenly wanted shot of Jimmy so that he could go and question Annie.

"You know Blair," Jimmy was saying. "It's a wonder he didn't arrest her on the spot, he's that keen to wrap up this case."

"Hamish Macbeth!" called an imperious voice from the kitchen.

"That's Mrs. Wellington, the minister's wife," said Hamish. "You'd best be off."

"Can I take the bottle with me?"

"No, you can't," said Hamish, seizing it and putting it firmly back in the bottom drawer. If Jimmy wanted more free whisky, then Jimmy would be back again and hopefully with more interesting information.

Having got rid of the detective, he went through to his kitchen and faced the tweedy bulk of the minister's wife.

"What I want to know," said Mrs. Wellington pugnaciously, "is what you're doing about it."

"The murder? There's not much I can do, Mrs. Wellington. I've been told to keep off the case."

"It hasn't stopped you before I can't stand that man Blair. You must go and see Annie Ferguson. He has reduced that poor woman to a shaking wreck. That beast, Duggan, seduced her and took her good name away."

Hamish blinked. "I didn't think in these free and easy days that women had any good name to take away at all."

"I'll have none of your cynical remarks. She sent me to get you. She feels if she does not get help soon, then Blair will arrest her."

"I'm on my way," said Hamish, delighted to have an invitation to see the very woman he was interested in interviewing.

"And if that pig Blair says anything to you," said Mrs. Wellington, "tell him I sent you to see her."

"Right," said Hamish. He ushered her out and then set off along the waterfront towards Annie's little cottage, which was situated just before the humpbacked bridge which led out of Lochdubh.

It was amazing, he marvelled, as he surveyed Annie when she opened the door to him, that you could think you knew someone quite well and then discover that you must hardly have known them at all. But who would think that Annie of all people, with her corseted figure and rigidly permed grey hair, would indulge in passion with a bit of rough like Duggan?

"Come in," said Annie. "I don't know what to do." Her voice trembled.

She led Hamish into a neat living-room filled with bits of highly polished furniture and bedecked with photographs in steel frames. There was an old-fashioned upright piano against one wall, with a quilted front and brackets for candles.

Lace curtains fluttered at the open cottage windows, and from outside came all the little snatches of sound of the normal everyday life of Lochdubh—people talking, children playing, bursts of music from radios, and cars driving past along the sunny road.

"So what's been going on, Annie?" asked Hamish.

"Sit down," she urged, "and I'll make us a nice cup of tea and I have baked scones. You aye liked my scones, Hamish."

Hamish was so anxious to hear what she had to say that despite his mooching ways, he would, for once, have gladly dispensed with the tea and scones, but one could not refuse hospitality in a Highland home. He waited impatiently as she fussed about, bringing in the tea-tray with the fat, rose-decorated china teapot, matching cups, cream jug and lump sugar. Then the golden scones, warm and oozing butter.

Hamish dutifully drank one cup of tea and ate two scones and then said, "So tell me about it."

"I think God is punishing me," she said. Her eyes began to water in the way of someone who has cried and cried for days.

"Now, now," said Hamish, wondering not for the first time why when things went wrong entirely through people's own making that they should wonder what God had against them. "Just tell me slowly and carefully. And remember. Nothing shocks me."

"You're a good man, Hamish. Randy and I fell into conversation in Patel's store. I was buying flour and he said he thought I was probably a good cook. I said, in the way we have in the village, 'Oh, drop by one day and I'll give you some of my scones.' So a day later, he did that and we got talking. I've never travelled further than Glasgow, Hamish, and his stories fascinated me. Also . . . he looked at me as if I were a woman, you know, and my ain husband didn't even do that in the later years afore he died, if you take my meaning. I wouldn't have let things get far, but he said he fancied me. I said I was a respectable body and a village was a hotbed of gossip and I had no desire to ruin my reputation. He pointed out that he came in the back way. No one had seen him. No one would know. So . . . I let him."

"You had an affair with him?"

"Yes."

"Well, you kept it quiet, I'll say that for you. So what went wrong?"

"He asked me to do a nasty and evil thing."

"You can tell me," said Hamish soothingly. "Now what was it?"

Her voice broke as she said, "I cannae tell anyone. Dirty, evil beast!"

"Now, Annie, it's a wicked world out there and we lead the sheltered life in Lochdubh. It may be nothing that horrible. Just spit it out and you'll feel better. I won't say a word to Blair."

"Do you mind not looking at me when I tell you?"

"I'll go and look out of the window."

He rose and went and stared through the lace curtains. The Currie sisters, Jessie and Nessie, were walking slowly past, arguing about something, shopping baskets over their arms.

"He came to me one night about three days afore the murder," said Annie in a choked voice. "He said he had bought me a wee present and he wanted me to put it on afore we went to bed."

"What was it?"

"It was a suspender belt, black stockings wi seams and . . . and . . . purple silk *crotchless* knickers. He wanted me to wear them in bed."

Hamish felt a sudden desire to giggle.

"I told him, I told him straight to his face, I was not a whore. I told him that my Hector, God rest his soul, had never even put the lights on once in the bedroom in all our marriage days, and the dirty animal had the nerve to tell me I was becoming boring and he felt like spicing things up a bit. I threw the filthy garments of Satan on the fire and told him to get out. He stood there laughing at me, like the demon he was. I said I would kill him. We were through ben the kitchen and I started to throw things at him. He left by the front and I threw a pot at his head, and now Blair will be hearing about it."

Hamish turned round. Annie's plain face was scarlet with shame.

"Now look here, Annie, you must not distress yourself. No one needs to know, although it is not very shocking at all. You just tell the police that he made a pass at you and you threw him out. Simple. I mean, you didn't exactly tell Blair that you had been sleeping with Randy."

"Oh, Hamish, I never thought of that."

"Did you tell anyone other than Mrs. Wellington?"

She shook her head.

"So don't. Just stick to the story I gave you. No need to say anything else. Tell me, what did Mrs. Wellington think of Randy's . . . er . . . behaviour?"

"She told me that men were like that, because she had read about it, and I wasn't to worry. She said they sold underwear like that in the city shops and Lochdubh must be the last place in the world where they sold knickers with elastic at the knee. But I found that hard to believe. What self-respecting woman would wear stuff like that?"

"Don't distress yourself further, Annie. I have to ask you this. What were you doing on the evening of the murder?"

"I was at home until the fight. I went to watch, for I hoped you'd beat the living daylights out of him."

"Might have at that," said Hamish, who didn't believe a word of what he was saying. "Do you know that Randy was drugged wi' chloral hydrate before he was shot?"

"What's that?"

"It's an old-fashioned sleeping draught. You wouldn't happen to know anyone who might still have some?"

"No, but Dr. Brodie would know. He's been the doctor here for some time."

Hamish silently cursed himself for not having thought of such an obvious thing himself. "I'll go and have a wee word with the doctor. So are you feeling better, Annie?" He stood up to leave and she rose as well. She kissed him on the cheek and looked up at him from under her sparse eyelashes. "Thanks, Hamish. Call on me anytime. Has anyone ever told you, you are a very attractive man?"

Hamish disengaged himself hurriedly and made for the door. "'Bye," he said and escaped outside and took a gulp of fresh air.

Annie went to the window and watched him go. "The big softy," she said, half to herself. "I hope I didn't lay it on too thick."

Hamish knew there was no surgery that morning and so went to the doctor's house. Dr. Brodie's wife, Angela, opened the door to him. "Come in, Hamish," she said, her thin face lighting up with pleasure.

"Is the doctor home?"

"In the kitchen."

Hamish went through to the cluttered kitchen, where Dr. Brodie was eating toast and drinking coffee.

"What brings you here, Hamish?" asked the doctor. "Apart from the free coffee, that is."

"Chloral hydrate," said Hamish.

"One of Blair's sidekicks has been round asking me that very question. I never prescribed it. In fact, I don't believe in sleeping pills either. I just tell them that lack of sleep never killed anyone."

"I thought lack of dreaming could do that," said Hamish. "I read this article . . ."

"It wouldn't kill anyone in Lochdubh. They dream with their eyes open."

"I want to talk to Angela about sexy underwear."

"Do you want me to leave the room?"

"No. Listen, Angela," said Hamish, "can you imagine a middle-aged woman in this day and age being horrified at the idea of wearing a suspender belt and crotchless panties?"

"If she's middle-aged, she probably wore a suspender belt in her youth, but the crotchless panties might come as a bit of a shock. What middle-aged woman have you been horrifying, Hamish?"

"Oh, nothing. Now about this chloral hydrate . . . ?"

"They could," said Dr. Brodie, "in this village, find it in someone's medicine cabinet left over from the old days. A lot of them have relatives out on the isles with medicine cabinets full of junk handed down from generation to generation. Do you know when I was last on Barra, I found someone with a cabinet full of old-fashioned drugs. What about the shotgun, Hamish? I suppose they're sifting through the records."

"I suppose they are. I mean, standard routine," said Hamish absent-mindedly. He glanced at Angela, who was putting fresh coffee in the percolator. She seemed such a contrast to Annie. Why? Hamish suddenly remembered a woman in Glasgow at the bus station pleading with him to lend her some money for her fare home to Inverness. She said she had been mugged. Hamish had generously given her the money for her bus fare home. She had seemed such a decent woman. Later that evening he had seen her lurching along Sauchiehall Street, dead drunk, and realized he had been conned. There had been something about that talk with Annie that hadn't rung true.

He wondered what Annie's underwear was really like. Turning the problem over in his mind while he talked of other things, he drank a cup of coffee and took his leave. The next call he made was on Archie Maclean.

How the fisherman appeared to fish all night and stay awake all day was a mystery, but there was Archie sitting outside his cottage in the sunshine, smoking a pipe. Hamish sat down on the wall beside him. "I've been to see Rosie," he said.

Archie's gnarled little brown face brightened, but he cast a nervous look over his shoulder at his cottage, where his wife could be heard scrubbing the floors. "How wass she?"

"Herself was just fine," said Hamish, "or as far as I could judge. She didn't seem all that friendly. A buttoned-down, closed-up sort of woman."

"Oh, now that iss the mystery aboot her," said Archie eagerly. "She's all wumman."

"It's an odd sort of friendship for a man like you to strike up," said Hamish. "Weren't you scared to death your wife would find out you had been going there?"

"She knew. I gave her Rosie's book, mind? She got it into her head that Rosie was an auld wumman and I didnae tell her otherwise."

"She'll find out."

"Don't care," said Archie bravely, but he cast another frightened look behind him.

"Did she talk about herself?" asked Hamish curiously. "Why she came here, that sort of thing."

"Aye, she said she wanted the Highland background, but also she said it was cheaper to live up here. She said . . . she said I wass a verra interesting man." And Archie gave a dreadful smirk.

To a wee henpecked man like Archie, thought Hamish, such flattery must have been like a drug. And yet, what had Rosie's purpose been in getting the little fisherman all steamed up?

He left Archie and went up to Tommel Castle Hotel. He drove past Blair on the waterfront, gave him a cheery wave and got a suspicious scowl in return.

"Now what?" said Priscilla as Hamish walked into the gift shop.

"Do you never think I might just want to see you?" demanded Hamish plaintively. "But yes, there is something."

"What now?"

"Could you invite Annie Ferguson up to the castle for tea this afternoon—say three o'clock?"

"I barely know the woman, Hamish. Why should I invite her?"

"Because I want a look inside her house. Because I think she's hiding something from me."

"You want me to assist you in breaking and entering?"

"There won't be any breaking and entering. She disnae lock her door. Come on, Priscilla."

"Oh, very well. What excuse do I give?"

"You won't need one. You're the lady of this manor. She'll be that flattered, she'll come like a shot."

"Give me her number and I'll ring now so you'll know if the coast is going to be clear."

Priscilla rang Annie and invited her. Hamish listened to the enthusiastic squawks of acceptance from the other end of the line. "Remember," cautioned Priscilla when she had replaced the receiver, "if you get caught it's got nothing to do with me."

After he had left her, Hamish walked across the hotel carpark to the police Land Rover. A small energetic-looking woman hailed him. "Where do you go in this burg for some fun?" she asked.

He pushed back his cap and scratched his hair. "It depends what you mean by fun," he said. "Are you here on holiday?"

"Yes." She held out a well-manicured hand. "I'm Betty John. I'm John Glover's fiancée."

Now here was sexiness compared to Rosie, thought Hamish. Betty exuded a sort of animal energy. "The banker?" he asked.

"The same."

Hamish smiled. "And why would you be here looking for fun when you are on holiday with your fiancé?"

"I've just arrived and the unromantic bugger's gone off somewhere on business. He never stops working. I work in the same bank. I tell you what, have dinner with me this evening. I've never had dinner with a copper before."

A malicious light gleamed momentarily in Hamish's hazel eyes. He wondered what Priscilla would think when she found out that he had been dining with John's fiancée. He wondered whether she even knew that John had this fiancée. But she was bound to know. Still, it would be nice if she didn't like the idea.

"That would be grand," he said. "There's an Italian restaurant in Lochdubh which is pretty good."

"I'll find it. Eight o'clock suit you?"

"Great."

"See you then."

Hamish went off, whistling.

Promptly at three in the afternoon, and keeping a sharp look out for Blair, he strolled along to Annie's cottage, going up the lane at the side and then vaulting the back gate. Randy could have come this way often without being seen. There was only old Mrs. Biggar on the one side of the lane and she was deaf, and then there were Mr. and Mrs. Gilchrist on the other side and they were unusual in that they never minded their neighbours' business.

As he had expected, the back door was unlocked. Lochdubh was one of the few remaining villages where people often did not bother to lock their doors or, for that matter, their cars.

He went through the neat, tidy kitchen and up the stairs to the bedrooms. He found one single one which had an unused air, a bathroom, gleaming with peach plastic, and then a double bedroom which was obviously where Annie slept. The bed was made, blankets tucked in hospital fashion. There was a photo of the late Mr. Ferguson beside the bed and a large Bible.

He opened a drawer on the bedside table. He found a packet of hairpins, a hairnet—what woman wore a hairnet these days?—and, tucked at the back of the drawer, a packet of condoms. Randy's?

Surely a respectable woman who had had a brief and, according to her, shameful fling, would have got rid of the things. He went to a large chest of drawers and slid the drawers open. The top drawer had papers and documents. He reluctantly left them and looked in the drawers underneath. Grimly respectable underwear, terrifying corsets, large sensible bras, wool knickers for winter, cotton knickers for summer, both of the old-fashioned kind sold in Lochdubh. Nylon petticoats, plain without lace. Thick stockings. He closed the drawers carefully after making sure that he had not disturbed anything. He turned and looked around. There was a wardrobe against the other wall. He crossed the room and swung it open. Serviceable suits and dresses, skirts and sweaters and cardigans, two tweed coats and one raincoat. On the shelf above, a selection of hats. Women in Lochdubh still wore hats to weddings, funerals, and on visits.

He was about to turn away defeated and feeling ashamed of himself for having been poking around a respectable lady's belongings when he saw that the wardrobe had two drawers at the bottom. He gave a shrug. Might as well do the job thoroughly. He knelt down on the floor and slid the top drawer open.

He stared down at a colourful jumble of sexy underwear. There were French knickers trimmed with lace, suspender belts, filmy black stockings, exotic nightgowns, and, underneath them all, three videos of the hard-porn variety. He sat back on his heels, amazed. The things that went on behind the lace curtains of Lochdubh, he marvelled. But one thing was certain. Here was a woman who would not have been alarmed in the slightest by any request to wear sexy underwear, nor would she have thrown it in the fire. But she had had a noisy fight with Duggan, because that was what she had told Blair, sure that he would hear somehow and wanting to get her side of the story in. So what had really gone on? He must find a way to talk to her again without letting her know he had been in her home.

The doorbell shrilled suddenly and imperatively, making him jump. He carefully closed the drawers and tiptoed down the stairs. Through the frosted glass pane of the front door, he could see the square bulk of a woman and guessed that the minister's wife had come calling.

He let himself out of the back door, jumped over the fence again and strolled down the lane. The lane led up the hill to the cottages at the back. In fact, if one crossed the fields from the top of the lane, one could reach Randy's cottage.

Mrs. Wellington hailed him as he came out of the lane. "Were you up at the scene of the crime?"

"Just taking a look," said Hamish. "I'm not supposed to be on the case."

"And more's the pity. I was just trying to call on poor Annie, but she's out. Did you have a word with her?"

"Yes, I did. I told her to tell Blair that Randy had made a pass at her and that was what the row was about."

"Clever of you. Her good name must be protected."

"Unless she's guilty."

"And I thought you were an intelligent man! Annie Ferguson a murderess! Don't be so daft!"

Chapter 5

If once a man indulges himself in
    murder,
very soon he comes to think little of
    robbing;
and from robbing he comes next to
    drinking
and sabbath-breaking, and from that to
    incivility and procrastination.

—*Thomas de Quincey*

Hamish decided to leave confronting Annie until he could think about it and decide how to go about it. He could hardly say to her something like, "A woman with underwear like yours would not be shocked by Randy's suggestion."

He found he was looking forward to dinner with Betty as an escape from Blair and the case. At least he was not bothered by the press, they confining their attentions to his superior. He saw a headline in a newspaper, "Murder Village," and shuddered. Lochdubh was getting a reputation. He was about to buy a copy and then decided against it.

He dressed carefully for dinner in a very well-tailored charcoal-grey suit and silk tie. Hamish had become a dedicated thrift-shop buyer. He brushed his red hair until it shone and then strolled along to the Italian restaurant.

Betty had not yet arrived. He let Willie Lamont usher him to a table for two in a quiet corner and then looked at him in surprise. Willie's fanaticism for cleaning was a legend. But in the candle-light, Hamish noticed that Willie's usually neat features were marred by stubble and there was a stain on his jersey. His glance fell on the checked table-cloth. There was a splash of spaghetti sauce on it which had not been cleaned away after the previous diners had finished. He looked again at Willie. In any other man he might have decided that the unshaved face was meant to be designer stubble, but this was Willie.

"What's happened to you?" demanded Hamish. "You look awful and there's a stain on this table-cloth."

"Oh, what's the point," said Willie wearily, but he went away and returned with a cloth and cleaned the plastic table-cloth. Hamish was then distracted by the arrival of Betty. She was wearing a white blouse with a deep V-neck and a black skirt under a loose coat and smelt of a strong, musky perfume. She had very fine eyes, he noticed, and a full, sensuous mouth.

"This is nice," she said, hanging her coat over the back of the chair and sitting down. Hamish started to worry about Willie again. He usually took the diners' coats and hung them up. Willie came up with the menus. There was a splash of candle-grease on the cover of the one he handed to Hamish. Hamish looked at him in pained surprise. "I won't have a first course," said Betty. "I'm trying to slim." She ordered an avocado salad and Hamish settled for lasagne and a bottle of Valpolicello.

"Priscilla all right?" asked Willie gloomily.

"She is just fine," said Hamish crossly. His engagement to Priscilla was long over but no one in the village seemed prepared to accept the fact, and Willie always made Hamish feel guilty if he was dining with some other woman.

"So how long have you worked in the bank?" asked Hamish.

"Since I was seventeen." She gave a husky laugh. "I'm not going to tell you how long ago that was. Mind if I smoke?"

"Go ahead," said Hamish, stifling the irritation the reformed smoker always feels when confronted by the unreformed.

She lit up a small cigar, puffed contentedly on it and then eyed him through the smoke. "So tell me all about policing. How's the murder case going?"

"I wouldnae know," said Hamish. "I'm just the local bobby. Strathbane's handling it."

"Don't you feel left out?"

"Aye, I do, but that's the way it goes."

"So you just do local stuff?"

Hamish wondered whether to tell her about murder cases he had been on outside Lochdubh but decided against it. "I want a night off from police work," he said. "Tell me about the bank."

"Well, I'm just a teller. Whatever they might say about this age of women's lib, it's hard to get promotion. But I look forward to seeing some of my customers, and if the bank is quiet, we can have a bit of a chat." She told several amusing stories about her customers.

"So how did you get to know John Glover?" asked Hamish.

"He was appointed bank manager from a branch in Motherwell, oh, about five years ago. We didn't have much to do with each other until the Christmas party last year. We both got a bit drunk and started swapping stories about our unhappy marriages. We're both divorced. And things just progressed from there."

"If I may say so," remarked Hamish, "neither of you looks like the kind of folks who would want to come to the Scottish Highlands for a holiday."

"Why?"

"You're a pretty sophisticated pair."

"Why, thank you, sir. I don't know what your friend Priscilla would think about that. You mean sophisticated people don't holiday in Scotland?"

"I meant, I see the pair of you in some five-star Continental hotel with a beach."

"Oh, we like the Highlands, John particularly. I think it was because his ex hated coming up here that he takes a particular delight in doing everything she would have disliked. Tell me about this village and what goes on, and you must have some views on the murder."

"I was rather hoping it would turn out to be someone like your John."

She threw back her head and gave a full belly laugh. "John! Why on earth would John want to kill anyone?" she said when she could. "Well, maybe some of the customers with huge overdrafts and no intention of ever paying them off. Why John? He's the least murderous person I've ever met."

"I want it to be someone outside of the village," said Hamish. "These people are all my friends."

"I see your point. But odd things happen in villages. I wouldn't like to be up here in the winter, when it's hardly ever light. What do you lot do for amusement? There's no cinema or disco or anything."

"Oh, the kirk organizes things. They show films in the church hall. Then we hae the television and Patel rents videos."

She leaned forward and he smelt her perfume, heavy and exotic. Her eyes flirted with him. "Anything else, copper?"

She was exuding a strong air of sexuality. Hamish smiled. "Anything else is my business and that's private."

Her voice when she next spoke was husky and intimate. "I'll soon be married. It's not only men who want a fling before they're hitched."

"Are you propositioning me?" asked Hamish.

"It's an idea."

"It iss the very fascinating idea," began Hamish, and then his eyes fell on dishevelled Willie, and again he felt a pang of alarm. "I dinnae like to go to bed on the first date," he said.

"What about the second?"

Hamish felt his senses stirring. It had been a long time. He never wanted to go back to being in love with Priscilla. Betty had a strong, sensual body and he was sure her breasts would be magnificent. "Perhaps," he said. "Wouldn't John be verra hurt if he found out?"

"I'd make sure he wouldn't."

"Can I think about it a wee bit? You make me feel like a Victorian miss. This is so sudden."

"Think all you like. What's bothering you? You're uneasy and it's not me."

"It's the waiter, there, Willie Lamont. He's always so neat and clean and now he looks a miserable mess."

"Probably had a row with the wife. Is he married?"

"Yes, to Lucia. She's a relative of the owner. If you don't mind, I think I'll go along after dinner and hae a word with her."

"Suit yourself. But wait until I have a coffee and brandy first!"

* * *

Willie and Lucia lived in a cottage just before the hump-backed bridge at the end of the waterfront near to Annie's.

Hamish made his way there after he had said goodnight to Betty. He found that as soon as he was out of her orbit, he was amazed that he had even considered going to bed with her. Banks must be terribly lecherous places, he thought naïvely. Maybe it was the monotony of the work.

Lucia answered the door to him. She had been crying recently. "It is time you came to see your namesake," she said. Her son was called Hamish. Hamish followed her in. The baby was asleep in a small bedroom, already crammed with stuffed animals and all the signs of doting parents. Hamish made suitable, admiring noises over the cot and then followed Lucia back into the living-room.

"What's up?" he asked abruptly.

She sat down heavily and looked up at a framed photograph of the Spanish Steps as if wishing she were back in Italy again. "Nothing's up," she said. "Would you like coffee?"

"I chust had some, at the restaurant. And there wass Willie, looking shabby and miserable."

"Nothing's up," she repeated, looking mulish.

"Lucia, it iss verra hard to keep things quiet in a village like this. I'll find out sooner or later."

"No one must know," she said, half to herself.

"Must know what?" demanded Hamish sharply.

"Go away," she said, her eyes filling with tears. "I'm tired."

"I don't want to distress you further," said Hamish, heading for the door. "I'll always help you and Willie, you know that, Lucia."

She turned her head away. Hamish went out into the night, feeling sad and worried. He had always considered Willie a bit of a joke but he hated to see him unhappy. He could not ask the restaurant owner what had gone wrong, for he was away. He went back to the police station and watched the clock until he decided that Willie would be closing up for the night and then made his way back to the restaurant. He peered in through the glass door. Willie, who hardly ever drank, was sitting alone at a table, his sad face illumined by a single candle. He was drinking wine. Hamish rapped on the glass. Willie looked up and waved a hand in dismissal. Hamish rapped again. Willie wearily got to his feet and went and unlocked the restaurant door.

"What is it, Hamish?" he asked. "Did you leave something?"

"Let me come in, Willie, I want to talk to you."

"Suit yourself." Willie returned to the table. Hamish followed and sat down opposite him.

"Come on, Willie. You know what friends are for. You look a mess. Out wi' it, man, and get it off your chest."

Willie, the normally abstemious Willie, took another swig of wine. "She's adulterated," he said.

"You mean Lucia's been having an affair?"

Willie nodded gloomily.

"I cannae believe that. Did she tell you herself?"

"No, but I followed her and I kent."

"Kent what?"

"That she was having the affair with Randy Duggan."

Hamish felt a cold clutch of fear at his heart. But then reason took over. Lucia, who looked like Lollobrigida in the actress's younger days, would hardly look at a man like Duggan.

"Havers!" he said roundly. "Chust not possible. Willie, Willie, Lucia is a bonny lassie and Duggan was an ape."

"She had been acting strange. I followed her one night when she thought I was in the restaurant and I saw her go into his cottage."

"But this was before the murder. You were as neat as a pin a few days ago. Why the sudden disintegration?"

"Och, it got to me, the poison seeping in and seeping in."

"So what did she say when you asked her about it?"

"She began to cry and said it was none of my business. She kept on saying I had to trust her. I was going to kill him, Duggan, but some kind soul got there first and I hope you never find out who did it."

Hamish shook his head as if to clear his brain. Then he said, "You're to stop drinking and you're coming home wi' me and we're both going to talk to Lucia if I haff to drag you there."

Willie protested and clutched the wine bottle fiercely, as if that would anchor him to the table. Hamish gave an exclamation of disgust, twisted Willie's arm up his back and marched the protesting man out of the restaurant and along the waterfront towards the cottage by the bridge.

He opened the door and thrust Willie inside and into the living-room. Lucia saw them and began to cry.

"Enough!" shouted Hamish, torn between exasperation and fear. "Now we'll sit down and you will tell us what you were doing with Randy Duggan, Lucia."

She mopped her streaming eyes with an already sodden handkerchief and said fiercely, "No! If my own husband can't trust me . . ."

"Och, lassie, if you were married to me and I saw you go to another man's house, a man like Duggan, I'd want to know the reason why. Think o' your bairn. It's bad for a child to hae an atmosphere like this in the house. You'd better tell us, Lucia, or I'll sit here all night. Don't you know I ought to report your visit to Blair?"

"You wouldn't," said Lucia, looking appalled.

Hamish saw his advantage and took it. "Oh, yes, I would. So out wi' it!"

Lucia found another handkerchief in her handbag, blew her little nose and stared at them both defiantly. Then she said, "It is Willie's birthday in a week's time."

Hamish looked puzzled. "So?"

"So when I was serving in the restaurant one night—we were busy and Mrs. Mulligan was baby-sitting for me— Randy came in for dinner. He was wearing a Rolex watch and I admired it. He said he could get me one, cheap. I thought it would make a good present for Willie. I told him to go ahead but to keep it a secret. He phoned me a week later and said that he had the watch. I went to his cottage. The watch was a copy, not the real thing. There are many like it in Italy. I told him it was a fake and he tried to make a pass at me. I slapped his face."

"Why didn't you tell me this?" howled Willie.

"Because you should trust me," shouted Lucia. "There should be trust between a husband and wife!"

Willie began to cry, hiccuping drunken sobs. "I thocht I had lost ye," he said between sobs.

Lucia crossed the room and knelt in front of him. "Oh, Willie, I did not know I had made you suffer so much. Oh, Willie." She began to kiss him. Hamish quietly left the room and, once outside, mopped his brow. Thank God that's over, he thought, but the nagging fear that Willie, believing Lucia was unfaithful to him, had murdered Randy, would not go away.

* * *

Hamish rose the next morning, his mind still full of worries. He felt he had to do something and so he decided to call on Annie again and try to find out why she had lied to him without letting her know he had searched her house.

Annie Ferguson answered the door to him. She looked delighted to see him and Hamish wondered whether she might have been telling the truth and that, although she considered it all right for herself to wear sexy underwear, she considered it indecent to wear it for love-making.

He refused an offer of tea and scones and sat down. "Annie," he said, "I am worried about you."

"Oh, there is nothing to worry about," she said cheerfully. "I told Blair what you told me to tell him and—"

"I think there's more to it than that," interrupted Hamish. "Annie," he lied, "you are a sophisticated woman of the world and well-travelled. I believe you have even been as far as Glasgow."

"I have that," she said, preening. "I've seen the world."

Hamish reflected that Glasgow was hardly an exotic place and that one trip to the south of Scotland hardly turned anyone into a world traveller, but he pressed on. "I really cannae see you being shocked by Randy's suggestion."

A flush mounted to her face, mottling her neck and leaving patches of red on her cheeks.

Very much the outraged matron, she said, "I took you into my confidence and you doubt my word! Me, who told the minister's wife, too!"

Hamish sighed. "Annie, lies in a murder investigation are dangerous things. The innocent have nothing to fear." Except with someone like Blair around, he thought gloomily. "I am trying to do my best for you and I will protect you if you are innocent, but when I thought about your story, och, it didnae make sense. Come on, Annie. The truth."

"You're all the same. Men," she muttered. "Take you. Look what you did to that lovely girl, Priscilla. She was better than someone like you deserved and you jilted her."

"We came to an agreement to separate. I didnae jilt her," said Hamish furiously. Then his face cleared. "That's it! He jilted you. Thon ape jilted you." She stayed mulishly silent, looking at the carpet, a faded Wilton covered in cabbage roses. "Yes, that's the way it was," said Hamish, his voice suddenly gentle. "And you despised him, too. That's what made the rejection so bitter. You were ashamed of your affair with him. Did he say why he'd dropped you?"

She gave a dry little sob. "He told me he had found better."

"Who?" demanded Hamish with again that clutch of fear at the heart.

"That slut, Lucia Lamont."

"Lucia is not a slut and you know it, Annie. That's the jealousy talking. Lucia would have nothing to do with him."

"Then why was she seen going into his cottage?"

Hamish groaned inwardly. There were few secrets in a village. Sooner or later, Blair might get to hear of it. Of course, the villagers were united against such as Blair, but some of the policemen combing the heather around Randy's cottage for clues were another matter. They drank in the pub in the evening. They might hear gossip and relay it to Blair.

"Randy had promised Lucia that he could get her a cheap Rolex watch for Willie's birthday. She went to collect it and found it a fake. He made a pass at her and she slapped his face. That's all there was to it. A man of his vanity probably thought he could get lucky."

"So what are you going to do?" asked Annie, suddenly frightened. "If you tell them I lied, that Blair will arrest me."

Hamish sat silent for a few moments, thinking hard. By not telling Blair what he knew, he was obstructing a police investigation. And yet Blair would come down on *him* like a ton of bricks for having held back information. At last he said, "Did you kill him, Annie?"

"No," she said. "But I wanted to."

"We'll leave it there, Annie, and hopefully none of this will need to come out. But unless I find the real murderer fast, then both you and Lucia are going to be in trouble!"

Chapter 6

Never make a defence of apology before
you be accused.

—*King Charles* I

Priscilla was closing up the gift shop at lunch-time the following day when John Glover suddenly appeared. "Back from your travels?" she said, feeling awkward because she felt that he might at least have told her he was engaged when he first took her out for dinner.

"Just got back, and pretty hungry."

Priscilla looked at her watch. "They'll be serving lunch in the dining-room."

"I don't want lunch in the dining-room and it's actually sunny. Come with me and we'll drive someplace."

"And what is Betty doing?"

"I don't know. She told me she had dinner with that copper friend of yours last night and then she disappeared."

"I suppose I could go," said Priscilla. "That is, if Betty wouldn't mind."

"Oh, she won't mind. I told her we were friends."

Priscilla knew she should not go with him, but if Hamish had become friendly with Betty, then Hamish would get to hear of it, and she suddenly wanted Hamish to know that other men wanted her company.

"If you tell me where we're going, I'll leave a message at reception."

"I was hoping you'd suggest somewhere."

"There's a hotel in Crask which serves quite good food in the bar and it's not too far. I have to be back here by two o'clock."

"Crask it is."

Priscilla left a message in reception that she could be contacted in Crask.

Hamish Macbeth opened the door to a thirsty-looking Jimmy Anderson. The detective sighed with pleasure as he downed his first whisky of the day and then smiled at Hamish. "I've a wee bit o' news that might make you sit up, Hamish."

"What's that?"

"Our local pathologist's in trouble. They're getting another one up from Glasgow."

Hamish looked interested. "He missed something important?"

"Very important. Duggan had had plastic surgery at some time, so all these pictures of him that have been running in the press with headlines 'Do You Know This Man?' are nae good at all."

"Who discovered the plastic surgery?"

"That's what was so shaming. A wee bit o' a lassie who works in the lab."

Hamish heaved a sigh of relief. "That begins to put the murderer outside Lochdubh."

"I don't get your reasoning."

"Plastic surgery, man! That puts Duggan in the big-class criminal league."

"But the man was vain!"

"Well, he cannae have been that vain because plastic surgery didn't exactly make him pretty."

"Maybe he thought it did. Then if it was a gangland killing, Hamish, surely they'd just blast him. A woman, now, would drug him first."

Hamish looked stubborn. "I still think it was done by someone outside. Any news on the chloral hydrate?"

Jimmy shook his head. "Could have come from anywhere. Brodie didn't prescribe it. There's another wee bit o' news."

"What?"

"We got the impression that Randy had nothing to do with the women. How could he? we thought, him bragging away in the pub at all hours."

"So there's a woman?"

"Aye, a writer, Rosie Draly. Some little bird told Blair that Randy had been seen going into her cottage."

Jimmy's foxy features suddenly sharpened with alarm at the sound of a heavy tread outside. He dived under the desk. Hamish opened the bottom drawer and put the bottle and Jimmy's half-full glass into it just as the door swung open and Blair walked in.

"If you tried knocking," said Hamish mildly, "I might know to expect you."

"This place stinks o' whisky," grumbled Blair.

"Then come ben to the kitchen," said Hamish quickly before Blair could sit down on the side of the desk under which Jimmy was crouching. He walked off and Blair followed.

"I've a wee bittie o' a problem." Blair sat down on a kitchen chair which squeaked in protest under his bulk. "Now you know you're not to be on the case. Daviot said so."

"And you liked that," commented Hamish.

"But as your senior officer," said Blair heavily, "and seeing as how you've naethin' to do but sit in yer office and drink whisky, I want you to do a wee job for me."

"If it's to do with the case, why should I bother?" Hamish leaned his back against the kitchen counter and folded his arms. "You tried to get me off the force."

"I was only doing my duty," said Blair belligerently. "Do you want to help or not?"

Hamish longed to be able to say no, but curiosity would not let him.

"All right," he said. "What do you want?"

"You should address me as 'sir' when you speak to me."

"Aye, but I think this is in the way of an unofficial chat."

"Here's what it is," said Blair. "Duggan was seeing that writer. Rosie Draly. I've tried to have a word with her, but all she does is tell me she was using him for local colour and then threatens me with a lawyer. You have sneaky ways with the women. Why not pay a call on her and see what you can find out? You let me know what you've got and I'll see if I can wheedle Daviot into letting you in on the case."

Hamish naturally did not want to say he had seen Rosie already and did not think he could get much further with her. He was also itching to be privy to all the research already done.

"Anything in her background?" he asked.

"She was married and got divorced ten years ago. No children. Schoolteacher who started writing and then found she could make enough at it to free-lance and give up teaching. Doesn't earn all that much but works hard. Sells in America and Germany as well. I thought all thae writers earned a fortune, but not in her case. Agent says she's quiet and efficient and delivers her manuscripts on time."

Hamish said, "I'll go and see her now and when I get back, I'll report to you and I expect you to fill me in on the background to the case."

Fury gleamed for a moment in Blair's piggy eyes. He wanted to use Hamish's flair for getting people to talk. And he would figure out a way somehow to make sure Hamish did not get any credit. He rose to his feet. "Get to it. Hae ye seen that layabout, Jimmy Anderson?"

"Aye," said Hamish, "he was walking past a while ago in the direction of the harbour."

"I'd better find him. See you later."

Hamish went into the office after Blair had left. "He's gone off looking for you, Jimmy, you can come out now."

Jimmy crawled out from under the desk, stood up and brushed himself down with his hands. "You could do with a woman to clean for you, Hamish."

"Well, I didnae think anyone would be crawling around under my desk. Blair wants me to have a word wi' Rosie Draly."

"That's because he's stuck as usual. He bullies and blusters and puts people's backs up and then he tries to be oily and wheedle, but by that time the damage has been done. Which way did he go?"

"I sent him off towards the harbour."

"I'll go that way myself, then, and say I was looking for *him*."

After Jimmy had left, Hamish was about to get into the Land Rover when he became aware that someone was watching him and swung round. Betty John was standing there, smiling at him.

"We all have telepathic powers," she said. "They say if you stare long enough at the back of anyone's head, sooner or later they'll sense you're there."

"And what brings you here?"

"Looking for you," said Betty. Once again he was struck by the sheer force of her personality, of her sexuality. There she stood, small, compact, plump, swarthy-skinned and black-eyed, and yet radiating femininity.

"And where's John?"

"John, the reception tells me, is off having lunch with Miss Priscilla Halburton-Smythe, and so I thought I'd come along here and see if you were free for lunch."

"I can't. I'm off on police business, and even if I weren't, Blair would not enjoy the sight of me entertaining a fascinating woman."

"I've been called a lot of things in my time but never fascinating. I rather like it. What about dinner tonight?"

"What about John?"

"I don't like him going off with Miss Toffee-Nosed Priscilla. I want to get even, if you want the truth."

"And here wass me thinking you wanted me for my beautiful body."

"That, too, copper."

"Och, well, a bit of dinner wouldn't harm anyone," said Hamish, who would not admit to himself that *he* wanted to get even with Priscilla. "Will I call for you at eight, say?"

"No, I'll call for you and leave a message at reception for John."

They both suddenly grinned at each other, two adults who knew they were behaving like children.

"See you," said Hamish, and drove off whistling.

Perhaps because the day was sunny and he still remembered the seemingly endless days of rain, perhaps because he was on the case, he exuded cheerfulness and goodwill when Rosie answered the door to him.

"Oh, it's you," she said. She turned away and he followed her in. The monitor of the word processor shone greenly in the dismal room. He looked for a place to sit down. The chairs were covered with magazines, books, papers and discarded clothes. She stood looking at him, her tight little features as closed as ever. Then she scooped up a handful of magazines and papers from a chair and said abruptly, "Sit down."

Hamish sat down and she leaned against the mantel of the fireplace. She was wearing a long skirt and those Edwardian tart's boots which had come into fashion, a shirt blouse and a cardigan. Her eyes, he noticed, were grey-blue with thin fair lashes.

"I don't suppose this is a social call," she said with a trace of weariness in her voice.

"In a murder investigation," said Hamish, "anyone who had anything to do with the murdered man is questioned over and over again. That's the way it works. I'd like to try a different line of questioning because we don't know anything about Randy Duggan other than the tall stories he told about himself."

"I don't think I can tell you anything other than what you have already observed and heard. He came across as a braggart and a liar."

"Would you say he could be attractive to women?"

She shrugged her thin shoulders, turned round and threw a peat from a bucket beside the fireplace onto the smoking fire. She took a packet of cigarettes from the mantel and lit one and then turned back wreathed in smoke from the cigarette and smoke from the peat fire behind her. "There's no accounting for taste," she said. "There's someone for everyone, or so they say." She crossed to the window and stared out. The Lochdubh bus lurched past on the road and whined off into the silence of moorland which lay for miles around the cottage.

"Let me put it this way," pursued Hamish, "you're a writer and you claim to have had Archie Maclean and Andy MacTavish up here as well as Duggan to get local colour. There must have been something about him you wanted."

"I told you. He was real material for a villain."

"And did you use it for a detective story?"

"I've got a historical to finish and a deadline to meet. The detective story was only an idea in the back of my head."

Hamish cast a covert look at the word processor from under his eyelashes. He would love to get a look at what was stored in there. But he could not go on burgling houses. That close shave where he had nearly lost his job had frightened him. From now on he would tread a strictly legal path. And then she said, "I've got to go down to London tomorrow to see my agent. Could you tell your superior that? As long as they know where I am, they cannot hold me here."

It was not that fate was tempting him from the straight and narrow, reflected Hamish, it was merely just too good an opportunity to miss.

"When folks are away," he said, "they often leave the house key at the police station. And I can keep an eye on the place for you."

"Thanks, but no thanks. I don't want you or any of the locals snooping around." She handed him a card. "That's my agent's name, address, and phone number. I'll only be gone four days."

"Did you get the impression that Randy Duggan might be a criminal?"

"I have led a sheltered life," she said. "I wouldn't know what criminals are like. That's your job."

Hamish sighed. He was going to have little to report to Blair.

He decided to go for the jugular. "But you had an affair with him. You must have known him better than anyone."

"Be very, very careful," she said in a thin voice, "or I'll sue you."

"But you did," said Hamish stubbornly.

"That's my business and none of yours. Now get out! "

Hamish rose to his feet. At least he had something to tell Blair. She had as good as admitted it. He did not feel like protecting her from Blair's questions either. On the other hand, if he gave Blair this nugget of information, then Blair would pull her in for further questioning and she would not leave for London and he would not have an opportunity to look at the word processor.

Her eyes were hard, implacable, and he realized with surprise that she hated him. Why? He was only another policeman doing his job. It was only when he was driving away that he realized he didn't know anything about word processors. Even if he succeeded in breaking in, he wouldn't know what to do with the damn machine. But Priscilla knew all about word processors and computers. He looked at his watch. It was nearly two o'clock and she was due back at the castle gift shop to open it. As he drove up the castle drive, he felt the air damp against his cheek through the open Rover window. Rain was coming in from the west to put an end to the brief glimpse of summer.

He parked outside the gift shop and waited. A car drove up. John was at the wheel and Priscilla was sitting beside him. She laughed at something he said. John stopped outside the gift shop and then drove on and into the castle car park.

She did not know that Hamish Macbeth was too keen to pick her brains about computers to feel any further anger at her date with John and so felt somewhat piqued to be met by a smiling Hamish who said he hoped she had enjoyed her lunch.

"Very much, thank you," said Priscilla, unlocking the shop door. "He's an amusing companion. I hope Betty doesn't mind when she finds out."

"I don't think she will, but I'll ask her over dinner tonight," said Hamish with a little spurt of malice.

Her eyebrows rose. "Lunch with an engaged person is one thing, dinner another."

"Oh, iss that a fact?" demanded Hamish. "Never heard o' love in the afternoon, Priscilla?" Her face took on a tight, closed look which suddenly reminded him of Rosie Draly. It also reminded him that he needed her help.

"Priscilla, the shop's quiet and I see you have the computer over there. I wouldnae mind a few lessons."

"It'll take ages, Hamish. That's the one for the shop and the way I check out what's needing to be replaced. Why the sudden interest?"

"I need to hae a look at someone's word processor and I want to know how to load the discs and read what's on them."

"What make?"

"A Harbley."

"That's the cheapest on the market. Did you see any number on it?"

"PCW 921."

"That's their bottom-of-the-range model. I have one upstairs. It was the first one I got. I used it for business letters and simple accounts."

"Could you show me?"

Priscilla straightened some goods on the counter. "The only time I've got free is from eight o'clock this evening."

"All right."

"What about your date with Betty?"

"That can wait. I'll tell her I'm off on police business."

"Then I'll see you at eight. What's it for? I mean, whose word processor?"

"I'll tell you later," said Hamish quickly, frightened she would refuse if he told her the truth.

He left a message for Betty at the reception desk of the hotel and drove back to Lochdubh and up to Randy's cottage. A few local reporters were standing around, the ones from the nationals having given up and gone home.

Blair came out of one of the mobile units and went to join Hamish as he climbed down from the Land Rover.

"Well?" he demanded. "Get anything?"

Hamish decided to improvise. "For a start she said to tell you she's off to London tomorrow to see her agent." He showed Blair the card Rosie had given him. "That's the agent's address and phone number. She'll only be gone four days."

"I don't like it," growled Blair.

"There's nothing for us to keep her. But there's a wee bit o' hope," said Hamish, looking at his superior and radiating honesty. "She's taken a bit o' a fancy to me and she said she would think of everything Randy had told her and give me a typewritten statement when she got back. She said if she had a few days to think about it, she might remember something useful."

Blair's face cleared. "Good work," he said reluctantly.

"So can I see some of the background?"

Blair looked for a moment as if he was going to refuse. But then he shouted, "Anderson, come here!"

Jimmy Anderson came slouching up. "Show Macbeth here the statements and background."

"Sure thing, Chief." Blair looked at him sharply for signs of insolence but Jimmy's watery blue eyes only showed respect.

Jimmy led Hamish into one of the mobile units where two policewomen and two policemen were working in the makeshift office. "Take a seat, Hamish," said Jimmy. "You've got a lot to go through."

After a long day, Hamish was disappointed. The bare facts were these. Time of death could not be pinpointed, but then it rarely could. The warmth of the body due to the central heating plus the two-bar electric fire put death at any time from five in the evening until after ten at night. Chloral hydrate had been found. The contents of the stomach revealed that he had lunch of hamburgers and then tea and coffee but no dinner. The chloral hydrate could have been given to him in a drink, but all glasses and cups in the kitchen were clean. Hamish frowned. He could not imagine such as Randy keeping a clean kitchen, or a sink free of dirty dishes. He had a shadowy picture of a murderer who could calmly kill and then take his or her time about cleaning up, for there had been no fingerprints at all, apart from Archie's. Everyone knew about fingerprints, but usually only the very cold-blooded managed to get rid of every trace. He thought of Rosie Draly. But surely this was no crime of passion, no outburst of rage. This had been a cold and calculated murder. But a scorned woman would have had time to think and brood and plot and plan. The statements revealed as little as possible, with the exception of the retired schoolteacher, Geordie Mackenzie, who had bragged that he could have well killed Duggan because he, Geordie, "was a lion when roused."

"Silly wee man," grumbled Hamish, rising and stretching. He glanced at his watch. Just time now to eat and visit Priscilla.

* * *

"Pay attention," admonished Priscilla that evening. "I'll go through it again. You put in the Logoscript disc and when it is loaded, take it out and put in the disc you want to read."

"Stop flicking your fingers over these damn keys. I cannae see what you're doing," complained Hamish, who was feeling stupid and backward and resenting it.

"Okay, now you've taken your programming disc out, put in that one, with the side you want to the left . . . the left, Hamish! Now press *e* for edit and then press 'enter.' There you are. Simple."

But somehow Hamish could not get the hang of it. "You're suffering from technofear," said Priscilla. "I'll type out a simple list of instructions and leave you to it. You'll learn easier if you do it yourself."

She switched off the word processor after she had typed out a list of instructions. "Now start at the beginning."

Left to his own devices, Hamish stared gloomily at the blank monitor. It was all the fault of modern society, he reflected, where people credited computers with independent brains. He couldn't, say, get the seat he wanted on a Glasgow-bound bus at the Strathbane bus station because the girl in the booking office said The Computer had allocated him another seat entirely. A cheque for a prize he had won for hill-running at one of the Highland Games took ages to arrive, and it was at a time when he needed the money badly. But every time he phoned the Games Committee, some official would say, "It's in the computer," as if only the computer could decide when one Hamish Macbeth would get paid.

He straightened the monitor with a vicious pull, pulled forward his chair, and switched it on. Nothing happened.

He looked at the machine in a panic and then struck the top of the monitor. The black screen stared back at him, reflecting his worried features. He tried switching it on and off. He found he was sweating slightly and marvelled that a mere machine could upset him so much. He did not want to call Priscilla. He was frightened that she would come and do something childishly simple and make him feel even more of a fool than ever. Time passed as he tried again switching it on and off. At last the door opened behind him and Priscilla came in. "How are you getting on?" she asked.

"Fine. Chust fine," said Hamish through gritted teeth.

"If I could make a suggestion . . ."

"No, I'm telling you, I'm getting the hang o' this thing chust great."

"Suit yourself. But, my darling, I think you would get on *chust* fine if you put the plug back in at the wall which you have pulled out."

She smiled at the back of his rigid neck and went out again.

Hamish plugged in the machine, which had become disconnected when he had jerked the monitor, and switched it on. The monitor shone greenly. Painstakingly following Priscilla's instructions, he worked away until he began to master it, and when she finally returned, he felt quite triumphant.

"You're not finished yet," she said to his dismay. "If you want to print something off, you'll need to learn to do that." Hamish groaned. It was half past eleven at night before he finally rose and stretched, thanked Priscilla and made to take his leave.

"Sit down, Hamish," she said quietly. "Now tell me why this sudden interest in the workings of a word processor?"

"Oh," he said shiftily, "the police force is all computerized these days. Got to keep abreast of the times."

Priscilla looked at him thoughtfully, at the open, honest expression on his face, and said, "You're lying. You're up to something. Out with it."

"Oh, all right. That writer, Rosie Draly, is off to London tomorrow and I want to get a look at what she's been writing."

"Didn't you read one of her books?"

"Aye, she gave me one, but, och, it could hae been written by a machine. I have a feeling in my bones that she had started work on a detective story. There might be something there."

"Hamish, you were as near as that"—she held up a finger and thumb to measure a tiny distance—"from getting fired. What if you're caught?"

"I won't be."

Priscilla surveyed him. She was worried in her mind about John Glover. She had enjoyed his company immensely. Despite the arrival of his fiancée, she knew he was still very attracted to her. She could feel herself being drawn to him. And yet there was Betty. They weren't married yet, but still . . .

"I'll come with you and keep guard," she said.

"That iss not necessary."

"I think it is. If you are caught, I will say that I thought I saw a light in the cottage and knew Rosie was away and so I called you in to investigate."

Hamish hesitated only for a moment. He knew Blair was frightened of Priscilla and her influence in high places.

"All right," he said. "I think about one o'clock in the morning the day after tomorrow. That's about as dark as it gets up here in the summer. I'll call for you."

They suddenly smiled at each other and Hamish felt that old treacherous tug at his heart-strings. "Good night," he said gruffly.

* * *

He spent the next day making various calls on people in the village, drinking endless cups of tea, listening to gossip, but the verdict was always the same. Someone from outside must have done it. He was relieved that no one seemed to have heard any gossip about Lucia and then wondered if he had been too soft on that pair. That prim Willie Lamont was still madly in love with his beautiful wife was evident. Would Willie crack out of his cleaning and orderly encased shell and commit murder?

He went reluctantly along to the restaurant. Willie was cleaning the brass rail which ran along the front windows and whistling to himself.

But his face darkened when he saw Hamish and he said, "I hope this is a social call."

"No, it's not," said Hamish crossly. "I wass that upset that you and Lucia were fighting that I couldn't think clearly. I want to know if you visited Randy at any time. I want to know if you threatened him."

"Well, I didn't."

Willie was a bad liar. "You did!" said Hamish. "My God, if Blair gets to hear this. You silly wee man, what did you do?"

"Mind your own business."

"Put down that rag and stop polishing and listen to me," howled Hamish. "If Blair gets wind o' the fact that you threatened Randy—and you cannae lie to me, Willie, you did, I can see it on your face—you'll need a friend."

Willie suddenly sat down at a table and covered his face with his long, thin, bony fingers. Hamish sat down opposite him. "You willnae tell Lucia?" said Willie at last.

"I'm not so worried about Lucia as about you. Out with it. it."

"I went to see him," said Willie from behind the shield of his hands.

"When?"

"The evening of the day afore the murder."

"And?"

"I told him if he ever went near Lucia again I'd break him in half."

"Go on. Take your hands away from your face!"

Willie slowly lowered his hands. To Hamish's dismay, Willie's eyes were shining with tears.

"He just laughed and laughed. He said awful things about Lucia. That she was hot for it and she'd be back. I tried to punch him and he just swung me round, got me by the scruff of the neck and threw me out. I've never been so humiliated in all my life. I shouted I'd kill him."

"It's a mercy nobody saw you or heard you."

Willie let out a broken little sob. "Only Geordie Mackenzie, and he won't be saying anything."

"Geordie! What was he doing?"

"He was walking past. I didnae think to ask him what he was doing, I was that upset. He made me feel more of a wimp than ever because he said he wasn't going to take any more rubbish from Randy. I said, 'The big ape'll massacre you,' and he said something about a man with brains could always get even with a man who was only brawn."

Hamish leaned back in his chair, digesting this new information. He had discounted little Geordie, had never even considered him. What a mess! He had initially thought that Randy was only dangerous as a man who bragged too much in the bar. Now all these nasty episodes were surfacing. He had humiliated Geordie, Annie, Andy, Willie and Archie, and probably Rosie Draly.

"But I didn't kill him, Hamish," said Willie. "I just didnae have the guts."

"I'm beginning to think it took guts not to kill Randy," said

Hamish moodily. "If we could get something on the man, on his background, anything to move the suspicion away from Lochdubh. What's Blair doing? He's probably put up the backs of the Glasgow police so much they're dragging their heels. I'll have another word with you, Willie, but I won't be saying anything to Blair unless I absolutely have to."

Hamish went along to the bar in search of Geordie Mackenzie. The retired schoolteacher was drinking whisky and water and chatting to a group of fishermen. Hamish tapped him on the shoulder. "Outside, Geordie."

Geordie looked up at him nervously but he obediently put down his drink and followed Hamish outside. "Walk away with me a wee bit," said Hamish. "I want a private chat." Geordie brightened visibly and trotted eagerly after Hamish, like a small terrier trying to keep pace with an afghan hound. "You need my help solving this case?" he panted.

"Aye, you could say that." Hamish stopped by the harbour wall. Neither man noticed the rain. The short period of sunshine was forgotten and so both had settled back into living with the rain and ignoring it. It was what the Irish with their usual talent for euphemism would call "a nice, soft day." Drizzle was blowing in from the Atlantic, veiling the hills and forests across the loch. The air smelled of a mixture of pine and tar, wood-smoke and fish.

"This'll do," said Hamish, resting one arm along the wall. "Now, Geordie, what's this I hear about you saying you could get even with Randy? You said something like that to Willie Lamont."

"He's got no call to shoot his mouth off," said Geordie angrily. "I'm disappointed in you, Hamish. A man of my intelligence could be of good help to you in finding the murderer."

"Aye, well, a man of your intelligence should know that the police most certainly want to talk to everyone who had anything to do with Randy, and that means people who threatened him in particular."

"It was just words," said Geordie sulkily.

"I think you had something in mind. Come on, Geordie. What was it?"

"I'm good at accents," said Geordie. "When he was drunk, Randy's voice became Scottish and I recognized a Glasgow accent. I've got a wee bit put by. I was going to hire a private detective in Glasgow to find out all about him."

Hamish looked at him with interest. "But you didn't?"

"I didn't have the time. Someone killed him, and good riddance," he said venomously, "and I hope you never find out who did it!"

"Was that why you offered to help me with the case?" demanded Hamish. "So that you could make sure I didn't find anyone?"

"Och, no," said Geordie. "You do twist a man's words."

"You twist them yourself. You must have hated the big man."

"Here now. It's no use trying to pin it on me," said Geordie, getting flustered.

"I'm simply trying to get at the truth," retorted Hamish wearily. "If you would all realize in this village that if you didn't do the murder, then you've nothing to fear. If you think of anything, come to me."

Geordie brightened. "I'll look around and keep my ear to the ground," he said. "But I think a woman did it."

"What makes you say that?"

"The chloral hydrate. That's a woman's trick."

"Not necessarily. A man, a small man, a weak man would just as easily have wanted a quiet and silent Randy to shoot."

Hamish made his way up to Tommel Castle in the rain, which had increased from a drizzle to a downpour. The castle, floodlit against the dark sky, loomed up as if under water. The windscreen wipers were barely coping with the flood. As soon as he had stopped outside the castle, Priscilla darted forward to join him. "What a night!" she gasped, shaking raindrops from her hair. "At least there will be no wandering poacher to see us."

They drove to Rosie's cottage. "Did you make sure she had left?" asked Priscilla.

"I phoned at regular intervals this evening, but there was no reply."

"How are you going to break in? If you smash the windows, that'll cause a fuss."

"I've got a wee gadget for picking locks."

"And where did a respectable policeman get this wee gadget from?"

"Fergie, over at the ironmonger's in Cnothan, made it for me. He's fair fascinated wi' lock-picking. People who forget their keys and can't get into their houses always come to him. I hope it's an easy lock, mind. If she's got a dead bolt or anything like that, I'm stuck."

He parked and they both got out. "I should have brought an umbrella," mourned Priscilla as the rain bucketed down on them.

"I'm glad the efficient Priscilla has slipped up for once in her life," he said.

"But don't you see, it means if we get in there, we'll drip all over the floor?"

"I'll deal with that problem when I get to it," said Hamish, starting work on the lock. Now he felt so close to finding out what was hidden in the word processor, he was determined to go ahead with his plan.

It was a simple Yale lock and he dealt with it quickly. They both crept inside, Hamish lighting a pencil torch. Then each put on gloves.

"Draw the curtains," hissed Priscilla. "When we switch on the machine, if anyone even passes in a car, they'll see the light from it."

He jerked the curtains closed. Floppy discs were scattered over the table. "Give me the torch," said Priscilla. "She's written titles of books on each one. *Lady Jane's Fancy*. Hardly the title of a detective story. This one's marked 'Letters' and this one 'Tax.' No good. Hamish, maybe she told the truth and never even got started."

"She didn't cultivate such as Archie and Andy for nothing. I do believe she did want local colour. Any notes, papers?"

There were notes and papers and bundles of manuscript but nothing relating to Lochdubh or its inhabitants.

The table which was supposed to serve as a dining one was where she worked. "Damm it," said Hamish after an hour's futile searching. "I'm going to put on the light. If anyone comes to investigate, we'll use your story about having seen a light. We'll say we found a door open." Priscilla switched on the light and they looked around the bleak room.

"She's been burning something in the fireplace," muttered Hamish, crouching down in front of it. "Come here, Priscilla. What's this?"

She knelt down on the hearthrug beside him. He pointed to some black melted plastic stuck to the grate. "That looks as if she'd been burning discs as well," said Priscilla.

Hamish sat back on his heels and listened to the drumming of the rain on the roof. "I don't like this," he whispered. "There's a bad feeling here. Wait! I'm going to look in the other rooms."

"What for?"

"I don't know. But I'm afraid."

"Of what?"

But he rose and left the room without answering her. Throwing caution to the winds, he switched on the light in the kitchen. There was a dirty plate, knife and fork and teacup on the kitchen table. He conjured up a vision of Rosie Draly. She could hardly be called a homebody, but she would surely not go off to London and leave dirty dishes. His mouth felt dry. He opened the kitchen door, which led out to the yard at the back, and drew in his breath in a hiss of alarm. Rosie's white Ford Escort was parked outside.

The cottage was tiny and all on one floor. What had been the parlour in the old days had been turned into this kitchen. There were only three other rooms, living-room, bathroom and the bedroom.

He went out into the small hall. Priscilla came and joined him. "You look awful," she said. "What's up?"

"Her car's out the back."

"Then we'd better go. She might be asleep in the bedroom. Hamish!"

Hamish opened the bedroom door and switched on the light.

Rosie Draly was lying across her bed. She was naked and she looked like the lurid cover of a "true life" crime magazine, for there was a large kitchen knife sticking out of her back.

He went forward and picked up one limp wrist and felt her pulse. But there was no life, no life at all. And the body was cold and rigid.

Priscilla stood silently beside him, one hand to her mouth.

"We'll need our story of having seen a light," said Hamish. "This hass got to be reported right away. Blair's over in Strathbane. I'll phone him at home first."

"We should clean up our prints," said Priscilla.

"We're both wearing gloves," pointed out Hamish. "You didn't take yours off at any time?" She dumbly shook her head.

"Do you want me to take you home first?"

"No, I'd better wait here with you, just in case anyone did see us. You'd better lie about the door and say it wasn't locked. I'll go and put it on the latch."

"Are you all right?"

"I'll probably have the horrors in the morning, but not now. Things have to be dealt with."

They went back to the living-room. Hamish used his handkerchief to lift the receiver. "Silly," he said. "There won't be a print in the place. Maybe they'll get something off the car. Whoever killed Rosie probably drove her car round the back of the house out of sight. Hallo, Mr. Blair?"

Priscilla stood, still wet and bedraggled. She stifled a nervous yawn. Oh, to get home to a warm bed and away from this nightmare. Hamish finished his report. "Let's get out of here and sit in the Rover until they arrive," he said.

Rain thudded down on the roof of the vehicle, rain streamed down the windows. Hamish switched on the engine and, after it had been running for some minutes, the heater. Priscilla began to shiver and he put an arm around her. "The ordeal is chust beginning," he said softly. "We're going to be here being asked questions all night. Then you'll need to keep away from the press."

"I've always found it a mistake to keep away from the press," said Priscilla through chattering teeth. "A few pleasant words mean a lot to them. Then they don't harry you so much."

Soon, in the distance, they faintly heard the wail of a siren.

"Here they come," said Hamish with a sigh. "Here they come."

Chapter 7

Do you think my mind has matured late,
Or simply rotted early?

—*Ogden Nash*

When Hamish finally got home to his police station, the rain had
returned to a damp drizzle. He was immensely tired but he wanted
to get in touch with Rosie's agent before Blair did and he remembered that there had been a home phone number on the card Rosie
had given him. Blair could not complain when he found out
because he had said Hamish was now officially on the case.

He found the card and went into the police office and pulled
the phone towards him. He dialled the home number. The
agent's name was Harriet Simmonds. It rang for a long time
and then a sleepy voice answered.

"Miss Simmonds," began Hamish. "This is the police in
Lochdubh, Sutherland. I am afraid I have bad news about your
author, Rosie Draly."

"What? How?" demanded Miss Simmonds. And then, by
the sharpening of her voice, he realized she had come fully

awake. "Come again," she said. "You are the police? From Lochdubh? That's where Rosie lives."

"Lived," corrected Hamish gently. "She has been murdered."

"Murdered? Is this some bad joke? Who are you?"

"My name is Hamish Macbeth, and I am the police constable in Lochdubh. If you do not believe me, I will give you a number to call back." As he said it, he realized it was a bit silly, because there was only he himself.

"No, no," said Miss Simmonds, "I've got myself together now. It's the shock. Rosie. Murdered! Why would anyone murder Rosie? How was she murdered?"

"Someone, we don't know who yet, stuck a knife in her back."

"Good God! I was expecting to see her today."

"There is another thing," said Hamish. "Did she tell you that there had been a murder here?"

"Yes, she did. She said it was interesting because she was going to write a detective story. I tried to dissuade her."

"Why?"

"It's a crowded market. I suppose they all are. She was competent, but I didn't think she could do it. But she said it would be faction."

"What's that?"

"It's where an author takes a real-life story and fictionalizes it."

"The trouble is," said Hamish, "I think that's what caused her death. Her discs and papers have been burnt, or rather, there's evidence of that, and I think the murderer was destroying her evidence. Did she tell you anything about it?"

"No, but she was going to . . . today. I told her if she knew anything, she should tell the police. But she said it was her chance to make big money. She was tired of being a library author and earning peanuts."

"What's a library author?"

"It's a writer who is well liked enough but never a best-seller. The books are bought by the libraries but hardly ever bought by the bookshops. Do you know there are a legion of writers in this country who never actually see their books on sale? And she was desperate for money."

"Was she in trouble? In debt?"

"No, but she felt very frustrated every time she read about some writer making a fortune. She wanted to travel. I'm her fourth agent. You see, at first she blamed the agent for her lack of success. I mean, she was always published, but she didn't earn much. She was always trying to band-wagon."

"You'll need to explain that as well."

"If a certain genre became fashionable—science fiction, spy, the occult, World War Two, that sort of thing—Rosie would try to write whatever she thought would hit the big time. Now when even a competent author tries to write in a field that first of all they haven't read much of and it isn't their thing, the writing becomes very bad indeed. That's what happened to Rosie. But she worked so hard! Always trying. She was so excited about this detective story."

"I cannae envisage Rosie Draly getting excited about anything," said Hamish. "She seemed so self-contained, almost colourless."

"I suppose I'm the only person she ever talked to. She never referred to any friends."

"Family? Lovers?"

"No lovers. She has a sister. I have the name and address."

"Can you give it to me? She'll need to be informed."

"Wait a moment."

After a few minutes she came back to the phone. "It's a Mrs. Beck, 12 Jubilee Lane, Willesden."

"Any phone number?"

"I don't have that. But the police down here will no doubt get it."

"Miss Simmonds, if there is anything you can think of, anything at all, that Rosie might have said about her life up here that might give us a clue to her murder, please let us know."

"I will, of course. But Rosie liked secrets. Not that she ever seemed to have anything to be secretive about, but that's the impression I got."

"Did you like her?"

There was a startled silence and then she said cautiously, "I don't want to speak ill of the dead . . . "

"Oh, please do," urged Hamish.

"Well, I didn't like her, and that's a fact. She had a way of watching me out of the corner of her eye, as if seeing something in me that caused amused contempt. It rattled me. She also kept implying, without actually putting it into exact words, that I was a failure as an agent, although after her failures with her previous agents she must have known that wasn't true. I feel awful talking about her like this. It seems such a lurid death. What kind of knife?"

"An ordinary big kitchen knife."

"Oh, poor Rosie! It might at least have been a mysterious South American dagger or something. Still, I suppose the press will all be there and she'll get the publicity she always craved, but hardly in a way she ever dreamt of getting it. Give me your number. I promise to call you if I think of anything."

"There's just one more thing. Rosie had been chatting up the locals for a bit of colour. Two of them seem to have been quite entranced with her."

"You lot must be stuck for women up there. I *am* being bitchy. Sorry. But I swear to God, Rosie wasn't interested in men. I always thought she was a lesbian."

"Now there's something. Anything concrete on that?"

"Nothing, I'm afraid. Just an impression. I used to spend as little time with Rosie as was decently possible."

Hamish felt he had got as much out of her as he possibly could for the time being. He said goodbye and rang off. Then he sat down to type out a statement of what she had said. He had just finished and was looking forward to going to bed when there was a knock at the kitchen door. He went through and answered it.

Betty John stood there, her large black eyes gleaming with excitement. "What a thrilling place this has turned out to be!" she said. "Another murder. Tell me about it."

"I can't now," said Hamish. "I've been up all night and now I'm going to bed."

She pouted. "I was hoping for a cup of coffee."

"There's instant in the kitchen. Help yourself, but chust let me go to bed. I'm weary."

He went into the bathroom, stripped off and washed down, put on his pyjamas, and then, stretching and yawning, went through to his bedroom and climbed into bed. What had Rosie found out? he wondered sleepily. The silly woman must have found out something from Randy. Randy's plastic surgery pointed to a high-level criminal. He dozed off. Then he awoke with a start. Someone was in the bed with him, someone's body was pressed against his own. He twisted round on the pillow and found himself looking straight into the lecherous black eyes of Betty John.

"For heffen's sakes, woman," groaned Hamish. "What do you think you are doing?"

"This," she said with a throaty laugh, and her hands became busy under the bedclothes.

Hamish was half drugged with sleep, but he had been celibate a long time. Making love to Betty John seemed part of an exotic dream. When he finally fell completely asleep, she buried her head on his chest and fell asleep as well.

Priscilla headed down to the police station at lunch-time with a basket of food from the hotel kitchen beside her on the seat. She was surprised that she had recovered so quickly from the sight of Rosie's dead body, but reflected that had Rosie been blasted to death or battered to death, it would have taken her considerably longer to get over it. There had been something so unreal, so theatrical, about that naked body with the knife sticking out of its back.

She planned to make Hamish lunch and discuss the case. As she parked the car and climbed out, she was hailed by the Currie sisters, Nessie and Jessie, and then immediately joined by Mrs. Wellington, the minister's wife. While the spinster sisters exclaimed about the murder and wondered volubly what had happened to the normally tranquil life of the Scottish Highlands, Mrs. Wellington boomed, "I want to see Hamish Macbeth and find out just what he is doing about this. This place is getting like New York!"

"He's probably very tired," said Priscilla. "He was up all night."

"It's his job to be up all night," said Mrs. Wellington, marching towards the kitchen door, which stood open. The Currie sisters followed, glasses gleaming, rigidly permed hair shining with raindrops. Priscilla reluctantly followed.

Mrs. Wellington looked around the kitchen and then went through to the police office. "Still in bed, the lazy man," she snorted. "Time he was up."

She pushed open the bedroom door and then let out a squawk of horror. The Currie sisters peered around her tweedy bulk and Priscilla, taller than the rest, looked over them. The naked bodies of Hamish Macbeth and Betty John lay tangled on the bed.

Hamish awoke, as if conscious of all the horrified stares directed at him. "Get out of here!" he shouted.

"Disgraceful," said the sisters in unison. They looked absolutely delighted.

The women retreated to the kitchen. "That man is not only immoral, he is amoral, Priscilla," said Mrs. Wellington. "Priscilla?"

But the slamming of the kitchen door was the only reply.

Hamish, in a most unloverlike way, told Betty to get lost. She took it with good humour, unselfconsciously pulling her discarded clothes over her sturdy, naked body. When she had left; he turned his face into the pillow and groaned aloud. What a disgrace! That he had been found in bed with Betty would be all over Lochdubh. He waited until he heard Mrs. Wellington and the Currie sisters, exclaiming their way out of the police station. And Priscilla! What did that chilly lassie expect him to do? Live like a monk?

He gloomily took a scalding bath, reflecting that he was behaving like a girl who had just lost her virginity.

He had just dressed in his uniform when Jimmy Anderson arrived. "How's the Don Joon o' the hills?" he greeted Hamish, a leer on his foxy features.

"You heard already?"

"Man, if you stick your nose out o' the police-station door, you'll see wee groups of people all along the waterfront and they're talking about nothing else."

"Damn this place," said Hamish savagely. "There's been two brutal murders and all they've got to gossip about is my private life!"

"Well, next time, lock your doors. Blair wants your report and your presence."

"He'll get both. Where is he?"

"Up at the mobile unit. Any whisky?"

"How you can drink at this time of day beats me."

"Come on, Hamish. The sun is over the poop deck, or whatever."

"You know where the bottle is. Help yourself."

Jimmy scurried off into the police office, rubbing his hands. Hamish followed him in. "And don't take all day about it."

Jimmy took bottle and glass out of the bottom drawer and examined the bottle with a critical eye. "Getting low," he commented, pouring a large slug. "You'll need to get more."

"I'll see," said Hamish. "So what's the latest on Rosie?"

"Dead. Knife in the back. Won't know about chloral hydrate till the results of the autopsy are through, but she certainly didn't have a peaceful expression on her face when she died."

"And what's happening down in Glasgow, for God's sake? They're looking through the mug shots, aren't they?"

"Sure. But the man had plastic surgery and we're pretty sure he changed his name."

"I would like to get down there and hae a look myself."

"Blair won't let you go and you must have run out of fictitious dead relatives."

"I'll think of something. You've just finished that bottle, so why don't you go off and keep Blair quiet while I see what I can dig up."

When Jimmy had left, Hamish plugged in the electric kettle and made himself a quick cup of coffee. He took a mouthful of it and shuddered. It was called Kenyan Delight and was being sold very cheaply at Patel's. Now he knew why it was being sold cheaply. He poured the rest down the sink. His stomach rumbled but he could not face the idea of making anything to eat. He straightened his peaked cap, braced his thin shoulders, and marched out to face the population of Lochdubh.

To his amazement and relief the waterfront was deserted, apart from a harassed tourist mother dragging along a screaming child and shouting, "I brung you here tae enjoy yourself, and enjoy yourself you will!"

Amazing, thought Hamish. Parents always say the same stupid things. He stopped by the woman and said mildly, "Don't be too hard on the wean, missis. It's all this rain."

"I wish I'd gone tae Spain," said the woman. She was fat and blowsy, with raindrops shining in the black roots of her bleached hair. Hamish crouched down in front of the screaming child, a small boy with a red nose and streaming eyes. The child stopped screaming and stared at him. "Now, laddie," said Hamish, "what's the matter? You can tell me. I'm the police and you've got to tell me the truth."

"I've peed my pants," said the boy dismally, wiping his nose on his sleeve.

"Why didn't you tell your ma?"

"She'd wallop me."

Hamish straightened up and looked at the woman severely. "You heard that," he said, "and you will not be hitting the boy."

The woman looked frightened. "Och, you'll no' be reporting me to the Social."

"Take him away and let him get changed." Hamish fished a fifty-pee piece out of his pocket. "Here, laddie, buy yourself an ice-cream."

He stood and watched them as they went off, the woman now cooing affectionately to her small son and flashing nervous little smiles back at Hamish.

He walked along, turning over the names of the suspects in his head. He decided to have another talk to Annie Ferguson.

She greeted him with, "Oh, Hamish. It's yourself. I don't think you should come here. I shouldn't be seen talking to you."

"Why?" he demanded crossly.

"I've my reputation to consider, and after what you've been up to—"

"Look here," said Hamish furiously, "I am here officially on a murder inquiry, and everyone in the village knows that."

"Everyone in the village knows something else about you now," said Annie with a flash of pure Highland malice. "Och, come ben."

He went into her parlour, took off his cap, placed it on the coffee-table and sat down. She sat down opposite him, tugging her skirt firmly over her sturdy knees in case the sight of them would drive this lecherous policeman into some mad act of passion.

"Now," began Hamish, "I want you to think carefully about any conversation you had with Randy. Did he mention anywhere in the States in particular?"

"I think he seemed to have been just about everywhere. New York, New Orleans, Los Angeles, places like that."

"Did he mention friends, any he might have known?"

She shook her head. "We didn't talk much," she said with a sudden roguish look, quite awful to behold.

"Did you know he had had plastic surgery?"

Her amazement looked genuine.

"Why would he do that? I mean, it's the women who go in for that. Although you wouldn't catch me getting any of that."

"We believe he was a criminal who had gone to great lengths to conceal his real identity."

"A criminal! Oh, you must be mistaken. I wouldn't have had anything to do with anyone like that!"

"But you didn't know he was a criminal," said Hamish patiently.

"And you don't either. You're just clutching at straws."

"Annie, try to be a bit less defensive. Think. What money did he have?"

"He always had wads of the stuff," said Annie. "You must have heard that. And he was always flashing it about in the bar."

Hamish asked her several more questions but could glean nothing of importance. He left and went up to the mobile unit and read the reports. The whole wrestling fraternity of America and Britain had been rigorously interviewed without success. Police artists in Glasgow were working on pictures of what Randy might have looked like before plastic surgery. Rosie's sister, Mrs. Beck, had been contacted and was travelling up to Lochdubh. The rain was still falling, and through the smeared and misted-up windows of the mobile home, Hamish could see groups of pressmen huddled together. Some tourists were also standing about, as if waiting for another murder to happen to enliven the tedium of a rain soaked Scottish holiday.

Mrs. Beck, he learned, was due to arrive from Inverness around five o'clock. She would be staying in Mrs. McCartney's bed and breakfast in the village. Blair was all set to interview her and Hamish wanted to be present at that interview. He knew that if he asked Blair he would be sent about his business and so he decided to wait until she arrived and just turn up.

He left and went to question Archie Maclean, Geordie Mackenzie, and then the barman, Pete Queen. The trouble turned out to be that all had accepted Randy's hospitality without paying any attention to what he had said. Randy had arrived among them, Randy had bragged, Randy had been murdered, and that was the end of it. When he returned to the police station, bending his head against the now wind-driven rain, he felt tired and dirty and miserable. He wanted to phone Priscilla and explain how he had happened to be in bed with Betty, but could think of no explanation which would appeal in any way.

He felt, too, that he ought, as a Highland gentleman should, to phone Betty. Although she had taken it well, there had been no reason for him to have been so rude. He phoned the Tommel Castle Hotel. At first he did not recognize the curt voice on the telephone as that of Priscilla and he asked to speak to Betty. And that was when he recognized her voice when Priscilla said coldly, "Your lady-love is out in the hills with her fiancé."

Cursing the fact that with servants at the castle always going off sick with bad backs or whatever other Highland excuse occurred to them, leaving Priscilla to fill their jobs, Hamish said, "That just happened. I woke up and found her in bed."

Her voice dripped icicles. "Indeed? I will tell her you called." The line went dead and he looked miserably at the receiver before slowly replacing it. Why, when he had done the right thing by getting himself out of a cold relationship, did he still get so dreadfully hurt? A psychiatrist would say it pointed to a lack of love in childhood that he should long for the unobtainable, and yet he had had a very loving childhood. Bugger analysis, thought Hamish Macbeth, and geared himself up instead to gatecrashing the interview with Mrs. Beck.

* * *

A furiously rolling eye in his direction was the only sign of Blair's displeasure when Hamish quietly followed the detectives into the bed and breakfast. Mrs. Beck was sitting in the front parlour under a sign which warned guests that the terms were bed and breakfast and no matter what the weather, they were expected to make themselves absent from the house immediately after breakfast was over.

Mrs. Beck did not look at all like her sister. She was small and plump with that brisk, no-nonsense look about her which often betrays a total lack of humour. We all adopt masks, thought Hamish dreamily. Somewhere along the line, Mrs. Beck had decided on the role of capable housewife who did not suffer fools gladly and would probably play it to the end of time. Did he have a mask? he wondered. Did he . . . ?

"Sit down, Macbeth, and stop gawping like a loon," snapped Blair. Hamish hurriedly retreated to a small chair in the corner of the parlour.

"Now, Mrs. Beck," crooned Blair, adjusting his truculent features into the oily expression he wore when facing the recently bereaved, "we are all shocked and saddened by your loss."

"Enough of that," said Mrs. Beck, clutching a large battered leather handbag on her knees. "You don't give a damn, so let's not waste any time."

Her accent was Scottish, which surprised Hamish. Rosie had had an almost accentless voice and he had assumed her to be English.

"Then we won't waste time," said Blair, returning to his usual bad-tempered character. "We believe your sister found out something about a man who was murdered here, Randy Duggan. We believe she wanted to use the information about this man, who was possibly a criminal, in one of her books, and that is the reason she was killed."

"She probably knew nothing about him at all," said Mrs. Beck. "Does it always rain here?" She shifted her bulk in her chair and glared towards the window, where fat raindrops chased each other down the glass.

"And what makes you say that?"

"Rosie always liked to hint she had secrets, that she knew something about you. It made her very unpopular at school, but she never really knew anything about anyone. She was too wrapped up in herself."

"Then let's begin at the beginning. Where were you brought up? Where did you go to school?"

She gave a crisp outline in an unemotional, flat voice. They had been brought up in Dumfries. Both their parents were dead. There had been no other children, only she and Rosie.

After school, she had married and left for the south. Rosie had gone to university and then become a teacher. They had never liked each other, and so, apart from exchanging cards at Christmas and on birthdays, there had been little communication between them over the years. She had seen Rosie last year when she had arrived unexpectedly to say that she had bought a house in Sutherland. Before that she had been living in Glasgow. She supplied the Glasgow address.

"What did you think of her books?" the quiet Highland voice of Hamish Macbeth came from the corner of the room.

Blair glared at him.

Mrs. Beck sniffed. "I never read any of them. I haven't time to read."

"You must have been verra jealous of her." Hamish again.

"What!" Mrs. Beck looked at him wrathfully. "What was there to be jealous of? I am married, she wasn't. What had she ever done with her life except write trash?"

"You not only were jealous of her," pursued Hamish, "you actually hated her. Why?"

"What is this? What kind of policeman are you?"

"Did she try to take your husband away from you?" Hamish's voice was suddenly sharp.

"How did you find out about that?"

Hamish remained silent. The wind began to rise outside with a low, keening, moaning sound which meant even worse weather to come. A puff of smoke belched out from the dismal little peat fire which was doing little to warm the room.

Blair, for once, had the wit to remain silent. "It was just after Bob and me were married," said Mrs. Beck. "She came on a visit. Bob was an overseer at an electronics factory and he was made redundant. I took a job in a shop because although he had his redundancy money, I knew it wouldn't last forever. So I was out all day. And then I found out they had been going to the movies in the afternoon when I was out and to lunch as well, spending that precious redundancy money while I slaved away selling women's underwear. There was a big scene. I gave Rosie her marching orders, and Bob said he was going with her. But I'd found out the night before from the doctor that I was pregnant. So I told him that and he stayed and Rosie went. That's all."

And what a wealth of bitterness "that's all" covered, thought Hamish. Rosie had probably not fancied Bob in the slightest but was determined to prove to her sister that she could do anything better, and Mrs. Beck had probably crowed over Rosie about being married.

"Where were you when Rosie was murdered?" demanded Blair sharply.

"I was at home."

"With your husband?"

"He only comes home at the weekends. He works in Birmingham."

Again Hamish's voice. "Do you know if he saw your sister at any time?"

Her eyes flashed. "He wouldn't dare."

"But then you wouldnae know," said Hamish, almost as if talking to himself. "He was away all week. He could take time off from work and go where he liked. Where was he the night of Rosie's murder, for example?"

She looked at this Highland tormentor with a slight air of triumph. "He phoned me from Birmingham that very evening."

"How did you know he was phoning from Birmingham?"

"Aye," put in Blair. "He could have been phoning from up here."

"That's where you're wrong! Bob's digs are next to the railway line. He always phones at nine in the evening and at nine a train always goes past on the line outside and shakes the very place. I heard it."

"That seems conclusive enough," said Blair heavily. "Mrs. Beck . . . or may I call you Beryl?"

"You may call me Mrs. Beck."

"Just write down your husband's address. That will be all for now. PC Black will take you to Strathbane now to formally identify the body. Do you know if Miss Draly made a will?"

She shook her head.

"We're still sifting through her papers. If we find anything, we'll let you know."

They all left and Hamish went back to the police station, made a cup of coffee and sat down and stared at the kitchen wall.

Here was a new scenario. What if the murders of Duggan and Rosie were not connected? He listened to the now screaming wrath of the wind outside and rose and went to light the wood-burning stove in the kitchen. When it was crackling merrily, he sat down again. He had come across many cases of sibling rivalry before, although none of them had amounted to murder. Here were two sisters—one bossy and sure of herself, and then there was the unknown quantity of Rosie. What did he know of Rosie? Possibly lesbian, but liked to get attention from men. Liked power. Perhaps that was it. Would she let Bob go just like that, or would she, over the years, try to keep him on a string? He thought of his past burning sexual frustration over Priscilla. He thought of the times he could cheerfully have murdered her. What if Rosie had never gone to bed with Bob, but had kept tugging his leash? Exciting secret meetings, always with the promise of sex held out. Did she do that? Had she done that? Was that what she did with Randy, and when he came on to her was that what had prompted the row? He suddenly wanted to see Archie Maclean. The fishing boats would not be out in such weather.

He went out and fought his way against the gale to the bar, but Archie was not there, so, with a certain reluctance, he called at his cottage. Hamish, like everyone else in Lochdubh, found Mrs. Maclean terrifying.

Mrs. Maclean was working ferociously over at the sink, scrubbing at a pot. Archie was sitting gloomily on a hard chair in the middle of the kitchen in his tight clothes. The floor had been recently washed and Archie's highly polished boots were resting on a square of newspaper.

"Like a dram, Archie?"

Archie brightened. "That would be grand."

Mrs. Maclean whipped round and brandished a pot-scrubber like a weapon. "You are not to be wasting good money on the drink."

"I'm paying," said Hamish mildly.

"Well, don't be long," she said reluctantly. "It'll give me a chance to wash that floor again. You should hae left your boots at the door, Hamish Macbeth. This is a clean house."

"Cleanest in Lochdubh," agreed Hamish.

"Wait!" she screeched as her husband got to his feet. She picked up a newspaper and, separating the pages, spread them out across the floor in front of him like stepping stones.

Archie took down a crackling black oilskin from a peg and shrugged himself into it, and together both men escaped into the howling night. Conversation on the road to the Lochdubh bar was impossible because of the vicious screaming of the wind.

The bar was quiet that evening, to Hamish's relief. Archie asked for a whisky and went to prop up the bar in his usual way but Hamish led him to a small table in the corner.

"Did you mourn Rosie?" asked Hamish.

Archie smoothed the sparse hairs over his head with a gnarled hand. "I'm right sorry she's dead," he mumbled.

"But you did not cry?"

"Och, come on, Hamish. Greetin's for bairns."

"Try to think clearly, Archie. This is important. Were you fond of her?"

There was a long silence while the fisherman struggled for words. At last he said. "The fact is, I was a wee bit flattered. Her being a writer and all. She told me I wass a highly intelligent man. But with her gone, it iss as if she neffer existed. Do you know what I mean?"

"But while she was flattering you and making you cups of tea, did you ever think of having an affair with her?"

Archie blushed deeply. "Och, Hamish, the thought neffer crossed my mind and that's the truth. I've only got to look in the mirror."

"You're a modest man, Archie, but you must have wondered *why* she flattered you and cultivated your company."

The little fisherman's eyes were suddenly shrewd. "I think she wanted me to fall in love with her," he said.

"And why would that be?"

"The ladies like the men to fall in love with them even when they're not interested. It's the way they are. Makes them feel good."

"She was right about the one thing, Archie. You are an intelligent man. I'll buy you another and then I've got to go. I've got a phone call to make."

Back in the police station, Hamish got through to Birmingham CID. He was lucky in that he got a clever and bored detective who was anxious for action. He was Detective Sergeant Hugh Perrin.

Hamish outlined the details of the murder of Rosie Draly and then said, "I was just wondering whether it would be possible to get a search warrant for Bob Beck's apartment. You see, when he made that phone call to his wife, she said he must have been down in Birmingham because she heard the nine-o'clock. Now all he had to do was make a tape recording of that train, take it up to Sutherland and play it."

"You've got a point there. But you say there was evidence that papers and computer discs had been burnt in the fireplace? Doesn't that point to the murderer of Duggan?"

"Beck could ha' been burning evidence of letters from him and letters back to him."

"Bit far-fetched. If that was the case, why didn't he just chuck this tape of the train going past in the fire as well?"

"I think when he murdered her, he might have got rid of any evidence of letters. Then he would sit down and phone his wife. Wait a bit. He wouldn't phone her from Rosie's because we checked the calls for that evening. Damn, we should have been checking back through the past few months. Think o' this. He needs a phone. He can hardly stand in a phone box and operate the tape recorder properly. He might be pressed for time. So he would go to some hotel or motel, on the road south and phone from there, not too far from Lochdubh."

"There's your answer then," said Perrin. "You get evidence he was anywhere near the scene and we can haul him in . . . easy. I'm going to be here all night."

With a fast-beating heart, Hamish said goodbye and reached for the battered phone book. He began to phone hotels and boarding-houses in the immediate area, asking if any stranger had checked in on the evening of the murder for one night and if there had been a London phone call on the bill. He gave Mrs. Beck's number. And then, just when he was about to give up, he remembered the new Cluny Motor Inn on the A9 and phoned there. He could not believe his luck. Not only was there a clear record of Bob Beck's having phoned home but he had even used his own name.

He phoned Detective Sergeant Perrin with the news. "We'll get him in," said the detective triumphantly. "But surely he hasn't still got that tape? Surely he chucked it out the car window or something."

"If you pull him in," said Hamish, "I'll go out to the Cluny Motor Inn and go through the trash. With any luck it hasn't been collected."

He stopped only to pick up his radio, which had a tape deck, from the kitchen table before driving off into the wild night. Sheets of rain battered against the windscreen and he thought bleakly of sitting in the Land Rover with Priscilla waiting for Blair and the others to arrive and experienced a stabbing pain of hurt and loss in his gut. He marvelled that the pain could still be so intense. He didn't feel like a drink or a pill to ease it, but rather thought of taking a shotgun and blasting a big hole in his stomach, not to kill himself, but, like a cartoon animal, to leave a nice clean round hole where the hurt had been.

At last he reached the motor inn and eagerly asked the manager if he could search through the hotel rubbish. "Suit yourself," said the manager. "It gets collected tomorrow. It's all round the back."

He led Hamish out to the back of the hotel, where two giant metal rubbish bins gleamed wetly in the lights from the inn. "You'd best leave me to it," said Hamish gloomily. "I'll need to take everything out."

"I'll make it easy for you," said the manager. "The bin on the left is the kitchen waste. The one on the right is mostly other stuff from the rooms, old newspapers, that sort of stuff."

The bin was so large that, tall as he was, Hamish had to stand on a box to reach down into the contents. The hours went past as he patiently sifted through cartons, newspapers, magazines, cigarette butts, condoms, sandwich wrappings and empty bottles. He threw everything out over his shoulder and then climbed into the bin as the contents grew lower and by the light of his torch ferreted around in the bottom. His hands closed on a cassette and he gave a whoop of triumph. He shouted for the manager, who came running out. "I want you to witness that I am taking this out o' the bin," said Hamish. "We'll take it into reception and play it."

Together they went back into the warmth of the reception, where Hamish had left his radio. He put the tape in the deck and pressed PLAY. After a few seconds, the throaty voice of Cher blasted around the room.

Hamish did not normally swear, but when he switched off the tape deck, his oaths resounded round the room. "Here! Enough o' that," said the manager. "If you're finished, take yourself off."

"I'm going for another look," said Hamish stubbornly.

He went back out into the wind and rain and climbed back into the large green metal bin, concentrating on the refuse from the hotel rooms which was in the small plastic garbage bags used to line the waste-baskets. He opened one at the bottom and shone his torch. An empty half-bottle of whisky, a crushed, empty cigarette packet, several butts, soiled tissues . . . and a tape.

Once more, he called the manager. "What is it this time?" demanded the manager with heavy sarcasm. "Dolly Parton?"

"I want you to witness I'm taking this out of the bin."

"Oh, sure."

Hamish climbed out. Together they went back into the hotel again. Hamish slotted in the tape and switched on the machine. At first there was silence, broken only by the hiss of the tape, and then suddenly the room was filled with the sound of an approaching train. A slow smile broke on Hamish's thin features.

He listened until the sound of the train had finished. "Is that what you wanted?" asked the manager.

"It's the very thing."

"Well, I'm short-staffed at the moment, so get out there and put that rubbish back."

But Hamish had had enough of ferreting through rubbish. "It's all police evidence," he said. "You'll need to leave it as it is until the forensic boys get here."

As he drove back to Lochdubh, Hamish's feeling of triumph began to ebb. He should have told Blair what he was going to do. Blair would be furious.

And sure enough, when he drove towards the police station, he saw the cars parked outside, and in the light of the blue lamp over the front door, swinging wildly in the wind, he made out the truculent features of Blair.

"What have ye been up to, pillock?" shouted Blair. "I got a call frae Birmingham telling me they were pulling in Beck for questioning and I didnae know a thing about it. Daviot'll get to hear o' this."

"I've got the tape Beck made of the train going past," said Hamish.

"How? What . . . ?"

While Hamish talked, Blair only half listened to him, his mind working busily. Somehow he had to claim this bit of detective work as his own. He became suddenly conciliatory and smiled horribly. "Aye, well done, lad. You'll be needing your bed. Just let's be having that tape."

Hamish meekly passed it over. He knew what Blair was going to do. Blair would tell Daviot that he, Blair, had instructed Hamish to phone Birmingham and had sent him out to look for the tape.

Which was what Blair subsequently did and was met with heavy suspicion. "What were you about," demanded Peter Daviot nastily, "to send one lone constable out on the search? And phoning the CID in Birmingham and giving them instructions is your job, not Macbeth's."

"I phoned them myself," howled Blair.

"That's not what I heard. I heard that Hamish Macbeth phoned."

"I mean," said Blair quickly, "like I just said, I told him to phone."

"Next time, do the job yourself."

"Yes, sir," said Blair meekly, and he hated Hamish Macbeth from the bottom of his heart.

Chapter 8

When love grows diseas'd, the best thing
we can do
is put it to a violent death; I cannot
endure the
torture of a lingring and consumptive
passion.

—*Sir George Etherege*

As a sign that Superintendent Peter Daviot knew who had uncovered Beck as the murderer of Rosie, Hamish Macbeth was invited to the interview in Strathbane when Beck was brought north. Blair was in a sour mood.

Hamish, in the corner as usual, looked at Bob Beck with a sort of wonder. He was a grey-haired man with a slight stoop, thick spectacles through which pale eyes looked out at the world with a childlike innocence, a rather large nose and a small mouth. He was wearing a well-pressed grey suit and black lacing shoes. He was hardly the picture of a man who, driven mad with passion, had plunged a knife into the naked back of Rosie Draly. Had it not been for the evidence of the tape, Hamish would have been tempted to think that he had merely been unlucky, that he had travelled to Sutherland to see Rosie on the very day of her murder.

Blair began the questioning, mildly enough for him. Beside Beck sat his solicitor, a thin, rabbity man who looked even more bewildered than the murderer.

"How long had you known the writer, Rosie Draly?"

"Years," said Beck, and then said firmly, "to save time I would like to make a full confession."

Blair smiled expansively. "That's the ticket, laddie. Go ahead."

"I fell in love with Rosie just after Beryl and I were married," he said in a rusty voice, as if he had not spoken for some time. "That was in nineteen sixty-four. I wanted to leave Beryl, get a divorce, but then Beryl told me she was pregnant and Rosie told me I must do the decent thing and stay with her. I've hated Beryl for a long time." He blinked round the room myopically. "But I coped, particularly after I got the job in Birmingham. Beryl did not want to move to Birmingham and that suited me. Rosie and I met . . . often. I wanted her, I wanted to have her, and she always held out that hope and I believed her because I was in the grip of an obsession. When I wasn't with her, I thought of her all day long. Some days I thought I would take time off from this madness, but then the day would be so black and empty, I would need to return to my dreams. In my dreams, I always made love to her as no man has made love to a woman. She wrote to me regularly and I saved all her letters. And then she moved to Sutherland, and the letters became less and finally stopped. When I phoned her, she always seemed to cut me off. May I have a glass of water, please?"

They waited while a policewoman fetched him a glass of water, which he drank in one long thirsty gulp.

"At last I couldn't bear it any longer," he went on. "She had told me that Lochdubh was a gossipy place and I was never to come up and see her. But I drove up. I took a tape recording of the train going past because I knew I had to phone Beryl.

When I set out, I had no thought of murder in my head. I did not need to ask directions to her cottage. When she first moved up to the Highlands, she had described it in every detail and where it was. I was stunned when she answered the door. She was harsh with me, abrupt. She said she had big things ahead of her, a good future. She was going to London to see her agent and couldn't waste any time on me."

His eyes filled with tears and he blinked them away. "She said she was going to have a bath and I could take myself off. She walked into the bedroom and she stripped off, insolent in all the nakedness I had dreamt so long about. I haven't much memory of what happened next. I hurt so dreadfully. All I could think of was hurting her as much as she had hurt me. I must have taken the knife out of the kitchen drawer. I went back to the bedroom. She was bending over the bed, still naked. I plunged the knife into her back. I'm no surgeon. I didn't know where to strike, didn't even think of it. But she died instantly. One minute she was alive and the next she was as cold as mutton.

"And then all the hurt and rage left me and I was looking back on a life ruined by obsession. All I could think was to save myself, not make myself a sacrifice for such a woman. I found letters from me and some of her letters to me still on a computer disc. She never handwrote letters, and I burnt them. The rest you've found out—how I went to the Cluny Motor Inn, phoned Beryl with the tape of the train playing in the background, and how I threw it in the rubbish."

His voice died away. Blair leaned forward, his beefy shoulders hunched, suppressed excitement quivering in every part of his unlovely body. "But you were up here afore," he said. "Tell us how you killed Randy."

Hamish leaned back in his chair and sighed and waited for the inevitable denial. To his horror he heard Beck say, "So you know about that, too?"

"Aye," said Blair triumphantly. "So tell us about it."

Hesitantly Beck said, "She said she had met this most interesting man. It was in one of her rare letters, but I read between the lines and I went mad with jealousy. I stayed at a bed-and-breakfast place on the road to Lochdubh; don't ask me what it was called, I was in such a passion, I can't remember. I bought a shotgun in Birmingham. They're easy to get if you know which pub to go to. I bought myself a wig and put on a pair of sunglasses and scouted around until I had identified him and then I followed him home. I had some chloral hydrate. It was my mother's. I called on him and said I was a friend of Rosie's and had dropped by for a chat. He offered me a drink. When he was out of the room, I poured the chloral hydrate into his glass and then, after he had drunk it, I waited for it to take effect. I bound up his hands because I was frightened he would wake up. I shot him, turned up the heating to conceal the time of death, just in case I had been seen, and then I drove south again, stopping only to throw the shotgun into a peat bog."

"You're lying," said Hamish Macbeth.

Blair's face turned purple with rage. Here he was on the edge of winding up the whole business and this rat, Macbeth, was trying to spoil it. Like every other human being, Blair judged other people's motives by his own. Hamish Macbeth was trying to take his success away from him.

"You!" he roared at Hamish. "Get oot o' here!"

And so Hamish left. Beck signed a written statement and the next day the newspapers were full of the solving of the two murders.

The press left Lochdubh, satellite dishes, cables, cameras and all. The rain continued to fall steadily and Hamish Macbeth was left alone with an unsolved murder on his hands. He believed that Beck had murdered Rosie—all that passion, all that obsession had been genuine. But why on earth had the man confessed to murdering Randy? All the details of the case had been published in the newspapers, so he would have known of every detail, from the tying of the wrists to the chloral hydrate in the drink. Blair, so anxious to believe the confession, would not check it thoroughly, would not find out who Beck's mother's doctor had been and whether he had ever prescribed chloral hydrate. Could it be that Beck might have been as burnt up with hatred for his wife as he had been with passion for Rosie? Was this his way of getting even, so that Beryl would find out she was married to a double murderer?

He sat down in his office and began to write out a short list of suspects. There was Geordie Mackenzie, who had been sorely humiliated by Randy; there was Annie Ferguson; there was Andy MacTavish, the forestry worker; and even Archie Maclean was suspect. And then there was Willie Lamont and Lucia. Beck had shown what a mild man in the grip of passion could do. He now could not interview any of them officially. But he could talk to them as friends. He could say that he did not believe Beck had murdered Randy and he knew that piece of gossip would go around the village like wildfire.

He had not seen anything of Betty and felt he ought to phone her but did not like to find that Priscilla was answering the hotel phones. He shivered. Not only was it still raining but the weather was turning colder. He lit the wood-burning stove in the kitchen so that he would have a warm room to return to, pulled on his raincoat, settled his peaked cap down about his ears and went wearily out into the deluge. He headed in the direction of Geordie's cottage, reflecting that he had never been there before. It was a trim, low-storeyed, whitewashed building. The garden was neat and orderly, with small flower-beds edged with scallop-shells. He rang the bell and waited.

After a few moments Geordie answered the door and smiled a welcome. Hamish thought that none of his suspects would feel they had anything to fear from the police any more. Geordie led the way into a small living-room. It was as soul-less and characterless as Rosie's and just as cold.

"Coffee?" asked Geordie. "I just put the kettle on."

"No, thank you," said the normally mooching Hamish and Geordie looked at the tall policeman with a flicker of unease at the back of his eyes. "Well, well," he said, rubbing his hands, "sit down, sit down. It was kind of you to call. What a business, eh? Here we all are thinking of international crime and gangsters and it was that man, Beck, all along."

"Aye," said Hamish, "but there's a lot still to be explained."

"Such as?"

"Who on earth was Randy Duggan, for a start? Why the plastic surgery? And why," said Hamish, leaning forward, "should Beck admit to a murder he did not commit?"

Geordie stared in dismay. "What are you talking about, Hamish?"

"I don't believe he killed Duggan. He killed Rosie, yes, but not Duggan. And this is Scotland, not England. A confession on its own isn't enough. They'll need to dig up some more proof, although, if I know Blair, he'll try not to."

Geordie protested, "But why would he admit to it?"

"I think his obsession with Rosie turned Beck's brain. I think he hated his wife with a passion because she would not give him his freedom when he wanted to leave her and marry Rosie. I think he thought he would confess to Duggan's murder to get revenge on her and also to make him look more macho, not some wimp dying of love for a woman, but an action man."

"That's guesswork. Look, Hamish, it's over and we can all return to normal. You're only trying to stir up things because you've got a hunch. Folks here say you're easygoing and would rather go fishing than solve crimes. What's come over you?"

Hamish's normally lazy expression vanished and a hard look came over his face. "I may be easygoing with small little crimes in the village that can be sorted out by me, Geordie, without bringing Strathbane into it. But when it comes to murder, then justice must be done, and justice isn't pouncing on some fellow who gives a convenient confession. I will continue to ferret away, Geordie, until I find the real killer. It could ha' been anyone." He let a little silence fall. The rain drummed steadily on the bushes outside the window. Then he spoke again. "It could have been you."

"Me!" squeaked Geordie. "Why me?"

"He humiliated you publicly."

"And you think that would make me kill the man? Because I was humiliated? Look at me, Hamish I was a schoolteacher, long years of teaching snotty little boys who took the piss out of me on every occasion. Teachers who were promoted over my head for no other reason than that they were rugger buggers or sleeping with the head's wife. I tell you, man, with me, humiliation's a way of life!"

Hamish got up to leave. "Chust remember, Geordie," he said quietly, "that I'm still looking."

After he had left, Geordie stared bleakly for a long time at the chair in which Hamish Macbeth had been sitting, and listened to the relentless sound of the rain.

Hamish glanced at his watch and then set off towards Lucia and Willie's cottage by the bridge. When he arrived, Willie was polishing the kitchen counter while the beautiful Lucia painted her nails bright red.

Willie came in from the kitchen, a cleaning rag in his hand. "Glad it's all over, Hamish," he said cheerfully. "Isn't this awful weather? They say there's more perception forecast for the morrow."

"Precipitation," corrected Hamish. "And it's not all over, Willie. You, as an ex-policeman, should know that Beck's confession to the murder of Randy is just a bit too pat."

"I think," said Lucia in measured tones and with a toss of her black curly hair, "that your nose is out of joint because Blair solved the murders."

"It wass not Blair," said Hamish crossly. "It was me that found out Beck was guilty of Rosie's murder. But I do not believe for a moment that he killed Duggan."

"Of course he did," shouted Willie. "It's over, all over, and you're just stirring up muck out of vanity."

"I believe," said Hamish, holding on to his temper, "that someone in Lochdubh killed Randy and I am going to find out who that someone is and my personal feelings for any of the inhabitants of Lochdubh will not get in the way."

"Meaning you still think I might be guilty!" exclaimed Willie.

"You or Lucia."

"Get out of my house . . . now!" yelled Willie, flapping the cleaning rag and filling the air with the smell of ammonia. He rushed and opened the door and stood by it. Hamish turned in the doorway and looked back at Lucia. Her eyes were wide with fear.

He turned his coat collar up against the rain and went back to the police Land Rover and got in. "Time to make someone else's life a misery," he said to the windscreen wipers as they slashed against the streaming rain. He drove off and around the loch to where the pine forest stood and then up one of the forestry tracks, rolling down the window until he could hear the crash of falling trees.

Andy and some of the other forestry workers were in a clearing. Hamish arrived just as another of those spindly, grey-trunked forestry pines, which never looked like real trees, came crashing down. It was not like the Brazilian rain forest, thought Hamish. Because of the demand for wood, the north of Scotland was gradually being covered by forest. The companies did their best, growing ornamental trees by the sides of the roads and setting out picnic tables and benches in the clearings, but these were bastard trees, crammed together, thin and dripping in the soft air.

Andy came forward to meet him. "Just taking a break, Hamish," he hailed him. "Going to brew up some tea."

"Not for me," said Hamish. "Can we have a chat?"

"Aye, come ower here. What's up? Can't be this murder business. That's all solved."

They walked slowly over a thick carpet of pine needles and sat down opposite each other on a pair of tree stumps.

"I am not satisfied it was Beck who killed Randy," began Hamish.

He was prepared for anger, denial, but Andy looked at him with mild eyes and said surprisingly, "Now there's the funny thing. Maybe it was because I was so sure that Randy was wan o' thae big-time criminals that I couldnae swallow the fact that it was done by Rosie's boy-friend. The thing is no one saw him round the village, although no one's been watching like they do in the good weather. Folks are mostly indoors of an evening, wi' the telly switched on. But I've got this feeling in my bones."

Hamish looked at him with relief in his hazel eyes. "I thought you'd start shouting at me like some o' the others."

Andy grinned. "I may have had a fight with Randy but at the time I thought I had lost fair and square. I only learned about the knuckledusters afterwards. At the time, I didn't feel mad, see. Just ashamed of myself. Told myself I should keep oot o' fights. Maybe if the fight had been public like the one he was going to have wi' you, I might have been madder."

"But have you any concrete reason for supposing that Randy was not killed by Beck?"

"Och, not really. When I heard about it, I just got this idea that it was all too pat. There's been people afore, you know that, Hamish, who've confessed to murders they didn't do to get a bit of the limelight. It's not as if we have the death penalty."

"Aye, but the silly folk who confess to the murders they did not do are people who haven't committed murder at all. There's no doubt in my mind that Beck killed Rosie."

"If that's the case, Hamish, I don't envy you the job o' finding out who really did it with the trail cold and you not allowed to use any of the services in Strathbane."

"I've managed before," said Hamish mulishly, "and I'll manage again on my own. I think I will have that cup o' tea, Andy."

They walked back to join the other men. "We'll all be getting webbed feet if this goes on," said Hamish. "And have you seen the forecasts for the south of England? Sunshine every day."

"That's the English for you," said a forestry worker who had overheard Hamish's last remark. "They take the best of everything."

Hamish drove round to Annie Ferguson's and parked outside. As he climbed down from the Land Rover, he saw Willie outside the Italian restaurant. Willie gave an odd little duck of his head and scuttled out of view.

Annie Ferguson opened the door just as he was raising his hand to knock it. "Oh, it's yourself, Hamish, come along in," she said cheerfully.

"So how's yourself?" asked Annie, once he was settled in a chair in the living room. "Isn't it grand they've got someone for these murders, and an outsider, too."

Hamish clasped his hands round his knees and looked at her steadily. "Annie, it is my belief that Randy Duggan was not killed by Beck."

Her mouth dropped open. "But . . . b-but . . ." she stammered, "it's all over. Nothing to do with us."

"It would be grand if I could believe that."

"If *you* could believe that! And just who are you, Hamish Macbeth? You're only a village copper. If your superiors in Strathbane are satisfied, then what's it to do with you?"

"It's to do with justice, Annie. I don't like the idea of a murderer going free, and neither should you."

"You've no right to come here and talk rubbish. Just because you wear a uniform, you think you can go around bullying poor widows." She began to cry. Hamish looked at her in frustration.

"Annie, Annie, pull yourself together, lassie. What's so awful about me thinking the murderer is still at large?"

"Because you're wrong," she shouted through her tears.

Hamish left. He had done what he had come to do, which was to start the gossip circulating fast around Lochdubh that he was still on the look-out for the murderer.

Two hours later, Priscilla was arranging a new consignment of paperweights on the shelves of the gift shop when the shop bell clanged and Lucia came in. She was wearing a gleaming red oilskin with bright-red Wellington boots.

"Hallo," said Priscilla. "Come to buy something, or just a chat?"

"Just a chat," said Lucia, taking off a scarlet rain hat and shaking out her dark curls.

"It's quiet today." Priscilla went behind the counter and picked up a jug of coffee. "Care to join me?"

"Thank you."

"So what's new in Lochdubh? Everyone must be feeling cheered up at the arrest of Beck. When these awful things happen, I'm always frightened it might turn out to be one of us."

"Someone still might be determined to make it one of us." Lucia perched on a chair at the counter and took the cup of coffee Priscilla was holding out to her.

"What do you mean?"

"Well," began Lucia primly, and Priscilla reflected that not only had the beautiful Lucia lost her charming Italian accent but was rapidly assuming the mannerisms of a Scottish village housewife of the gossipy variety, "Hamish Macbeth is going around tormenting everyone and saying this man, Beck, did not murder Duggan but one of us did."

"And why should he say that?"

"It's his pride. He's begun to believe he solved all those past cases himself."

"He did!"

"We have only his word for it."

"Oh, no, I was there at some of them, and believe me, if it had not been for Hamish's brains and Highland intuition, some criminals would still be at large."

"Willie says there's another reason."

"That being?"

"That if it's Strathbane that's not convinced that Beck did the murder, then it stands to reason that Hamish should go around accusing one of us."

"I don't follow your reasoning."

"Don't you see, *Hamish* is the one who is the most likely suspect. He was the one who was saved from being beaten by Randy because of his death."

"I know Hamish Macbeth very well," said Priscilla severely, "and he would never harm anyone, let alone kill them."

Lucia dropped her long eyelashes and looked thoughtfully at her coffee cup. "I sometimes wonder if any of us really knows Hamish. I mean, I was shocked when I heard he had been found in bed with that Betty woman, and her someone else's fiancée, too."

Priscilla reached across the counter and firmly took Lucia's coffee-cup from her. "I can't spend any more time gossiping," she said. "I have work to do." Lucia picked up her rain hat and put it on. She walked to the door. With her hand on the door-knob she looked over her shoulder. "Poor Priscilla," she murmured, and then she left.

Priscilla grimly went back to stacking the shelves. Damn the philandering Hamish Macbeth. Because of Lucia's last remarks about Hamish and Betty, she had forgotten the earlier ones about Hamish's not believing Beck was the murderer.

John and Betty were still at the hotel. They were not due to leave until the end of the following week. She would be glad to see them go.

Towards evening, the rain eased off and a watery sun turned the sea loch to gold. Hamish, who had completed some long-neglected paperwork, stretched and yawned. He went outside and leaned on the garden gate.

He saw the Currie sisters approaching and wished he could turn and run indoors, but that would show guilt over having been found in bed with Betty, and what he did in his own bed in his own home was his business. Or so he told himself as both approached, with identical shopping baskets over their arms and the pale sun glinting on their glasses.

"You should be ashamed of yourself, ashamed of yourself," said Jessie, who had an irritating habit of repeating everything.

"What I do in my own bedroom is nothing to do with you."

"We're talking about you going round the village throwing suspicion on everyone so you don't get suspected of murdering that Duggan yourself," said Nessie.

"What!" Hamish looked every bit as bewildered as he felt.

"Accusing folks, accusing folks," snapped Jessie.

"You're the only one that has to worry," said Nessie. "Weren't you the one that stood to get a pounding from Randy Duggan and weren't you the one who was saved by his murder?"

"His convenient murder, his convenient murder," said Jessie.

"That's daft," said Hamish. "And who's been saying such a thing?"

"It's self-evident," said Nessie smugly.

Both sisters moved on.

Hamish stared after them and scratched his head. Now who had been putting that idea into their heads?

He had a sudden sharp longing to see Priscilla, not, he told himself severely, for any romantic reasons, but simply to toss around a few ideas.

He changed out of his uniform into a shirt, sweater and jeans, and drove up to the Tommel Castle Hotel. He parked the Land Rover, and as he was walking across the gravel of the forecourt, Betty came out.

Hamish blushed. "I'm sorry I haven't called you, Betty," he said awkwardly, vivid memories of what they had done together rushing into his head. "I did try once, but you were out."

"That's all right." She reached up and kissed him on the cheek. Hamish drew back hurriedly. "Where's John?"

"Around," she said carelessly. "Let's go up to my room and have a . . . chat." She wet her lips.

"No, no," babbled Hamish, backing towards the castle and stumbling as he went. "I'm on business."

He mopped his brow as soon as he was indoors. He went through to the hotel office where Priscilla was working at a computer. She gave him a closed look but said, "Take a chair and help yourself to coffee. I'll be through with this in a minute."

He poured coffee, sat down and watched as she competently typed out hotel accounts. The bell of her fair hair shone golden in a shaft of sunlight. He thought briefly of the dark swarthiness of Betty with a sudden stab of revulsion.

At last, she switched off the computer and said quietly, "Well, Hamish?"

"Well, Priscilla, I'm not going to chew over why I was in bed with Betty. I want to talk about the case."

"What case?"

"The murder of Randy Duggan, lassie."

Priscilla's face cleared. She suddenly remembered all that Lucia had said. "Oh, I heard you didn't believe Beck did it. It was Lucia who told me."

Hamish's features sharpened. "Since when have you been on gossiping terms with Lucia?"

"Since never. She dropped by for a chat, Hamish. She said you were going around saying you didn't believe Beck had done it, and she said as you were the prime suspect, you were trying to throw suspicion on everyone else, and probably the idea that Beck hadn't really done it would have come from Strathbane."

"If it had come from Strathbane, this village would still be crawling wi' policemen."

"Of course! Why didn't I think of that? I'll put that about and that will scotch that story."

"Will you?" Hamish looked at her gratefully.

Then he frowned down into his coffee-cup. "I think Willie's behind this. He probably sent Lucia around to spread the gossip. But why is Willie scared? It wouldn't surprise me if Lucia fears that Willie might have done it and Willie thinks she might be the guilty party."

"Do you think that's possible? I find it hard to believe. Can't they find out anything about Randy Duggan? If we knew who he was, we would then have a better idea as to why he was murdered and by whom."

"Nothing that I've heard," said Hamish gloomily. "If it was because he was a criminal and a Scottish criminal, Glasgow would be the place to start. But I'd need to go at my own expense, and money's a bit low at the moment."

Priscilla hesitated and then said, "I could lend you the money, Hamish."

"It's kind of you, but I'll manage somehow."

"What about the bank? You've a regular salary. Wouldn't they advance you something?"

He shook his head. "I've an overdraft as it is."

"Are you fit?"

"Why?"

"There's a prize for a thousand pounds over at Cnothan games. For hill-running. You used to be champion at that."

"A thousand pounds! When is it?"

"Tomorrow."

"Och, all the entries are in."

"You can still register. Colonel Darcy was telling Daddy that a lot of people were dropping out because of the bad weather."

Hamish brightened. "I'll go over to Cnothan and see what I can do. Care for a drive?"

Betty's coarse laugh sounded from the hall. Priscilla's face took on a closed look. "I'm too busy." She switched on the computer again. Hamish left, walking quickly through the reception area. He heard Betty call to him but he rushed out of the castle and leaped into the Land Rover, driving off at such speed that he sent a burst of gravel up against the windows of Priscilla's office.

He found, on reaching Cnothan, that he could still enter, and scraped together the necessary five-pound fee for doing so out of loose change in his pockets. Then he studied the course on a map. It looked gruelling and he wondered dismally whether he would be up to it or not. It ran across boggy tracts of moorland and then straight up the side of towering Ben Loss to the summit, down the other side, back round the flanks, and across the moorland again to the finishing line.

But he had a purpose to drive him on. Without that thousand pounds, there would be no money to go to Glasgow, and perhaps the real identity of Randy would remain lost forever along with that of his murderer.

Chapter 9

But at my back I always hear
Time's wingèd chariot hurrying near

—*Andrew Marvell*

Priscilla told one of the maids early that evening that Hamish Macbeth was to take part in the hill-running at Cnothan the following day, and the maid told the rest of the staff, who told the guests, and so in an hour's time the news had reached the village of Lochdubh and spread all over the place.

Many were determined to go over to Cnothan to see Hamish run. Ian Chisholm, the local garage owner, got out his carnival-coloured Volkswagon bus, painted bright red and yellow with the remainder of left-over paints to cover the rust, and put up a handwritten poster advertising a service to the Cnothan Highland Games.

The weather was calm and still, with a low sun shining on the waters of the loch. People were standing outside their cottages, gossiping. After the days and weeks of rain, Lochdubh was drying out and coming to life. Old resentments were forgiven and even Hamish's affair with Betty was forgotten as the villagers prepared to go to Cnothan to cheer their champion to the finishing line. The fact that Hamish was still looking for the murderer of Duggan had mostly been forgotten and was generally put down to a sort of mental aberration on Hamish's part. Murder had left Lochdubh, and the sun was shining.

Hamish took his kilt out of the wardrobe, but the moths had chewed several holes in it and the pleats badly needed pressing and there was an egg stain near the hem. He took out a pair of shorts instead and a pair of running shoes. Then he put any thought of the race to come firmly out of his head.

It was only when he awoke on the day of the race that he experienced the first real stab of apprehension. He had done no training at all. He was not particularly fit. He could only hope that the other runners were as ill-prepared. Cnothan was one of the small Highland games, not a big event the likes of Braemar.

Archie Maclean called round as Hamish was getting ready to depart. "I chust thought I would tell you," he said, "that the water bailiff over at the Cnothan estates is entering. His name is Bill French."

"So?" demanded Hamish impatiently.

"Himself was in the Special Air Service. Fit as a fiddle, made o' wire and steel."

"These ex-army men let themselves go to seed pretty quickly," said Hamish.

"Not this one. Heard he can run like the wind."

"Och, away wi' ye, Archie. You're trying to make me scared afore I even get to the starting post."

"Not me," said Archie. "My money's on you, Hamish, and don't you forget it, and the whole village is turning out to cheer you on."

And that made Hamish feel worse than ever.

It got even worse. As he moved off in the police Land Rover, the multi-coloured bus full of cheering villagers moved onto the road behind him, along with a long cavalcade of cars, and when the procession reached the gates of Tommel Castle Hotel, it was joined by even more cars. Hamish saw John and Betty and then Priscilla. He had a gloomy feeling that he was going to let everyone down and make a fool of himself into the bargain.

The sun shone remorselessly down and you could see for miles. No hope of the event being cancelled because of mist or rain. When the marquees and flags of the games appeared down in the valley and Hamish through the open window could hear the skirl of the pipes, he began to feel weak and helpless. He would not get near that prize money and he would have no hope of getting to Glasgow. Why had he been so stiff-necked and proud? Why hadn't he accepted Priscilla's offer of money?

He drove slowly into the large field reserved for parked cars and climbed down feeling stiff and old. It was because he no longer had a dog, he thought sadly. Towser had loved long walks in the hills.

Priscilla walked over the still-spongy grass to join him. "You don't look exactly confident," she said.

"It was a daft idea," muttered Hamish in a low voice. "I havenae done any training, and there's an ex-SAS man competing."

"You could always cancel."

"What! With the whole village here to see me! Don't be daft, lassie."

"Then just think of the money."

Unluckily for Hamish, the hill-running was the last event of the day. By the time he had watched the piping championships, caber-tossing, pigeon-plucking, ferret-chasing and all the other many activities, his heart was in his running shoes.

But at last the loudspeaker called for the competitors in the hill-running race to go to the starting line. Priscilla felt sorry for Hamish as his long lanky figure in a brief pair of shorts and a T-shirt sloped up to the starting line, where about fifteen tough and fit-looking men were waiting.

Hamish took up his position and waited with a dry mouth. "All the best, Hamish!" shouted some Lochdubh-ite and the rest of the village spectators began to cheer. He gave a limp wave and a weak smile.

They all crouched ready. Silence fell on the crowd. A curlew piped from the hillside. Then the starting pistol fired and they were off. Hamish set himself an easy pace, determined to do his best. He gained a good bit of advantage over the moorland, having run the course years before, knowing which treacherous bogs to avoid. Ben Loss was not a rock climber's mountain. Family parties often climbed its heathery flanks to picnic on the top. But for men running flat out, it was a gruelling climb. Hamish could feel his breath getting ragged and hear his heart pounding against his ribs, and to each heartbeat a voice cried in his brain, "Failure, failure, failure." And then, as he reached the summit and started the downward run, he saw the rest were ahead of him, with the powerful man he had earlier identified as Bill French, the water bailiff, leading the pack. All at once, he wanted to give up and sit down in the heather. His pace lagged. Then he decided to give it his best effort. He took a deep breath and prepared to run down that mountain and back across the moor as fast as he could. And then, just as he paused and stooped to retie the lace of one of his running shoes, there was the crack of a rifle from the heather over to his right and a bullet whizzed over his bent head. In a flash he realized that if he stopped any longer to find out who was firing at him, the marksman would take another shot at him.

He set off, this time running for his life.

* * *

"Here they come," cried Archie, who had sharp eyes. Priscilla peered through a powerful pair of binoculars and then lowered them and said in a sad voice, "Hamish is nowhere in sight."

"He never did any training, never any training," said Jessie Currie. "He's too lazy to run, and that's a fact."

The villagers gloomily watched the runners coming closer, with Bill French at their head.

Priscilla, worried now that Hamish might have collapsed, raised her binoculars to her eyes again.

And then she shouted to the villagers, who were turning away in disgust, "It's Hamish! He's coming! He's catching up!"

Startled, they all turned back and stared across the moorland.

And sure enough, there came Hamish Macbeth, long red-haired legs pumping like pistons. They started to cheer, at first tentatively and then hysterically, as Hamish pounded on.

"My God," said Ian Chisholm, "I haff neffer seen the like, and my money was on French!"

Hamish hurtled on. Bill French, hearing the cheering and cries of "Hamish," turned round, stumbled and fell in the heather and Hamish cleared his body in one great leap and went flat out over the finishing line, where he fell on the grass with his hands over his head.

Priscilla rushed to him. "Well done, Hamish."

"Shot," he gasped. "Up the Loss. Someone tried to kill me."

Priscilla gave a startled exclamation and ran towards the mobile police trailer. When she reported what Hamish had said and brought several policemen back with her, Hamish was sitting with his head in his hands. He quickly told the police what had happened. Soon police could be seen fanning up over the mountainside. Hamish, in a daze, accepted the prize money which, he was vaguely pleased to note, was in cash. A cheque would have disappeared into his overdraft. He then went over to the police trailer and led a second party up the mountain to show them where he had been shot at. But there was no evidence of anything, no spent cartridge cases, no sign anyone had been there, although there was such an expanse to cover, he knew they could well have missed something.

"Probably imagined it, Macbeth," said Sergeant Macgregor from Cnothan.

"I didn't," said Hamish stubbornly. "And I think it's tied up with the murder of Randy Duggan. Someone knows I don't believe Beck did it and someone wants me out of the way."

"Well, we cannae dae any mair but put in a report," said Sergeant Macgregor sourly, thinking of the paperwork and what Strathbane would say about all these policemen charging overtime looking for a supposed murderer.

Hamish arrived back at the police station at ten that night. The phone in the office was shrilling away and he was tempted not to answer it. At last he reluctantly picked it up.

Blair's voice snarled down the line. "Look here, pillock, stop trying to screw up my nicely solved case by wasting police time saying someone's trying to murder you because you know better than me."

"I don't think Beck murdered Duggan," said Hamish wearily.

"Well, it's time you did. In fact, I did you a favour. I told Daviot your poor auld brain is a wee bit strained these days and you need a break. Take a week off, he says. I say, do it."

Hamish opened his mouth to protest and then closed it again. Here was a perfect chance to go to Glasgow. He had the money and now he had the time.

"All right," he said meekly.

"Tell Macgregor over in Cnothan to cover for ye," said Blair, and rang off.

Hamish dialled Sergeant Macgregor's number. "Oh, the hell with it," said Macgregor when he heard Hamish's request. "I don't know why they bother keeping you on the force, and that's a fact."

"Anything up?" asked Hamish, hearing an odd note in the sergeant's voice.

Macgregor looked moodily at the shiny surface of his desk, where a single rifle bullet lay. A small boy had picked it up out of the heather at the top of Ben Loss, just where Hamish Macbeth had said he was shot at, and had brought it to Cnothan police station ten minutes before Hamish's call. But if he told Macbeth, then it would mean more paperwork. And anyway, it was probably from a deer rifle and had been lying there for ages. Besides, Blair had let him know forcibly that he considered the murder case of Randy Duggan solved and closed.

Macgregor picked up the bullet and then tossed it into the waste-basket. "Nothing's up," he said. "Good night to you."

Hamish wearily ran a hot bath, stripped and climbed into it and promptly fell asleep, waking to find the water stone cold. Cursing, he climbed out, aching in every bone, and towelled himself down. He went through to bed. The last thing he heard before he fell asleep again was a rhythmic pattering on the window.

Rain had returned to Lochdubh.

He awoke the following morning, thinking that he should pack up and head south to Glasgow. But there was something nagging at the back of his brain. And why go to Glasgow when the murderer was surely still around Lochdubh? And yet, in Randy's background lay the vital clue to the identity of the murderer. Then the fact that had been niggling away at him suddenly sprang into his brain and he cursed himself for a fool. Blair had said that Rosie Draly had been married and divorced ten years before. Yet Mrs. Beck had given the impression that her sister had never married. Bob Beck had said nothing about any husband. He scampered through to the police office in his pyjamas and dialled Mrs. Beck's number. With any luck she would be back in London and not yet at work.

Mrs. Beck's sharp voice answered the phone. "This is Police Constable Hamish Macbeth in Lochdubh," began Hamish.

"Why don't you stop persecuting me?" said Mrs. Beck. "Haven't I suffered enough? My husband a double murderer! I'm afraid to face the neighbours."

"It's just one wee thing," said Hamish soothingly. "Your sister was married?"

"That wasn't a marriage!"

"Well, was she married, or wasn't she?"

"Yes."

"Who to? When? Where?"

"Let me see, it would be in nineteen eighty-five. I didn't go to the wedding. It was in Inverness."

Hamish said patiently, although he felt like shouting at her, "What was the name of the man she married?"

"It was a Henry Beale. He was a journalist on the *Inverness Daily*."

"And when were they divorced?"

"He filed for divorce two days after the wedding." Her voice was full of bitter satisfaction. "That's why I never think of Rosie having been married."

"Have you an address for him?"

"Wait a bit."

And so Hamish waited, listening to the far-away sounds of Willesden. The windows must have been open, for he heard traffic passing and children playing. Then she came back on the line. "Number 423, Tipsel Road."

"Thanks," said Hamish quickly, after writing down the address. "I'll let you know if there's anything else."

He sat back and studied the address. Going to Inverness would mean precious time taken off his free week. But he could not ignore the fact that Rosie had been married, however briefly. She had managed to drive Bob Beck to murder. It was a long shot, but could this ex still have strong feelings for her, could he have decided she was having an affair with Randy and killed him? It just had to be checked out. Also, there was still the enigma that had been Rosie. Had she really known anything about Randy's background?

He packed a suitcase, deciding to drive to Inverness and, if there was nothing interesting there, drive on to Glasgow.

He wished it would stop raining. Nothing had had a chance to dry out. The air outside, he noticed as he slung his case into the Land Rover, was muggy and close. His bones ached abominably after the hill run. He felt weary in mind and body. He wished the sun would shine again and this wretched case would be solved. He hesitated for just a moment before climbing into the driving seat. How easy it would be to let it go. Beck had murdered Rosie. Why not let him take the rap for the murder of Duggan? But the murderer was still here, polluting the very air of Lochdubh, and he would never be able to find out who it was unless he found out exactly who Randy Duggan had been.

All the long way down to Inverness he turned over what he knew about the case in his mind. Perhaps the only reason he was really going to Glasgow was in the hope that there would be something in Duggan's background which meant that the murderer came from outside, that the murderer would not turn out to be someone in the village whom he knew.

Inverness was busier than ever. Where did they all come from? he marvelled, as he left his Land Rover in the multistorey by the bus station. Crowds everywhere, shopping, shopping, shopping, while the dingy seagulls screamed overhead. He walked up the Castle Wynd. The statue of Flora Macdonald still stared out blindly looking for the return of Bonnie Prince Charlie.

The office of the *Inverness Daily* was to be found up a stone staircase between two shops. It had a small circulation and ran to only two or three pages of mostly local news. A prize sheep, for example, took precedence over any atrocity in Bosnia.

In a large dusty room were two reporters and two typists, hammering away at computers. Hamish asked for Henry Beale, half expecting to be told the man was either dead or had moved on. A typist with her hair gelled into spikes said laconically, "Isnae here. Sheep sales at Lairg."

Hamish left quickly and weaved his way through the crowds back to where the Land Rover was parked. Now he had a weary wet drive back to Lairg. He took the Struie Pass after leaving Inverness, through Bonar Bridge, and then up through the heathery hills to Lairg.

The annual Lairg sheep sale was a huge event, the biggest sheep sale in Europe, and as he approached he realized with a sinking heart that there would be plenty of police on duty. He remembered he had a crofter friend in Lairg called Iain Seaton. He, Hamish, was officially on holiday and if asked, he could say he was looking for Iain. The air was full of the cries of sheep. There was a hectic air, almost of gambling fever, as each crofter hoped for a good price. A lot of them were dressed in the sort of clothes that people often believed only incomers, trying to be Highland, affected: knee-breeches, lovat socks, brogues, kilt jacket and tall stick. Hamish went into the shed where the bidding was going on and scanned the crowd. He did not know what Beale looked like but Hamish usually found reporters easily recognizable, as reporters, however Highland, carried about with them the same raffish air of their counterparts in London. And then he spotted a man at the edge of the ring, staring with weary boredom out of a pair of bloodshot eyes. He had an air of slightly drunken resentment as if he felt he were meant for better things and better places than the Lairg sheep sale. Hamish then spotted other reporter types nearby, but for some reason he could not explain, he felt sure the man with the bloodshot eyes was Henry Beale. He waited patiently until he saw Beale say something to the photographer next to him and then start edging his way out. Hamish was across the ring from him but he felt sure that Beale would make straight for the bar.

Sure enough, that was where he found him. It was a sort of café-cum-bar, selling coffee, tea, beer, whisky, hamburgers and bacon sandwiches.

Hamish saw Beale's broad tweed back and tapped him on the shoulder. "What d'ye want?" demanded Beale, swinging round. Hamish was not in uniform. "Mr. Beale? I wonder if I might hae a word."

"Oh, aye, but wait till I get a drink or I'll never get one, not with this crowd." Beale ordered three whiskies and when he was served poured them into the one glass. Hamish ordered one as well and then they shuffled outside into the soft rain, all the tables being taken. "I never bother to get water in this," said Beale gloomily. "There's enough o' the stuff falling out the sky."

"I am PC Hamish Macbeth from Lochdubh," began Hamish.

"So why the plain clothes?"

Hamish thought quickly. "I am assigned to the CID for this case."

"What case? Someone buggering their sheep?" sneered Beale. He took a gulp of whisky.

"Rosie Draly," said Hamish quietly.

"You've got someone for that," he said in a low voice, his drunken pugnacity suddenly leaving him.

"Aye, but we're just tying up the loose ends."

Beale gazed mournfully out at the milling throng. "You've already questioned me," he said. Of course Strathbane would have questioned him, thought Hamish.

"No one seems to have given us a verra clear picture of what Rosie Draly was really like," said Hamish. "Could you talk about her for a little?"

He gave a sigh. "Come over to my car," said Beale. "This rain's getting to me."

He led the way across the road to where a rusting old Volvo station wagon stood with a press sign in its window. He unlocked the doors. Hamish got in the passenger seat. "So," said Beale, after climbing carefully in the other side so as not to spill any of his drink, "what can I tell you that I havenae told the others?" No use asking him where he had been on the night of the murder. That would have been covered.

"How did you meet her?"

"She was giving a talk to some writers' circle in Inverness on creative writing. Why do they call fiction creative writing? What's uncreative writing?"

"Lairg sheep sale?"

"Aye, you could say that."

Beale took a sip of his drink before saying, "I wanted just a few paragraphs for the paper. We wouldnae normally have touched it but the editor's wife was a member of the writers' circle. Rosie talked a load of crud. She went on in Open-University–speak about linear progression. Know what she meant? The plot, man, the bloody plot. I remember thinking, why didn't the silly bitch say so?"

"Anyway, I was all set to escape at the end when the editor's wife insisted on introducing us and then left me with her over the tea and buns. She smiled at me and said those magic words, 'I've got a bottle of Scotch back in my hotel room.'

"So of course I went with her. Well, she filled me up with Scotch and then she said, 'I want you to marry me.' I got such a fright I nearly sobered up. I wanted to lie, to say that I was married already, but she went on talking. She said she had good contacts in newspapers in London and could advance my career, she said she had a good income. And so on. And the more she talked, the more I realized how lonely I was. I'd been married before but she'd run off and left me. I drank more and thought Rosie really looked a bit of all right. We didn't go to bed and I said yes, I'd marry her. And three weeks later and only meeting for a few lunches and dinners, we were married. I don't think I was sober for a moment. She paid for everything. She'd said a honeymoon wasn't necessary, she'd just move in with me. After the wedding we'd go and get her stuff from Glasgow. I sobered up all right on the wedding night. She wouldnae let me near her. She said it was too soon. Give her time. When she went to sleep, I got up to see if there was any whisky left. I found a letter to her sister she had been writing and hadn't finished and it was all about, 'You thought I couldn't get married, did you? Well, this is just to let you know . . .' That sort of crap. I sat down and had a long thought. I realized the bitch had coerced me into marriage to get even with this sister. I faced her with it next day and she didn't say anything, just sat and stared at me. I began to get scared of her. I thought she had a slate loose. I said either she make it a proper marriage, that is sleep with me, or get lost, and she said in a prim little voice—I'll never forget—'Then you had better file for a divorce.' "

There was a heavy silence while Beale nursed his glass and stared out at the rain.

Hamish turned the scene over in his mind and then said softly, "So you struck her."

"How did you know that!"

"What any man in those circumstances would do," said Hamish, who could not envisage raising his hand to any woman.

"Aye, well I slapped her about a bit and then I got drunk and then I went to see a lawyer. When I got back, she'd gone and so had the letter to her sister.

"From what I gathered from the police, she had in fact married me just to prove something to her sister. Och, women!"

He drained his glass, choked and wiped his mouth. He made restless movements as if to leave. Hamish fished in the capacious pocket of his waxed coat and produced a half-bottle of whisky he had had the forethought to buy in Inverness. He unscrewed the top and filled Beale's glass right up.

"Thank you," said Beale.

"I hope I'm not keeping you from the sheep sale."

"Och, no. The usual. I find out who got the highest price and then run a wee bit about the other prices. I've been doing it for years. That's where Rosie got me. Money. Promise o' security. Someone to warm my slippers in my old age. What was up wi' her?"

"Her agent thought she might be lesbian, although there is no proof of that at all."

"God, I wish there were some proof. Know what I mean? I've never felt so rejected and humiliated in my life! I could have killed her."

Another silence. The rain, increasing in force, drummed on the roof of the car.

"Someone murdered Duggan," said Hamish quietly.

"Here! What d'ye mean? Beck did it."

"I don't think so. I think Beck wanted to get even with his wife. He had done the one murder. Why not confess to the other? The police are all too happy to have it all wrapped up. What do you think?"

"I never knew Duggan." His eyes were sharp. "So you think it was someone else?"

"Aye. Did Rosie ever contact you again? Did she ever hint she might know something about this Duggan?"

"Never heard a word from the bitch and didn't want to."

Hamish, seeing he had finished his drink, poured him another, felt obliged to tell him to be sure and sober up before he drove back to Inverness, and then left him. Afterwards, he was to think that the rain must have affected his brain. It did not dawn on him at the time that he had told a reporter that he did not believe that Beck had murdered Duggan.

Blair was summoned to Superintendent Peter Daviot's office the following morning. Mr. Daviot had a copy of the *Inverness Daily* spread out on his desk. "Have you seen this?" demanded the superintendent in a thin voice.

"No, sir," said Blair curiously, wondering what a paper which specialized in stories no less dramatic than "Beauly Ferret Bites Housewife" could contain that should be so upsetting.

"Macbeth has been shooting his mouth off to some reporter called Beale about how he is looking for the murderer of

Duggan, how he does not believe that Beck did it. Dammit, isn't that the very Beale who was married to Rosie Draly? This is *sub judice*, apart from anything else. Where the hell is the bastard?"

"We gave him a week off."

"Then get him and bring him back, and I don't care if it takes every man on the force to do it."

Blair went out with a solemn face, but once outside began to whistle a jaunty tune. Macbeth was in deep shit. Life was good.

An hour later, Priscilla Halburton-Smythe, icily splendid and splendidly null, faced Blair and Anderson and Macnab in the office of the Tommel Castle Hotel. No, she did not have the faintest idea where Hamish Macbeth had gone. No, she could not even guess. Now, they were very busy, so if there was nothing else . . . ? In a fury, Blair crashed around Lochdubh, bullying and threatening. Then he went over to Cnothan to see Sergeant Macgregor. Hamish might have gone to see his stand-in.

Sergeant Macgregor had not seen the *Inverness Daily*, so when Blair said curtly, "Macbeth is missing. Have you seen him? Any idea where he is?" the sergeant suddenly thought guiltily of that spent rifle bullet lying in his waste-basket. If Macbeth was found dead and that wee boy came forward to tell the police about the rifle bullet, he would be in trouble. He surreptitiously pulled the waste-paper basket forward with his foot. "It's funny you should say that," he said. "I hae something here I was just going to phone you about." He bent down and jerked open the bottom drawer and then scrabbled quickly in the waste-paper basket, straightening up, holding out the bullet. "A wee boy found this up on Ben Loss where Hamish says he was shot at. I would hae reported it right away, but you said Macbeth was making it up."

Blair stared at that bullet. The policeman in him warred with the man who would have liked to ignore the whole thing. "What," he demanded wrathfully, "are you doing handling the thing with your great fat, stupid fingers? Anderson, take it from him and put it in an envelope."

Jimmy Anderson took out a pair of tweezers and lifted the bullet from Macgregor's now sweating hand and dropped it into a plastic envelope. "You'll hear further of this," said Blair. "Now where's Macbeth?"

"I don't know. He just said he was off for a week."

"I'll get that bastard," growled Blair. But no one thought of calling the Glasgow police.

And Hamish could have continued his investigations quietly when he got to Glasgow had it not been for the reaction of Peter Daviot when he heard about that rifle bullet. He had just heard of Hamish's view that Beck did not murder Duggan. He remembered all the times Hamish had been right when all the evidence pointed the other way. Then Hamish was missing and there was that bullet.

He shuddered to think of the scandal if Hamish Macbeth were found dead. An official photograph of Hamish was dug out of the files and issued to the press. An all-stations alert was put out. They could not rouse Hamish on his radio, for he had switched it off.

Hamish, however, had his car radio tuned into a pop-music station and was whistling along to it as he approached the outskirts of Glasgow. Then the music died away and a serious announcer's voice said, "We interrupt this broadcast for a special announcement." In a sweat, Hamish listened to the voice which went on to say that Constable Hamish Macbeth was to report to the nearest police station. He pulled into a garage by the side of the road and sat staring miserably through the windscreen. He remembered what he had said to Beale, a reporter, of all people. It was too good a story for Beale to ignore. And then he turned and looked out at the rack of newspapers outside the garage. No photograph of himself stared out from the pages; but he climbed out and bought a copy of the *Daily Record*. There it was in the stop press. "Highland cop who believes Beck currently under arrest for the murder of Randy Duggan did not do it has gone missing. All-stations alert."

There would be a photograph of him in the papers the next day, he was sure of it. It was a miracle his conspicuous police Land Rover had not been spotted.

He drove to Bearsden on the outskirts of Glasgow, a wealthy suburb, and drove to a trim bungalow owned by some cousin, so distant on the Macbeth family tree, a mere twig, that he had not seen her in years. Her name was Josie Sinclair. To his delight he saw a wooden garage at the end of the small drive next to the bungalow. It was empty. Without checking at the house first, he drove the police Land Rover straight into it, lifted out his suitcase, walked out and closed the garage doors behind him.

A dog barked sharply from within the house, Josie appeared at the back door, shouting, "Who's there?"

"It's me, Hamish." He strolled forward, carrying his suitcase.

Josie was a small, dark-haired woman with a chinless face and prominent nose.

"Heavens," she said. "Hamish! I've just been hearing about you on the radio. But come in. Tell me what on earth is happening."

Hamish followed her into the bungalow. He felt suddenly weary. He wondered whether to start to tell a series of whopping lies, but one look at Josie's worried honest eyes made him settle for the truth. "Sit down, Josie," he said. "It's a long story."

Josie listened while he outlined the murders of Duggan and Rosie and then explained what he was doing in Glasgow.

She listened carefully without comment, but when he had finished, she said, "My son, Callum, is away in the Gulf, so you can have his room." Hamish remembered suddenly her husband had died three years before. "There's only one thing. Even if you find the real murderer, or anything leading to who the right murderer might be, you're not going to have a job to go back to."

"I'll take that risk. Look, Josie, I think there might be a picture of me in the papers tomorrow. I'll need to change my appearance."

"I'll do my best for you, Hamish. I'll always do my best for the family. But you'll need to keep me out of it."

"I promise, Josie."

"So how are you going to get about? You can't drive that police thing."

"I'll think o' something."

"I've still got my poor Johnny's driving license. You could use that to rent a car. If you're caught, you must say you broke in here and stole it."

"You're a brick, Josie."

She gave a reluctant laugh. "I'm a daft fool. Well, let's get started after we have a cup of tea. It's a good thing for you that I dye my hair. The first thing to do is to get rid of that red hair of yours."

By late afternoon, Hamish had short black hair, a black moustache made from cuttings of his own hair, and a pair of wire-rimmed glasses. Wearing one of the late Johnny Sinclair's business suits and in possession of a hired car, he drove into

Glasgow. He parked the car and went to a phone box and called an old friend of his, Detective Sergeant Bill Walton.

"Don't say my name," said Hamish when Bill came on the phone. "Don't shop me, Bill, I need to see you."

"I'm off duty in half an hour," said Bill in his usual flat voice. Bill, Hamish remembered, never seemed to be surprised at anything. "You'd best come round to my flat. It's in Bath Street, next to that new hotel." He gave Hamish the address.

Hamish left the car where it was and then slowly walked to Bath Street. He stood in a doorway opposite Bill's flat. His heart sank when a police car screamed up, seemingly full of policemen. But only Bill got out and the car drove off. Still Hamish waited until he saw Bill go upstairs.

After a few more cautious moments, he crossed the road and rang the bell. The door buzzer went and he let himself in and climbed the stairs. Bill was waiting at the top.

"You look like a bank clerk on a bad day," he commented. "It is yourself, is it not?"

"Aye," said Hamish.

He followed Bill into a dark and dingy flat. Bill switched on a two-bar electric heater in the grate and pulled the curtains closed and then switched on the light. Landlord's furniture, thought Hamish, looking round the dismal living-room, but no sign of any woman. Good. Just Bill.

Bill Walton was a tall middle-aged man with a face like Buster Keaton. "So you're on the run, are you, Hamish? And in disguise? You'd best have a dram and tell me all about it before I send for the wee men in the white coats."

So for the second time that day, Hamish talked and talked about the murder cases while Bill listened patiently.

"I've never doubted your intelligence before, Hamish," said Bill when Hamish had finished. "But, man, what were you about to tell a reporter all about it?"

"I don't know," said Hamish miserably. "It must have been the damn rain."

"What are you talking about?"

"You don't know. You don't live in the Highlands," said Hamish obscurely.

"So I'm supposed to turn you in and if I'm found out helping you in this, I'll lose my job and I haven't long to go before retirement. But a lot of what you've said makes sense, don't ask me why. This Randy had plastic surgery. How can you pick his face out o' the rogues' gallery when the experts couldn't?"

"I'll bet they werenae looking hard enough and dropped the whole thing when Beck confessed," said Hamish. He added shrewdly, "And I'll bet Blair managed to put up so many backs in Glasgow that they didnae really bother."

"Dreadful pillock, that man, Blair. I remember when he was a copper down here. Yes, you're right, he did put backs up. You know how it goes. We don't like being bossed around by another force, and a Highland one at that."

"So is there any way I could get a look at the rogues' gallery?"

"Looking like you do, no one would recognize you. I can just march you into the station. But what rogues' gallery do you want to look into? Murderers, muggers, rapists? What?"

"If it were a revenge killing," said Hamish slowly, "then there would be money involved, possibly a lot of money."

"So you're looking for a big-time robbery?"

"Something like that."

"I've got a date tonight," said Bill and then blushed.

"I neffer thought of you as a ladies' man."

"I'm not. This is someone special. You're in for a late night. Off with you now and meet me at headquarters at one in the morning. It'll be real quiet then. People are always looking through photos. I'll meet you outside and take you in."

"Thanks, Bill. I'll never forget this."

"I've a feeling I won't either. Now remember, if you're caught, I didn't know who you were. You tricked me."

"I promise."

"Okay. See you later."

Hamish went out into the evening. He did not want to go back out to Bearsden. He phoned Josie from a call-box and told her not to expect him back that night. He then went to a cinema. He was never quite sure afterwards what the film was that he saw. The enormity of what he had done was seizing up his brain. Why on earth had he not believed Beck? Why had he not gone to Strathbane with his doubts? Why had he assumed they would take Beck's word for it without checking thoroughly?

Away from his native Highlands and here in this vast, bustling city full of uncaring people, he felt like the Highland idiot people often thought he was. He could not seem to think clearly any more.

He had a dismal meal in an all-night café and then went back to the car-park and sat and waited for one in the morning. He nearly fell asleep but jerked himself fully awake and glanced at the clock on the dashboard. Ten to one.

He hurried out of the car-park and raced round to police headquarters. Bill was standing outside, waiting impatiently. "Come on," he snapped. "I'm beginning to regret this."

He led the way upstairs after signing Hamish in as Mr. Sinclair. He put Hamish in a bleak cubby-hole of a room and said sternly, "Wait here." So Hamish waited, listening to the night-time sounds of the city, trying to clear his brain, which was becoming even more fogged with anxiety. After some time, Bill came back carrying heavy books of photographs. "You can start with these," he said curtly. All his previous friendliness had gone. Bill was obviously regretting his decision to help Hamish.

Hamish took off the glasses and blinked for a moment myopically to get his own very good eyesight back into focus. He began studying the faces in the books while a white-faced clock on the wall ticked away the minutes and then the hours. What would Randy have changed about his features? Nose? Chin? Hairline? He wouldn't have had plastic surgery for beauty, that was for sure, but simply to hide his identity. At six in the morning, Bill came in and thumped a cup of coffee in front of Hamish. "Going to be much longer?" he asked curtly.

Hamish sighed and ran his thin fingers through his short dyed hair. His brain suddenly seemed to clear up. He tapped the books. "Which of these villains has been involved in major robbery? Or, look, let me put it another way. Let's go for the big time. What was the biggest robbery of cash in Glasgow in recent years?"

Bill sat down, suddenly curious. "I suppose you mean unsolved robbery. Well, let me see, there was the break-in at the Celtic Bank. No, wait a bit, we got someone for that. I know, nineteen eighty-nine. Another bank."

"The Scottish and General?" asked Hamish, suddenly remembering John Glover.

"No, it was the Clyde and South-Western Bank. The head office in Hope Street."

"What happened?"

"They hijacked the manager from his home. One man stayed behind with a gun held at his wife and children. Manager did what they said. Opened up the bank. Opened up the safe. Got away with over two millions pounds."

Hamish fingered the books eagerly. "Who was suspected?"

"There's a villain we've only heard about from our under-world contacts. Known as Gentleman Jim. Supposed to have been the brains behind it. We pulled in several of the usual low life who might have done this but couldn't crack any of them. This Gentleman Jim seems to run a reign of terror. But unlike the Kray brothers, no one on the force knows who he is. Villains get drunk, villains brag, but no one will give us a murmur about him."

"So who did you pull in to question on this robbery?"

Bill pulled forward the books and began to skim through them. "Usual lot. All of them with alibis. Where are they?"

"Holding a gun on a woman and kids," mused Hamish. "Who have you got that would be nasty enough for that?"

"I'll scribble you a list of names and leave you to it. But one hour more, Hamish, and that's your lot."

Hamish stared at the list of names and then the books. Forget about what Randy had looked like when he knew him. Think of really bad villains. His brain now very sharp and clear, he opened the books again. The door opened. Bill came in and put a photo of Randy on the desk. "You might need that," he said.

Hamish looked at the photograph. It was not one made up from the cleaned-up corpse of Randy. It had been taken by someone of a group standing in the Lochdubh bar. It was a good clear shot of Randy. He couldn't have known the photograph was being taken, for he was not looking at the camera but talking to a group of locals, including Andy MacTavish and Archie Maclean. For once he wasn't wearing his ridiculous slatted glasses and his hat was tilted back on his head.

Keeping the photograph beside him, Hamish studied the list of names again and began to find photographs in the books to match them.

His eyes kept returning to one photograph. It was of a thin-faced man with short straight hair. His very shoulders were thin. He had had previous convictions for armed robbery and inflicting grievous bodily harm. His name was Charlie Stoddart. But there was something about that face, about the arrogant, malicious gleam in the eyes that the camera had caught.

He looked from the photo in the file to the one of Randy beside him on the desk. What if Randy had gone in for body-building as well as plastic surgery? What if he had become a big heavy-set, powerful man?

He became aware that Bill was standing in the doorway, watching him curiously. "Got anything?"

"Come and have a look at this," said Hamish.

Bill walked forward and peered over his shoulder. "That's never Duggan!"

"There's something about it," said Hamish. "Same way o' looking. Think, man. He could have gone in for body-building or taken steroids. Then the plastic surgery. Is he currently under arrest?"

"No, I remember we pulled him in for questioning over that bank robbery, but he had an alibi and we had to let him go."

"Can you get me his last known address?"

"Sure."

Bill left and Hamish waited impatiently. When Bill returned, Hamish seized the address.

"I should keep clear of you," said Bill, "but I'm off duty and I'll go with you. But if anyone recognizes you, I'll swear I didn't know it was you."

"All right," said Hamish with a grin. "Let's see if we can find Charlie Stoddart."

The rain continued to fall in the Highlands, dampening the souls of the inhabitants of Lochdubh, causing general depression, which meant that the staff of the Tommel Castle Hotel kept falling "sick," with the usual Highland-excuse ailments of bad backs and viruses.

John Glover and Betty John would be leaving the following morning. Priscilla, who was manning the reception desk, had said she would have their bill ready for them before they left. John had issued no more invitations to lunch or dinner and Priscilla was glad of that. She had taken a hearty dislike to the couple. She gave a little start when she realized both were standing before her.

"I see your Hamish has his photo in the newspapers this morning," said John. "It says he's gone missing. Know where he is?"

"Not a clue," said Priscilla.

"Do you believe someone really shot at him at the Cnothan games?" asked Betty.

Priscilla gave her a long cool look. "Yes, I do. Hamish is never mistaken in things like that."

"Someone in the village said he had been told to take a week off because they thought he was suffering from stress," said John.

"He suspected that Randy Duggan had not been killed by Beck," remarked Priscilla, "so I think Strathbane wanted him out of the road."

"Well, let's hope he's all right," said Betty, taking John's arm in her own. "The bar's open. Let's have a drink."

Priscilla watched them as they walked away. She had thought her dislike of them was because of Betty's fling with Hamish, but now she decided she did not like either of them just because of the way they were. There was a cockiness about them, an insolence, and she began to wonder if John had briefly courted her as some sort of joke.

Willie Lamont ran home from the restaurant and waved a newspaper in front of Lucia. "Do you see this? Hamish has gone missing."

"Let's hope he stays missing," she said coldly. "He was causing a lot of trouble with his stupid suspicions."

"But he could be dead!" wailed Willie. "He could have driven over a cliff."

Lucia gave a little curved smile. "Good," she said, and tossed the paper away.

Annie Ferguson was serving tea to Geordie Mackenzie. Annie had made one of her rare visits to the Lochdubh bar the night before. It had been nearly empty, as the fishing boats were out and the forestry workers were all at Andy MacTavish's birthday party. But Geordie had been there and she had issued the invitation to tea.

"I cannot understand this business about our Hamish going missing," said Geordie primly. "It bothers me. Look at it this way. Hamish goes around saying Duggan was not killed by Beck, Hamish gets shot at, and then no one can find him."

"Och, our Hamish is a bit o' a drama queen," said Annie. "He says he was shot at but we've only his word for it. Take it from me, Geordie, that man is sulking because he won't admit he was wrong about Randy's murder. Forget about him. Hamish Macbeth has a slate missing, if you ask me. Have another scone."

Chapter 10

O villain, villain, smiling, damned villain!

—William Shakespeare

Charlie Stoddart's last known address was in a depressing block of tower flats on the south side of the city.

Bill said it was due for demolition, and it had such a cracked, rusted, deserted air that it looked as if the demolition process had already started. Children did not play on the scrubby, balding, litter-strewn grass outside. At some point an attempt had been made to plant trees, but they had been savagely destroyed and only a few cracked, white shattered stumps lay around for mangy dogs to pee against.

The entrance hall was covered in graffiti. The lifts did not work and Bill said gloomily that they probably had not worked for some time. From checking the flat number in his notes, he said with even more gloom that Charlie lived on the top floor. They climbed onwards and upwards. There were occasional sounds of life to show that some flats in the block were still tenanted: a baby cried, a dreary, lost wail of sound; a man swore suddenly and violently; a woman shouted abuse.

Nobody wanted to live in these tower blocks, and so gradually the decent people had left and the flotsam and jetsam of humanity stayed behind, corrupting each other with their violence and misery and filth. No one, reflected Hamish, had such a talent as the bottom rung of the Scottish social ladder for sheer filth and decay. There were smells of urine and vomit, stale beer, and the cooking diet of the poor: fish fingers, chips and baked beans.

By the time they reached the outside of Charlie's flat, Hamish was beginning to feel light-headed with fatigue. He took off the late Mr. Sinclair's glasses and tucked them in his pocket. The lenses were beginning to give him a headache. The balconies outside the flats with their rusted railings were open to the salty, muggy, wet air blowing up from the river Clyde. Litter blew along the passageways. A dirty newspaper wrapped itself around Hamish's legs and he impatiently tore it away.

"Well, here it is," said Bill, stopping outside a chipped and scarred door. "But if there's anyone still here, it'll be a miracle."

He knocked loudly on the frosted glass of the door and they waited while the wind shrilled through the metal railings. Hamish leaned against the wall and wished it were all over and he was back home again.

Bill knocked loudly again and shouted, "Police! Open up!"

The door next to the one he was hammering on opened suddenly and a woman looked out.

"You'll no' get anyone in there, Jimmy," she said. "Hisnae been anyone there for a bit. Mrs. Stoddart left wi' the weans last month."

Hamish found the Glaswegian way of addressing everyone as Jimmy highly irritating. "Where did she go?" he asked.

"Ower Castlemilk way, Jimmy," said the woman laconically.

"And what about Charlie?" asked Bill.

"Och, that one went off a few years ago. Meant fur better things." She screeched with laughter.

"Have you an address in Castlemilk?"

"Wait a wee bit. Sharon, come here!"

The woman was small, stunted and ill-favoured. Sharon, on the other hand, was a giantess with dyed blond hair, thick lips, and vacant eyes. "Whaur in Castlemilk did Jeannie Stoddart go?" asked the woman, who seemed to be Sharon's mother.

"Lenin Road," said Sharon. "Nummer 52. I ken 'cos I wrote it doon. I always remembers what I write doon."

Bill and Hamish left and made their way down the miles of stairs and back out again. On the road to Castlemilk, Hamish fell asleep in the car, and when he awoke for a few moments he did not know where he was or what he was supposed to be doing.

Lenin Road did not seem to be any improvement on the tower block. Although it consisted of a row of two-storey houses with gardens, most of the windows were boarded up and the gardens were untended, and practically all had either no fences or the ones that had had wooden ones were contained now by only a few smashed pieces of wood.

They knocked at Mrs. Stoddart's door. To Hamish's relief, there were sounds of movements inside.

Bill shouted, "Police, Mrs. Stoddart."

The door opened suddenly. A woman stared at them. She was middle-aged with thick hair dyed yellow-blond. She was heavily made up, wearing ski pants and a low-cut cotton top. A tom, thought Hamish. Whatever she was before, Jeannie Stoddart is on the game, a prostitute.

"What d'ye want?" she asked sullenly.

"Where's Charlie?" asked Bill.

Two women stopped behind them at the garden gate and stared curiously. "Come inside," said Jeannie. She led the way into an overcrowded, fussy living room which seemed at first glance to be full of stuffed toys, magazines, and dolls from different countries.

She sat down and lit a cigarette and then said evenly, "I don't know where Charlie is and that's a fact."

"When did you last see him?"

"Nineteen eighty-nine."

The year of that bank robbery, thought Hamish, waking up again.

"Where did he say he was going?"

"I'm telling you, Mac, by that time he wasnae even speaking to me. I wasnae good enough fur him any more. Went off with his posh friends."

Bill looked at her cynically. "Charlie with posh friends? Pull the other one."

"It's true! Man wi' a big Mercedes used tae drop him off."

"And who was this man?"

She gave a half-ashamed sort of laugh. "It seems daft now. But I believed it at the time. Charlie said he was working for British Intelligence."

"Why would British Intelligence want to employ a toe rag like Charlie?" Bill's tired voice was heavy with sarcasm.

"He made it sound very convincing," she said defensively. "He said they got hold of him during his last stretch in prison, and they said if he worked for them, they'd shorten his sentence. There wus a play on the telly about that."

"Probably where Charlie got the idea from," said Hamish. He was sitting opposite Jeannie, his knees nearly touching hers. "Look," he coaxed, "you must have got a glimpse of the man in the Merc."

"Whit's in it for me?" she demanded truculently, her accent thickening.

"A hundred," said Hamish, cutting across Bill's exclamation that it was Jeannie's duty to tell the police everything that she knew.

"Let's see it."

Hamish turned away and peeled five twenties from the prize money in his inside pocket. She reached for it but he held it away. "Description first," said Hamish. "And make it a good one."

"Charlie told me never to look. He said the man in the posh car was the big boss. The boss dropped him back late one night when I couldnae sleep. I took a peek out o' the window. As Charlie got out, the man lit a cigarette. He had black hair, going grey, face like an executive."

"What do you mean by that?" asked Bill impatiently.

"Sort of tanned, well shaved, good suit, silk tie."

"Any distinguishing marks?"

She shook her blond head. "Nuthin' important. Big thick gold wrist-watch, cream shirt." She looked hungrily at the money. Hamish slowly passed it over. The beginning of a dreadful idea was forming in his brain. He nodded to Bill and got to his feet. Bill followed Hamish out. "What's the matter?" he asked.

Hamish leaned against the car and said slowly, "Look here. Think about this. I've described all the suspects to you. But there's one I didn't really concentrate on. At the time of the murder, there was this banker, John Glover, staying at the Tommel Castle Hotel. He said he was the bank manager of the Scottish and General Bank in Renfrew Street. Credit cards matched, car registration matched. Phoned the bank. Yes, Mr. Glover was on holiday in the Highlands. Nothing to worry about there. Fiancée called Betty John arrives. Romances me and tells me stories about the bank. Seems to know what she's talking about. But we never called at John Glover's home or asked for a photo of him."

"You think Charlie's posh boss could be someone posing as this banker?"

"It could be, and his boss could be this mysterious Gentleman Jim you've all been looking for."

"Hamish, Hamish, this is all a wee bit far-fetched. Och, I tell you what we'll do. We'll go to the Scottish and General and put your fears to rest. If I could nail this Gentleman Jim before I retire, it would be the height o' my career, and things like that just don't happen."

They drove in silence back into the centre of the city and stopped outside the bank.

They were received by the deputy manager, a Mr. Angus, a small, portly man with a pompous air.

"You've already asked all the questions," he said impatiently. "Mr. Glover is due back Monday. He always holidays up north and no, he doesn't leave an address, says he doesn't want to be bothered. I am perfectly able to handle things here in his absence." Mr. Angus looked as if he believed that he could run things better than Mr. Glover any day.

"And you have his fiancée, Betty John, as an employee?"

"Yes," said Mr. Angus testily, dashing Hamish's hopes.

Faint but pursuing, he said, "We would like to see a photograph of Mr. Glover."

"Oh, for heaven's sake. I don't carry photos about with me."

"Perhaps," ventured Bill, "there might be one taken at a staff function?"

"Oh, one of those." Mr. Angus's face cleared. "There's one taken at the Christmas party on the wall of his office next door."

He led them through and into a wood-panelled room with a large desk and the gloomy air of a million rejected bank loans.

He lifted a framed photograph down from the wall and held it out to them.

Hamish looked at it and then said in a voice sharp with alarm, "Which is John Glover?"

"Why, there, next to Miss Betty John."

It was Betty all right, but the man next to her was thin and stooped, with glasses and a tentative smile.

"That's not the John Glover who's been holidaying in Lochdubh," said Hamish bleakly. "Get us his home address, *now*!"

"You mean someone's been impersonating him?" said Mr. Angus, looking flustered.

"Just get the address," howled Bill.

"Are you going to call for back-up?" asked Hamish.

"We'll do that from the car on the road there."

Mr. Angus came back with an address in Hyndland Road in the west end of the city.

Priscilla, thought Hamish, as they raced through the streets. As soon as we see what's happened, I'd better warn Priscilla.

"There's your bill, Mr. Glover," Priscilla was saying.

"Thank you." He handed over a gold credit card. "We've enjoyed our stay. We'll just have a last cup of coffee and then we'll be on our road. Back to the unexciting life of banking, hey?"

Betty, standing beside him, let out a snort of laughter. Then both headed in the direction of the restaurant, looking, thought Priscilla suddenly, more like conspirators than lovers. Maybe lovers look like conspirators, jeered a voice in her head. How would you know, Priscilla?

She gave a little sigh. Still short-staffed, rain still falling. She may as well check their rooms and see if they had left anything behind. She took down the pass key and went upstairs. She went into Betty's room first. A suitcase and a hold-all stood packed and ready on the floor. She went into the bathroom. Nothing there. She went next door to John's room with a certain reluctance. She had an uneasy feeling John had *used* her. But why should she think that? They were obviously an immoral couple. Just think of Betty and Hamish! No, better not think of that. John had two suitcases—very expensive, Gucci—packed and ready. Nothing left in the bathroom. He had made his bed. How odd! He did not look the sort of man to bother making up his bed. And so neatly, too. Hospital corners. He must surely know the beds would be stripped the minute they had left. And who was to strip the beds? Me, thought Priscilla grimly, thinking of the absent maids. Might as well make a start.

She wrenched off the duvet and threw it on the floor, took off the cover, and then tugged at that firmly tucked-in under-sheet. She placed it on the floor. Then the pillowslips. She went to the linen cupboard at the end of the hall and took out a fresh duvet cover, sheet and pillowslips and returned to John's room. She knew she was being over-efficient. The next person who would take this room was not expected to arrive until the following morning. She knew she was playing the martyr. Some of the missing maids would surely soon be back on duty. Still, may as well use martyrdom to get some necessary jobs done.

And it was this wretched martyrdom of hers, Priscilla was to think later, that had made her decide to turn the mattress as well.

She heaved it up and over and then drew in her breath in a sharp exclamation of surprise. For under the mattress lay two leather gun cases. She backed away from the bed, her eyes flying to the phone on the bedside table.

And then a voice behind her said grimly, "Leave the phone alone, Miss Halburton-Smythe."

Hamish and Bill arrived outside John Glover's flat, which was in a tall sandstone building. They rang all the bells until the buzzer went on the door. "Who is it?" called a voice from the top of the stairs.

"Police!" shouted Bill. "Which is Mr. Glover's flat?" There had been no cards next to the bells.

"Number one, ground floor," quavered the voice from above.

"I hope to God we're right about this," said Bill, "for I'm about to smash in a good piece of Victorian stained glass." He took a small, unofficial truncheon out of his trousers pocket and smashed at the glass. Brightly coloured shards flew everywhere. He reached through the hole he had made and removed a chain and clicked the safety catch off the lock. "Easy," he said. "You'd think a bank manager would be more security-conscious. Jesus! Smell that, Hamish!"

There was a rank, sweetish smell, only too familiar to both men. In the distance they could hear the wail of police sirens. They did not have far to look for the real John Glover. Recognizable—just—from that photograph in the bank, he lay dead on his living-room floor among the ransacked debris of emptied drawers and cupboards. He had been strangled.

"Where's this fake John Glover now?" asked Bill.

"Tommel Castle Hotel. I cannae wait," said Hamish. "I've got to get there."

"Man, you may as well take a back seat now," said Bill. "They'll call out Strathbane."

"I've got to try," said Hamish. "There's someone I know might be in danger. I'm in enough trouble as it is. Give me the keys to your car, Bill. I did this for you."

Bill tossed him the keys as police burst into the room. "Let him go," snapped Bill as the police tried to grab hold of Hamish. "He's one of us."

"So what do we do with her?" Betty John was asking. Priscilla was gagged with sticking plaster and bound to a chair in the fake John's room.

"We wait," said "John" easily. "You go downstairs and tell that manager that Miss Halburton-Smythe has taken off for Inverness, then we wait until the lunch is over and the hotel is quiet again and then we take her out."

"What are we going to do with her?"

"Take her up in the hills and lose her," he said. "By the time she finds her way back and alerts the police, we'll be long gone."

"Why didn't we just clear off after you had got rid of Duggan?" fretted Betty.

"Then they would have guessed right away. Don't worry, we'll still get clear."

Betty's next words horrified Priscilla.

"When Glover doesn't turn up at the bank on Monday, they'll start searching for him."

"I thought of that. I'll phone in sick on Monday and then we'll disappear for a bit."

Priscilla listened with her eyes half closed. There was no Hamish to ride to the rescue. She did not believe for one moment that "John" meant to let her go. He would kill her as callously as he had killed the real bank manager and Duggan.

All she could do was wait and pray for a miracle. Betty went out. "John" surveyed her with a smile. "You're a silly, interfering bitch," he said. "It amused me to stay on here and play games with you and that loon of a boy-friend of yours. No one crosses me and gets away with it. You know what Duggan did?"

And you're going to tell me, thought Priscilla, because you're going to kill me, so it doesn't matter what I know now.

"He was told to stash a haul from a bank robbery and then report to my house for the share-out. We waited and waited. His name isn't Duggan, it's Charlie Stoddart. I couldn't believe the little bastard had made off with the money, but that's what he did. I kept a wait and watch. I traced him as far as America. I had all the planes watched, all the flights from America. There was a rumour he'd gone in for weight-lifting and plastic surgery. Then, by some fluke, the bastard got drunk one night in Houston, Texas, and shot off his mouth. The fellow he talked to knew I had a reward out for information, phoned me up and gave me his new name. He'd sobered up the next day and taken fright and got on a plane to Scotland. I missed him in Glasgow, but picked up his trail north. Probably thought the last place I would look for him was back in Scotland. I've got my reputation to think of. The underworld has to know that no one; *no one*, crosses Gentleman Jim and gets away with it."

He is nothing but a common criminal, thought Priscilla bleakly. How could I be so *stupid*?

Betty came into the room. "Okay," she said. "Thank God for the rain. No one will be hanging outside when we take her out. But to make sure, I've parked the car at the foot of the back stairs. Listen, you are going to let her go? I mean, there's been enough killing."

"Of course," said John. "Now, let's wait."

There was a mobile phone in the car but Hamish decided not to phone Priscilla. If she knew the real identity of the murderer, she might betray herself. Anyway, Strathbane would soon be racing over to the hotel, but just in case there was any hold-up, he had to try to get there.

He phoned the airport manager and asked if there was any plane about to take off to Inverness and was told only a private jet belonging to Mr. Morton of the Hillington Electronics Company. Hamish asked to be put through to him and Mr. Morton listened intrigued to Hamish's urgent Highland voice telling him why he had to get north in a hurry. "I'll take you," said Mr. Morton. "Come straight out on the runway. Then I can take you up by helicopter from Inverness."

He told Hamish how to get to the runway he was on. Hamish turned on the blue light and the siren and weaved his way through the traffic on the road to the airport.

He looked at his watch. Only ten in the morning! A lifetime seemed to have passed since they went to that tower block.

"What's the time?" asked Betty. "John" looked at the heavy gold watch on his wrist. "Early yet," he said laconically.

"I'm worried," said Betty. "Someone's bound to come."

"Did you hang the 'Do Not Disturb' sign outside the door?"

"Yes."

"Well, we've got the room until twelve. We'll wait until their lunch is over and then take her out."

"What if we meet someone in the corridor? You can't keep a gag on her."

"She'll have a gun in her ribs. She won't even squeak if she wants to stay alive." He smiled at Priscilla. "Will you, sweetie?"

Priscilla looked at him with hate. She was so sure he was going to kill her that she felt she ought to be brave enough to go down in flames. But such a villain would simply shoot anyone who tried to come to her aid.

* * *

They tried to prevent Hamish Macbeth from driving onto the tarmac: police car or not, he was told he needed clearance. A pig-faced policeman at the barrier leading to the runway said pontifically, "You jist wait where you are, laddie, while I make a few phone calls."

Hamish watched his fat retreating back in a fury. At the far end of the runway, he could see a Learjet, Mr. Morton's jet. He made up his mind. He got out of the car, dived under the barrier and began to run, running as he had run at the Cnothan games, pounding along the runway, deaf to the shouts behind him. He gained the jet and climbed in next to Mr. Morton, who was just getting the all clear for take-off. As the plane roared off down the runway, Mr. Morton said uneasily, "There seems to be a lot of activity."

"Don't pay any attention," urged Hamish. "Urgent police business."

But Hamish expected any minute that there would be a message from the control tower to turn back. When no such call came, he could only assume that the police, determined to catch this Gentleman Jim, had told the airport authorities to let him go. Thanks to Mr. Morton, he would get there quickly, in under an hour; but even so, Strathbane would be there and Blair would be desperate to claim the credit.

* * *

Blair had phoned the manager of the hotel and told him that John Glover was a dangerous criminal and not to be approached, as he was armed and dangerous. Staff should keep out of his way. They would shortly have the hotel surrounded. But the excited Blair in the race to Lochdubh from Strathbane put on the police siren. Up in the hotel room, John heard that distant wail.

"Trouble," he said to Betty. "Untie her, ungag her, and let's get her down the back stairs."

"We don't need her," hissed Betty, her face a muddy colour with fright.

"We may need a hostage. Leave the luggage. Leave the guns. I've got my pistol."

"But there's a fortune in clothes in my bags!" wailed Betty.

He slapped her so violently across the face that she went staggering across the room. "Do as you're told," he said.

Tight-lipped, Betty got to work, ripping the gag from Priscilla's mouth and untying her bonds.

With a pistol shoved into her side, Priscilla was hustled out and along the corridor. Betty's breath came in ragged gasps. Priscilla heard that wail of the siren in the distance and prayed the police would arrive in time.

Outside the back door, she blinked in the blaze of sunlight. The rain had stopped. "Sit in the back of the car with her," John ordered Betty. "Here, take the gun and keep her covered."

Priscilla kept her eyes on the gun now in Betty's hand. There was no sign of that hand wavering or Betty becoming distracted.

They raced off down the drive and swung out through gates and along the one-track road.

"They'll have road-blocks," said Betty.

"I know," he said calmly. "But while you were romancing that idiot of a copper, I've been doing my homework. There's plenty of places to hide out, and the closer to the hotel, the better." The car sped up into the hills and then John suddenly slowed. "This is the place," he said. He turned off to the left along a farm track. "There's a deserted building along here," he said. "We'll wait until dark. I've got one of those three-wheel dune-buggy-type vehicles they use for rounding up sheep. We can take off across the hills and avoid the roads."

"Where to?"

"You'll find out."

He stopped finally outside a deserted farm building. "Out," he commanded.

He urged them into the building. "Now keep her there a minute, Betty," he said. "I'm going to take a look around outside."

Betty and Priscilla faced each other across the bare room. Sun slanted through the broken windows.

"Did you really work in that bank?" Priscilla asked. She thought furiously: get her talking and she might drop her guard.

"Oh, yes," said Betty. "For fifteen years."

"Fifteen years!" exclaimed Priscilla. "Then that means you weren't a criminal until this."

Betty stared at her mulishly.

"Why?" pursued Priscilla. "Why now? You may as well tell me because he's going to kill me."

"No, he's not," said Betty contemptuously. "He'll set you free as soon as we decide to move."

"He'll kill me, just the way he killed the real John Glover."

"Jim didn't kill Glover."

"Oh, and how did you get his credit cards and bank-book? Ask him to hand them over?"

"Jim got one of his friends to keep a guard on him while we came up here. He'll be released as soon as we get back to Glasgow."

"Do you know this for a fact? He killed Duggan. You can't be naïve enough to think he let Glover live, or that he's going to let me live . . . or even you!"

Betty laughed. "Don't try and pull that one on me. Jim and me are an item."

"But you were engaged to John Glover, the *late* John Glover," said Priscilla, hoping to frighten her, hoping to get her angry.

"Stop saying that! Duggan deserved to die. He was nothing more than a common criminal."

"And your Jim is an uncommon criminal?"

There was a long silence. The wind of Sutherland howled around the deserted farmhouse like a banshee. The police would have reached the hotel, thought Priscilla. Surely they would search the surrounding countryside. But Blair would be in charge and Blair would think only of road-blocks. But surely they would bring dogs.

Betty gave an involuntary shiver. "I don't know how anyone can live up here," she complained. "Nothing for miles and miles, and the weather's dreadful."

"It can be just as dreadful in Glasgow," said Priscilla. "Look, we may as well pass the time until he gets back. Tell me how you got into all this."

Betty gave a shrug and walked to the window and looked out. The moorland fell away in front of her. Thin curtains of rain were trailing over the mountains in the distance although the sun shone where they were.

She turned back. "As I said, I'd been working in that bank for years. I got engaged to John Glover because I decided I'd better start making provision for my old age. I used to go to a bar near the bank after work. One evening, Jim came up to me and asked if he could buy me a drink. We got talking. He seemed rich and sophisticated, everything John was not. We began to see each other. Then we started an affair. I told him I would tell John the engagement was off. He asked me why I'd got involved with such a dry stick of a man in the first place and I told him, security. He said he'd a proposition to put to me. He said for a start I had to stay engaged to John. He said he loved me and was going to marry me."

"And you believed him!" exclaimed Priscilla.

"He does love me and he wants to marry me and I love him," said Betty passionately.

"In fact you love him so much, you end up in bed with Hamish Macbeth!"

"Oh, that! That was Jim's idea. Tie that copper up, he said, and he'll look elsewhere for suspects."

In all her misery and dread Priscilla suddenly wished she could stay alive if only to tell Hamish Macbeth what Betty had said.

"Let me get this straight," said Priscilla. "You're a respectable bank clerk for years. This Jim comes on the scene and you agree to his taking the identity of your fiancé and conspire to murder Duggan."

"His name wasn't Duggan. He was some rat of a low life called Charlie Stoddart."

"And that makes it all right?"

"Look, you snotty bitch, you don't know what it was like working in that bank, year in and year out, handling all that money that didn't belong to me. Jim said we could have everything I'd ever dreamt of—fancy clothes, fancy holidays, visit all the places I'd only seen in the movies." She turned back to the window. "What's keeping him?"

Jim checked to make sure the three-wheeler was still there and ready to drive. Then he walked away across the moorland, the wind tugging at his thick hair. He did not feel afraid, only felt a rush of adrenaline. He knew in his bones he was going to get away with it. He felt the gods were on his side. Beck confessing to the murder of Duggan had been an amazing bit of luck.

The jealousy that fat pig Blair had for the local Lochdubh copper had been another. There had been no need to try to kill Hamish, but he had felt it would have been a way of tying up loose ends. It had been amazingly simple to leave the crowd at the Cnothan games and climb up that mountain and be ready and waiting when Hamish came into view, finding the rifle he had buried in the heather the night before. So he had missed— so what? No one had believed Hamish's story, his rifle had not been found, and he had been able to get it back in the middle of the night after the games. It was a pity he'd had to go off and leave the rifle and shotgun in the hotel room, but it was a small price to pay for freedom. He had no intention of heading off during daylight. They would have helicopters up there soon, searching the surrounding countryside. He took a last look around. As he had previously found, the moorland was surprisingly dry and heathery despite all the rain: no sinister peat bogs. He had a man waiting for him in a cottage near Bonar Bridge, complete with a ready disguise for him and a set of fake identity papers. Now to clear up the remaining loose ends.

Blair was in a bigger fury than he had ever been before. It was he who had poured scorn on Hamish Macbeth's belief that Beck had not killed Duggan. But he could have saved the day with the arrest of this man masquerading as John Glover, believed to be the famous Gentleman Jim. But Jim was gone, together with that Betty John. And, worse than that, the staff had been told to keep clear, but a maid watching from one of the upstairs windows had seen the pair forcing Priscilla Halburton-Smythe into a car and driving off. The normally urbane Superintendent Peter Daviot was on the scene, and his language was worse than Blair's. Radios crackled as orders went out to block every road leading out of Lochdubh.

Colonel Halburton-Smythe, supporting his weeping wife, was shouting that they were all a bunch of dangerous incompetents.

Press cars were beginning to drive up and Blair was howling at his men to "get the buggers away."

Adding to the confusion were the villagers of Lochdubh, who had heard about the trouble at the castle before the police arrived and were huddled in groups in the hotel car park.

"So it wasn't you, Willie," said Lucia.

Willie looked at her in amazement. "You mean you thought I might have murdered Duggan! Why, for God's sake?"

"You're such a tiger when you're angry."

And Willie promptly forgave her everything.

Mrs. Wellington, the minister's wife, was addressing some of her husband's parishioners, her booming voice reaching Blair's infuriated ears. "We should have listened to Hamish Macbeth. Did he not say that Beck had not done the murder?"

"Yes, but how do we know this armed man here did it, tell me that?" cried Geordie Mackenzie.

Mrs. Wellington gave him a withering look. "Use your brains. We may be getting a reputation here, but it's hard to believe we have two murderers in Lochdubh."

"If you're right, then we have," said Geordie triumphantly. "Beck murdered Rosie and this fellow murdered Duggan."

Mrs. Wellington ignored him and went on, "It's all the fault of this hotel, letting rooms to murderers. Money greed, that's what it is. I shall tell my husband on Sunday to preach a sermon on the subject. They would let rooms to apes here provided the apes had enough money."

"Shut up, you old bag," screamed the colonel, beside himself with worry and fright. "What are all these policemen doing here, for God's sake? Why aren't they out looking for my daughter?"

Mr. Daviot approached him. "We have men blocking every road," he said soothingly.

The colonel clasped his trembling hands. "And if they take to the hills?"

"We're waiting for the dogs," said Mr. Daviot and turned away.

"Nearly there," said Mr. Morton. He was not piloting the helicopter, which had collected them from Inverness airport, as he had done the Learjet. "We'll set you down in the car-park at the Tommel Castle Hotel."

In that moment, Hamish looked down at the moorland below, purple with heather. He saw the little figure of a man and then saw that figure plunge into the heather for cover.

"Put me down in the nearest field," shouted Hamish above the noise of the helicopter. The helicopter began to heel and go downwards. "Have you a gun?" asked Hamish.

"My deer rifle's behind you," said Mr. Morton, who was beginning to feel he was beyond being surprised at anything. Hamish took the gun from its case, then found the bullets and loaded it. When the helicopter landed he was off and running again, the gun slung over his shoulder, heading to where he had seen that figure. Buckie's farmhouse, he thought. Empty. He was close to it.

Jim stumbled to his feet and ran towards the farmhouse. He was sure he hadn't been seen, but, just in case, he would need to change his plans and make his escape in daylight.

Betty gave him a relieved smile. He walked over and took the gun from her. "Outside," he said.

"He's going to kill me," said Priscilla to Betty. "Don't let him do this."

"Silly fool," said Betty. She said to Jim, "She thinks you're going to kill her."

Jim jerked his head at the doorway. "Outside," he repeated. He jabbed the gun in Priscilla's side.

They stood in the sunlight in the deserted farmyard. Jim had moved away from them, keeping Priscilla covered.

The smile had left Betty's face and she looked at Jim anxiously. The wind soughed through the skeletal branches of a dead ash tree over their heads, a curlew piped from the heather. The wind had dropped in that uncanny way of Sutherland winds, and all was still.

Jim pointed the pistol directly at Priscilla's heart. "Goodbye, Miss Toffee-Nose."

"NO!" screamed Betty and stood in front of Priscilla with her arms spread wide.

Priscilla in that split second should have tried to escape, but she seemed rooted to the spot, staring at Betty's dead body, spread-eagled at her feet.

She looked up and across at Jim. "You meant to kill her anyway."

"Well, well, Miss Clever-Clogs, how right you are." He raised the pistol again.

Hamish Macbeth raised the deer rifle to his shoulder. He knew, as any policeman should, that he should shout a warning. He saw Jim's grinning face in the telescopic sight and took careful aim.

Priscilla had decided to run for it. She darted to the side, tripped on a rusting piece of farm machinery, and fell panting on the ground. She heard a shot. She twisted round and looked at her tormentor. He was standing, swaying, his face a mask of blood.

And then he fell headlong and lay still.

Priscilla tried to stand up. But her legs would not hold her. Hamish found her kneeling on the ground, retching miserably.

He passed her a handkerchief. She finished vomiting and looked at him, her eyes widening. "Hamish?"

"Aye."

"Black hair doesn't suit you." She began to giggle weakly and then she began to cry. He took her in his arms, talking softly as he would to a hurt child.

"There now, there now. Hamish is here. It's over. You're safe. It's all over."

Police sirens wailed from the road in the distance. The shots had been heard.

"Listen tae me," said Hamish urgently as he heard cars start to bump down the long rutted road that led to the deserted farm, "you heard me shout a warning. Right? Got that? You heard me shout a warning."

She nodded dumbly.

Cars screeched to a halt. Blair's thick Glaswegian accent shouted, "You there! Leave the woman alone and walk towards us with your hands on your head."

Hamish stood up. "It's me . . . Hamish Macbeth," he said. "Ower there's your Gentleman Jim. I had tae shoot him. I gave him a warning."

Blair's face was purple and thick veins stood out on his forehead. Hamish stood swaying on his feet with fatigue. There he was with his dyed-black hair and his scraggly black moustache and Blair suddenly saw him through a red mist. Macbeth had caught the most wanted criminal in Scotland, Macbeth had found the murderer of Duggan.

He stumbled forwards, his thick hands groping blindly for Hamish's neck. It took the full efforts of Macnab and Anderson to stop Hamish Macbeth being strangled by a superior officer.

Chapter 11

We have learned to whittle the Eden Tree to the shape
   of a surplice peg,
We have learned to bottle our parents twain in the yolk
   of an addled egg,
We know that the tail must wag the dog, for the horse is
   drawn by the cart;
But the Devil whoops, as he whooped of old: "It's clever,
   but is it Art?"

                —*Rudyard Kipling*

Hamish Macbeth was on sick leave—by orders. He was told
not to talk to the press. Strathbane was wondering what to do
with this maverick policeman.

He was so tired, he did not care. He was also suffering
from delayed shock. He knew that if he had shouted a warning to Jim, the man might have swung that gun away from
Priscilla, but that had been a chance he had not been willing
to take. He had killed a man who had murdered without conscience, and yet the dead face of Gentleman Jim haunted his
dreams.

There was a sign on the police-station door referring all
calls to Cnothan, and yet the press, knowing that he was in

there, rang the doorbell and telephoned constantly. He began to feel he was under siege. During the night, under cover of darkness—for the light nights of mid-summer were over— he put out food for his hens. Then, packing up a bag, he began to walk along the deserted waterfront. His police Land Rover would be delivered back to him the next day. He knew that he was shortly about to be tangled up in miles of red tape. He would need to explain why he had taken off for Glasgow on his own, why he had not told Strathbane what he was doing, why he had spoken to a reporter, and why and how he had shot a man, not with a gun issued by the police but with a deer rifle.

He still felt incredibly weary and his bones ached from all the running he had done. His dyed hair was showing glints of red at the roots and there was a sore mark on his face above his mouth where he had ripped off the moustache which Josie had helped him to stick on so well.

He walked towards the humpbacked bridge. The cottages of Willie and Annie Ferguson were in darkness. He wondered if his friendship with Lucia and Willie would ever be the same again.

He stood for a moment on the bridge and stared down at the rushing waters of the river, swollen with all the recent rain. For the first time, he wondered if he was really suited to the police force. His pig-headed desire to do things on his own was not what was expected of a good policeman. But it was a life he loved, a life he was used to. He turned and looked back at the sleeping village strung out along the waterfront. Had he been born with some sort of ambition by-pass? He had not travelled very much, had not really wanted to. He was an arm-chair traveller, content to watch exotic countries from the comfort of his armchair. By modern-day standards, he was a failure, a drop-out.

He trudged on up the hill. Priscilla would not be awake, but there would be the night porter on duty and he would ask for a room for the night and be able to rest up away from the press, and gear himself up for the horrendous amount of paperwork that lay ahead of him.

Priscilla awoke with a cry. In her dream, Jim was once more facing her with the gun, but this time he had shot her, and when she awoke, her heart thudding against her ribs, she could still feel the impact of that dream bullet.

She climbed out of bed and went and stood by the window, hugging her shivering body. As she looked down from the castle window, she saw the weary figure of Hamish Macbeth trudging up the drive.

She scrambled into a sweater and jeans and ran down the stairs to find Hamish arguing with the night porter, a surly individual, who was telling him he would need to return the next morning to get a room.

"Never mind him," said Priscilla. "Come with me, Hamish. I'll find you something. Would you like coffee or a drink?"

He ran his hand through his dyed hair. "I could murder a whisky."

"Whisky it is." Under the disapproving stare of the night porter, she reached under the counter and unhitched the key to the bar, went across to it and unlocked the grille. She poured two fine old malt whiskies. "Let's sit down. Come to escape from the press?"

"Aye," said Hamish, sinking gratefully into one of the large chintz-covered armchairs in the bar. "It's a wee bittie late for me to start obeying orders, but I may as well try. I think I'll soon be out of a job."

"You were very unorthodox," said Priscilla. "But with all this media attention, I don't think they would dare fire you."

Hamish brightened. "I hadn't thought o' that." Then his face fell. He took a gulp of whisky. "I was thinking on the road up here that maybe I am not suited to the force at all. Is there something badly wrong wi' me that I don't want promotion or travel or anything like that?"

Priscilla looked at him with a sudden rush of affection. "Oh, Hamish, the number of times I've wished you'd get off your Highland arse and do something with your life! But maybe you've got something the rest of us could be doing with. Who was it said that a truly happy man is the one who accepts and enjoys what he has?"

"It would be grand to think I was like that. But this last case has shaken me. I suppose I should have given Jim a warning."

"If you'd followed correct police procedure, I'd probably be dead," said Priscilla. "Every time I think of giving your career a push, I'll think of that."

There was a companionable silence and then Priscilla said, "I wonder what Mrs. Beck is thinking now. That her husband was so obsessed with Rosie and hated her, his wife, so much that he was prepared to hurt her further by admitting to a murder he did not commit?"

"I think she'll get over the shock pretty quickly. She'll probably sell her story to a tabloid and it'll appear with screaming headlines after the murder trial and she'll begin to enjoy the notoriety. Then she'll marry again, some poor sod who actually likes being bullied, and live happily ever after. She won't suffer long. Think of the selfishness of keeping a man tied to you even though you know he hates your guts. Maybe if she's that selfish, she pretended the hatred wasn't there."

"And Lucia! She used to be so fond of you, named the baby after you; how could she go around spreading nasty stories about you?"

"Och, the silly lassie thought Willie had done it and it wouldn't amaze me if I found out that Willie thought she had done it. That's the terrible thing about murder in a small community, it turns one against the other and everyone starts suspecting everyone else. In the city, where people often don't know their own neighbours, it would be different, I think. Mind you, sometimes I wonder what it would be like to live in a place and be completely anonymous. I love Lochdubh, but sometimes I feel I'm living under a magnifying glass."

"Yes," she said drily, "being found in bed with a woman wouldn't be such a topic of gossip. Do you know she told me she had done that on instructions from Jim? It was to keep your mind off them?"

"The thing that kept my mind on them was I desperately wanted it to be the fake John Glover. I didnae want it to be one of the villagers." His hazel eyes gleamed with malice. "You must be feeling better, Priscilla. You enjoyed telling me that."

"I'll get us another drink," said Priscilla quickly, picking up his now empty glass and walking over to the bar, "and then I'll find you a bed. Oh, something good's come out of it all—or rather, I suppose it's good news."

"What's that?"

She filled their two glasses with a generous measure and walked back to join him and sat down.

"Geordie Mackenzie and Annie Ferguson are an item."

"Well, well, hardly love's young dream, but nice all the same. Has he been married before?"

"Don't think so. There's something else . . ."

"What? This whisky is grand."

"Archie Maclean has rebelled. The worm has turned."

"Never! What did he do? Throw his wife in the washtub?"

"She found out about his visiting Rosie Draly and called him a silly fool. The thing that evidently hurt Archie most was that she did not think for a moment he had been having an affair with Rosie. So he told her he had just as she was about to hit him with the potato masher. The yells were so loud that a lot of the villagers were crowded at the kitchen door to listen, which is why I got hold of all this. But I think what Archie did next was more shocking in her eyes than any affair."

"Go on. The mind boggles."

"He pushed through the people watching and ran into the garden and he jumped up and down in the garden until his boots were well and truly muddy and then he rushed back into the kitchen and pranced all over the floor to cheers from the crowd, shouting, 'Take that, you auld bitch.' And that's not all."

"She must have gone mad," marvelled Hamish. "That woman would consider mud on her kitchen floor worse than rape."

"Well, you know how Mrs. Maclean always boils and cleans his clothes so they're tight and shrunken? He rushed over to Patel's store and bought a pair of loose jogging trousers, a T-shirt, and a bright-red polyester jacket with a skull on the back. Everyone had followed him over. He stripped off down to his underwear right in the middle of the shop and put on his new clothes, then he smiled all round and went off to the bar."

"What on earth did Mrs. Maclean do?"

"She rushed round to Dr. Brodie, screaming her husband had gone mad and demanding men in white coats with a straitjacket. But Dr. Brodie sat her down, evidently, and told her a few home truths, including the fact that he had gleaned from the police that Rosie Draly had probably been a lesbian."

"And what did she say to that?"

"She said, 'Thae Greeks hae no morals.'"

Hamish laughed. "She'll win in the end. She'll get these new clothes off Archie's back soon enough and shrink them." Then he stifled a yawn.

"Drink up," said Priscilla, "and I'll show you your bed. I don't suppose you really meant to pay for the room, but in case you did, you don't have to. It's comfortable enough, but it's not being let to any guests until we get it redecorated."

She led the way upstairs to the top of the castle. "It's along from mine." She pushed open a door. "The bed's made up. All you've got to do is fall asleep."

He kissed her cheek. "Thanks," he said gruffly. "I'll need all my strength to cope with the wrath o' police headquarters."

"Don't worry," she said, "you won't be alone. I suppose Blair will be in more trouble than he's ever been in the whole of his life!"

Another day dawned sunny and clear with just a hint of early-morning frost in the air. The bracken on the hillsides was beginning to turn golden and the rowan trees were heavy with scarlet berries. Most of the cottages had a rowan tree at the gate. It was supposed to keep the fairies away, and although all would scornfully say that they didn't believe in fairies, all privately thought it was a good idea to have a rowan tree outside the house . . . well, just in case.

Mrs. Wellington was standing on the waterfront outside Patel's store with the Currie sisters when Detective Jimmy Anderson sloped along. "Day, ladies," he said. "Where's Hamish?"

"He's probably asleep," snorted the minister's wife. "That man must be the laziest policeman on the beat."

"Not to say the most immoral . . . most immoral," said Jessie Currie.

"Well, I shouldn't think you'll have to put up with him for much longer," said Jimmy, lighting a cigarette and puffing the smoke in the direction of Mrs. Wellington, who coughed stagily and flapped the air with her hand.

"What d'you mean?" asked Nessie.

"Our Hamish is all set for the high jump."

"Do you mean the games over at Lochinver?" asked Nessie, looking puzzled.

"No, fired, sacked, given the boot, that's what."

"Wait a minute," boomed Mrs. Wellington. "He solved the case, he killed that murderer, he saved Miss Halburton-Smythe's life; why on earth should he be given the sack?"

"For talking to a reporter," said Jimmy, ticking off the offences on his fingers, "for investigating on his own and not reporting in when his photo was in the papers and calls on the radio, for hiring a car with a dead man's driving license, for having driven a police vehicle to Glasgow without permission, for having borrowed a gun and shot someone without permission, and I think all that's just for starters."

"But if he had done everything by the book," said Mrs. Wellington, "you'd never have caught this Gentleman Jim; in fact, you'd probably never have known who he was!"

"Could be, but tell that to Strathbane."

"This is dreadful, dreadful," said Jessie, as much for Hamish now as she had so recently been against him. "Something must be done."

Customers coming out of the shop were hailed and told the bad news about Hamish and by lunch-time everyone in the village knew that Hamish Macbeth was due for the chop. Feelings began to run high. Hamish was *their* policeman, and no one from the "big city" was going to dictate to them whom they should or should not have.

At three o'clock that afternoon, Superintendent Peter Daviot was hosting an emergency meeting of all senior police officers in the Highlands.

"So you see," he said, after reading out a list of Hamish's iniquities, "although we are very glad to have this case wrapped up, we cannot possibly have a police constable who goes on like a Wild West sheriff. I think we should wait until the fuss has died down and then quietly tell him to leave the force. I have quite a good fellow lined up for the job in Lochdubh, PC Trevor Campbell."

"Let me see the report on him," said a chief constable. Mr. Daviot reluctantly handed a folder over.

"Dear me," said the chief constable and Mr. Daviot looked at him impatiently. The man had a fat, round, red face above a tight shirt collar. Mr. Daviot thought it looked like a face painted on a balloon.

"Campbell seems to be accident-prone, to say the least. Added to that, he barely reaches regulation height and he just scraped through his exams."

"We don't exactly need anyone brilliant to police a Highland village," said another.

A thin man with a clever face raised his voice. "What you must realize," he said, "is that we are all sitting round this table deciding to get rid of a constable who, by his own initiative, caught Scotland's biggest and most wanted criminal. I say, let's keep him and promote him. If you don't want him, I'll take him back to Glasgow with me."

"We have thought of promoting Hamish Macbeth before," said Mr. Daviot wearily. "He was actually promoted to sergeant."

"Oh, big, fat, hairy deal," commented the thin man.

"And," continued Mr. Daviot, "we had to demote him over that business of Pictish man. Macbeth caught the murderer, yes, by confronting her with a dead body. But it was the wrong body, if you remember. A fine example of Pictish man, and we were under fire from every professor and archaeological buff in the country over disturbing a rare corpse and removing it from its burial site. But the main difficulty, and I think this explains why Macbeth is such a maverick, is that he has no ambition to be other than a village policeman."

There was a startled silence while a roomful of men who had clawed their way to the top digested that bit of information.

"No, I say," said Mr. Daviot, "that we simply wait until the fuss has died down and then get rid of him."

"On what pretext?" demanded the thin man.

"I'll think of something," snapped Mr. Daviot.

"It won't answer," said his tormentor. "You cannot dismiss a policeman without a full inquiry, which would bring Macbeth back to the attention of the press. This detective, Blair, now, who appears to have been motivated by a certain degree of stupid spite—what has happened to him?"

"Nothing," said Mr. Daviot. "He did his job. He had a confession from Beck. The man was most convincing. He was prepared to stand up in court and plead guilty to both murders. We need good, obedient detectives like Blair on the force. He may be a bit truculent at times, but surely, gentlemen, you must admit that Macbeth's methods are enough to try the patience of a saint. I suggest we have discussed this long enough. I shall put it to the vote. You will find paper in front of you. Helen will go round with the box and collect the results and then I will count them." His efficient secretary waited until they had all scribbled on pieces of paper and folded them, and then she went round with a square wooden box with a slot in the top, collected them and placed the box in front of Mr. Daviot, who opened it. He separated the "For" and "Against" into neat piles. His secretary watched avidly. She loathed Hamish.

"That's that," said Mr. Daviot finally. "Macbeth is to be dismissed at a convenient moment."

Helen slipped out of the room. Blair and several others were waiting at the end of the corridor outside. Helen grinned at them and turned her thumb downwards.

"Oh, happy day," said Blair. "The drinks are on me." But the others shuffled off with long faces, leaving him standing glaring after them.

Inside the conference room, the men moved on to other business until at last Mr. Daviot said, "That's that." He rose to his feet. "Refreshments in the adjoining room, gentlemen. A drink before you leave."

They all rose and followed him through to a room where a long table of drinks and canapés was laid out. Soon the air was thick with smoke and conversation.

Helen opened a window to let some of the cigarette smoke out. The day was sunny, the rain had stopped at last, and she felt happy. No more would Hamish Macbeth look at her with that mocking glint in his eye as if he found her somewhat ridiculous.

Bertie Laver, a detective chief inspector from Caithness, cocked an ear. He was an old friend of Daviot's. "Is that the pipes I hear?" he asked. "Got a parade today?"

"Not that I know of," said Mr. Daviot. "Helen, has any group asked for permission to hold a parade?"

"No, sir."

The skirl of the pipes sounded nearer, followed by the sound of a band. Men began to move to the windows.

Mr. Daviot joined them and looked down, an amused smile fading from his lips.

Down the street towards police headquarters marched the villagers of Lochdubh, led by a piper and the school band murdering "Scotland the Brave." They were carrying placards:

SAVE OUR POLICEMAN. WE WANT HAMISH. And, worse than that, two press photographers were running down the street, cameras at the ready.

"You didn't tell us this Macbeth was so damned popular," said Bertie.

"I didn't quite realize . . ." said Mr. Daviot miserably. "I mean, Blair said . . ."

Bertie eyed him cynically. "Man, man, that Blair'll be the ruin o' ye, Peter, if you listen to any more he says."

The crowd gathered below them.

"I'll go down and see what they want," said Mr. Daviot.

Backed by Bertie, he hurried down the stairs.

At first he thought the large tweedy woman addressing the villagers and all the curious of Strathbane, who were gathering in increasing numbers to listen, was using a megaphone. But then he recognized Mrs. Wellington, the minister's wife, and realized it was her own booming, unaided voice.

"They have no right at all," Mrs. Wellington was saying, "to take our constable away from us without consulting our wishes. Are we going to be dictated to by Strathbane? By London? By Brussels?"

"NO! NO! NO!" howled the crowd.

A camera flash went off in Mr. Daviot's face.

"Do something," hissed Bertie.

"But the vote . . .!"

"Damn the vote. Use your initiative, man. Tell them the bugger's staying."

Mr. Daviot stepped up to Mrs. Wellington, tapping her on the arm and halting her in mid-flow.

He gave a weak smile. "I am afraid you are mistaken, Mrs. Wellington," he said. "There is no question of Hamish Macbeth being dismissed."

Her eyes raked him up and down, then she turned back to her audience. "He says there is no question of Hamish being dismissed," she shouted.

There were loud cheers. She held up her hands for silence. "But just to make sure," she cried, "I think we should have that in writing." Another cheer.

"Please wait here, Mrs. Wellington," said Mr. Daviot bleakly, "and do try to keep these people quiet."

He retreated back up the stairs, striding ahead with Bertie scurrying after him. The top policemen were back in the conference room and round the table.

"So," said the thin man, "we heard that bit about wanting confirmation in writing. I say, give it to them and be nice, very nice, to this Macbeth. He's got miles of paperwork to get through, hasn't he? Send him a secretary. What about Helen there?"

Helen shot him a look of horror. "I can't," she protested. "My mother's sick."

Mr. Daviot gave a sigh and once more took charge. "I think we will give that lot down below their written confirmation and then I will arrange for a woman to go over to Lochdubh to help Macbeth with his paperwork. He is not due back on duty for a few more days."

It was Helen who had the task of taking the written confirmation downstairs and handing it to Mrs. Wellington.

Mrs. Wellington read it out to the crowd. Cheers and yells. Then three cheers for Mrs. Wellington. Then the band struck up. "All the Blue Bonnets Are Over the Border" and the procession began to head out of Strathbane.

In the quiet coolness of a bar, Blair, unaware of the change in events, was celebrating the end of Hamish Macbeth's career. He dimly heard the pipes, the band, the cheers.

"Whit's that?" asked the barman.

"Who knows?" said Blair with a shrug of his fat shoulders. "Some demonstration. Some bunch o' pillocks. Animal Libbers, Save the Trees, Ban the Bomb." He raised his glass. "Up the lot of them and Hamish Macbeth as well."

"Who he?" asked the barman, who only read the sporting pages in the tabloids.

"Some creep who isnae around to plague me any mair," said Blair. He pushed his empty glass forward. "Whisky . . . and make it a double."

A few days later, Priscilla went on a visit to friends in Invernessshire. They were eager to hear about her adventures.

When she had finished, one of her friends, Bunty, said, "This Hamish Macbeth is no end of a hero. Didn't you nearly marry him? What happened?"

"We just didn't suit," said Priscilla vaguely, "but we're still friends."

"I'd like to meet him," said Bunty. "Any chance of you bringing him here?"

"I'll see," said Priscilla. "He doesn't go out of the village much."

"Well, he went all the way to Glasgow to chase that criminal. He must be very brave."

"More like a terrier," said Priscilla with a laugh. "When he gets his teeth into something, he doesn't like to let go."

"He'll surely be promoted after this."

"More likely in danger of losing his job. In any case, he doesn't want promotion. He avoids it every which way he can. He says he's quite happy being a village policeman. He's not ambitious."

Bunty, plump and black-haired, raised her eyebrows. "I would have thought that a copper who defies all the rules and regulations to get a criminal was very ambitious indeed. Hardly a laid-black approach."

"I never thought of that," said Priscilla slowly. "But if they moved him to the city, he would be miserable and he would find there was even more red tape to cut through."

When she went to bed that night, Priscilla lay awake for a little, remembering all the adventures she had shared with Hamish. He certainly was a very special man. Perhaps . . . perhaps when she returned to Lochdubh, they could take up their romance where it had left off. Well, not where it had left off, for that had been sad, but maybe get back to the way it had been before.

She fell asleep with a smile on her lips.

A week later, WPC Hetty Morrison drove competently over the winding road to Lochdubh. She was the strictest and most efficient woman police officer in Strathbane. She also had excellent shorthand and typing. Her portable computer and printer were beside her on the seat. Hetty had jet-black hair confined at the nape of her neck in a severe bun. She had a fine pair of brown eyes, a sharp nose and a thin mouth. Her figure in her well-pressed uniform was trim and neat. Her shoes shone like black glass.

She had never met Hamish Macbeth but had been fully briefed on the behaviour of this maverick constable and she disapproved of him. She actually enjoyed the rules and regulations of police work and her typed reports were miracles of efficiency. Hetty did not know why this village copper should be so favoured. She felt her talents were being wasted, and that just because she was a woman, she had been temporarily reduced to the rank of secretary.

She was from Perth originally and disapproved of the Highland character, which she considered devious and lazy.

As she drove down into Lochdubh, she did not see the beauty of the waterfront, or the little cottages, of the sea loch glittering in the sun; she only thought it looked a dead-alive sort of place. No wonder it had a reputation for murder, she thought. If I were stuck up here all year long, I'd feel like murdering someone too.

She drove up to the police station and parked behind the Land Rover at the side. She had seen a figure in a deck-chair in the front garden and opened the side gate and went in. Rambling roses in scarlet profusion rumbled round the blue police lamp over the front door, nearly obscuring it. I'd get those things cut down for a start, she thought.

Hamish Macbeth lay back at his ease in a striped canvas deck-chair, his eyes closed. His black-and-red hair glinted in the sunlight.

She coughed loudly and he opened his eyes and smiled up at her. "WPC Morrison, reporting for duty," she said.

"They told me you were coming," he said lazily. "It's a grand day. Wait and I'll get another chair and make us both a cup of tea."

"That will not be necessary," said Hetty crossly, "We have work to do and I would like to get started right away."

Hamish gave a little sigh and stood up. "All right," he said reluctantly. "Come on."

She collected her notebook and computer from the car and followed him into the police office.

"I trust we will not have any interference from the press," she said. "There's been quite enough of that."

"Oh, they've gone," said Hamish, "I wass the seven-days wonder."

Priscilla could have told Hetty that the sudden sibilancy of Hamish's Highland accent meant he was becoming angry, but Priscilla was not there.

Hamish sat behind his desk. Hetty sat on the other side, pencil and pad at the ready. He began to dictate rapidly. He was concise and efficient in his reports. But Hetty was the one who was beginning to become angry. The way this Hamish Macbeth was putting it, he had had no alternative but to do the detective work on his own or the wrong man would have been charged with the murder of Duggan. She reflected that when she typed it out, she would be able to find flaws in it. After a long afternoon, Hamish said, "Would you care for a cup of coffee or tea?"

"No, thank you," said Hetty. "If we have finished for the day, then I will type these up. I have a portable printer in the car, I can run them off and then we can go over them."

"Suite yourself." said Hamish laconically, "but I haff no intention of changing a word."

"I am not just a secretary," said Hetty, snapping her notebook shut, "I am also here to help and advise you."

"Nice of you," said Hamish with a tinge of mockery in his voice. "Now if you don't mind, Constable, I will go out for a walk while you type out the reports." It was five o'clock.

By eight o'clock, Hetty had typed out the notes and gone over them. Try as she would, she could not think of any way of changing them. And thanks to her own stubbornness, she had not eaten or drunk anything all day and she was very hungry and thirsty.

Hamish was strolling back along the waterfront after having called at several homes, Mrs. Wellington's among others, to say thank you for the demonstration outside police headquarters in Strathbane on his behalf. As he passed the Italian restaurant, Willie came out and stood there, looking rather sheepish. Then he held out his hand. "Sorry, Hamish," he said, "I should have known better than to doubt you."

"Och, that's all right," said Hamish, taking his hand and giving it a firm shake. "You were not in your right mind, what with you thinking Lucia might ha' done it, and herself thinking the same about you."

"I think we all went a wee bit crazy," said Willie. " "It's right good o' ye to take it like this. In fact, why don't you step inside for a meal on the house. You could bring Miss Halburton-Smythe. I hear she's back."

"I'll be along in a wee bit," said Hamish. "Thanks."

He went reluctantly back to the police station. Hetty silently pointed to the sheaf of notes. Her stomach gave an unmaidenly rumble. Kindness warred with dislike in Hamish's breast and kindness won. "I've been offered free food at the Italian restaurant," he said. "Care to join me?"

She never knew later why she had accepted, any more than Hamish knew why he had asked her instead of phoning Priscilla. Perhaps it was because this police station with the scent of roses coming in the open window in the soft evening air seemed so divorced and far away from the noise of Strathbane, but she found herself saying, "Yes, thank you."

"Right! I'll just change. The bathroom's outside on your left if you want to put any make-up on."

Hetty picked up her handbag and went into the long narrow bathroom. She washed her face and then surveyed her prim, neat features. She took out a brush and brushed down her hair until it waved on her shoulders. She had put her hairpins in the handbasin and, twisting her hair back into its bun, she scrabbled to retrieve the fine black pins, which promptly fell down the gaping open plug-hole and disappeared. She stared down crossly into the sink. Only a Highlander would have an open plug-hole like that without any sort of grid to prevent things from falling down it.

She brushed her hair again. She would just need to wear it down.

Hamish looked at her with something like surprise when she finally appeared. He was dressed in one of his well-tailored thrift-shop finds and a striped tie.

"We'll walk," he said. "It's just a wee bit along the front."

They walked along in the calm evening. People stood by garden gates or over at the sea-wall. "Evening, Hamish," they called, "grand evening," while Highland eyes curiously studied Hetty walking at his side.

Willie and Lucia gave Hamish an effusive welcome, as if to make up for their previous bad behaviour, and Hamish was given the best table at the window. Willie was determined to do them proud, as was Lucia. They were given Negronis to drink and then a bottle of Chianti. They had crisp mixed salads sprinkled with fresh basil to start with, followed by penne in a cream sauce, followed by large portions of chicken breast in a white-wine sauce, and then zabaglione.

It must have been the wine, Hetty was to think later, that had made her laugh so hard at Hamish's tall stories. But she found she was enjoying his company immensely. She had been out with police officers and detectives and usually the evening had ended with coarse jokes, innuendoes, and then the inevitable proposition. But Hamish just seemed happy to chat. She found herself telling him about the difficulties of coping with her mother and father, who always seemed to be shouting abuse at each other, about her sister, who had gone to

Glasgow and disappeared and never phoned, about how the police force and living in a policewomen's hostel had seemed so wonderful after the mess and violence of home. She had planned to drive back to Strathbane that evening, but time drifted by and she found herself asking Hamish if he could put her up for the night.

Two days later, Mr. Daviot buzzed Helen and said, "Is Hetty Morrison not back with that report yet?"

"Not that I have heard," said Helen.

"Phone Lochdubh police station and find out what's going on."

Helen disappeared and then returned some minutes later. "I spoke to WPC Morrison," she said primly, "and she said that the reports were taking longer than she had expected."

"That's strange. There's a mountain of work, but it would take our efficient Hetty no time at all, and she did not intend to stay more than a day in Lochdubh."

"She is probably trying to knock some sense into that idiot's head," said Helen crisply. "Hetty Morrison is a woman of iron."

Mr. Daviot looked at her doubtfully. "If you say so."

Priscilla emerged from Patel's with a shopping basket over her arm. It was another glorious day. She slung the basket into the passenger seat of the car and decided to go along for a chat with Hamish. She had rather hoped that he might have phoned her but perhaps he thought she was still in Inverness.

She walked along until she had nearly reached the police station when she heard the sound of Hamish's laughter. Disappointed that he was not alone, she approached slowly and looked over the hedge.

Hamish and a woman with long, glossy black hair were sitting in deck-chairs in the garden, drinking chilled white wine.

She backed away before they could see her and turned on her heel and walked back to her car.

It was just as well the engagement to Hamish had been broken off, she thought as she drove quickly and competently out of the village. He would never have been faithful.

Perhaps she needed a break, perhaps she needed to go back to London.

Perhaps she would go the following morning . . .

Please Turn the Page for a
Special Bonus Chapter
from the Newest
Hamish Macbeth Mystery

Death of a Dentist

Available in Hardcover from
The Mysterious Press
At Bookstores Everywhere

CHAPTER ONE

For there was never yet a philosopher,
That could endure the toothache patiently.

—William Shakespeare

It was a chill autumn in the Highlands of Scotland when Police Constable Hamish Macbeth awoke in hell.

The whole side of his jaw was a burning mass of pain.

Toothache. The sort of toothache so bad you cannot tell which tooth is infected because the pain runs through them all.

His dentist was in Inverness and he felt he could not bear the long drive. Lochdubh, the village in which his police station was situated, did not boast a dentist. The nearest one was at Braikie, a small town twenty miles away. The dentist there was Frederick Gilchrist.

The problem was that Hamish Macbeth still had all his teeth and meant to keep them all and Mr. Gilchrist had a reputation for pulling out teeth rather than saving them, which suited the locals, who still preferred to have their teeth drawn and a "nice" set of dentures put in. Also Gilchrist, in these days of high dental charges, was cheap.

One summer visitor complained bitterly that Gilchrist had performed The Great Australian Trench on her. Australian dentists had gained the unfair reputation for casually letting the drill slide across as many teeth as possible, therefore getting themselves a lucrative and steady customer. And although Mr. Gilchrist was Scottish, he was reputed to have performed this piece of supposedly Australian malpractice. Mrs. Harrison, a local widow, alleged nastily that she had been sexually molested by Gilchrist while unconscious under gas, but Mrs. Harrison was a strange woman who always seemed to think every man was lusting after her and so her charge was not taken very seriously, and as she had not reported it to the police, but only to everyone else who would listen, there had been no excuse for Hamish Macbeth to take the matter further.

And yet the pain was so fierce that by the time he had dressed, he had argued himself into sacrificing one tooth.

He dialled Gilchrist's number. Gilchrist's receptionist, Maggie Bane, answered the telephone and to Hamish's frantic appeal for help said sourly he would just need to come along and take his chances. Mr. Gilchrist was very busy. Come at three and maybe he'll fit you in.

Hamish then went to the bathroom and scrabbled in the kitchen cabinet, looking for aspirin and found none. He petulantly slammed the cabinet door shut. It fell off the wall into the handbasin, and cracked the porcelain of the handbasin before sending large shards of glass from its shattered glass doors onto the bathroom floor.

He looked at his watch through a red mist of pain. Eight o'clock in the morning. Dear God, he wouldn't *live* until the afternoon. A sorry, lanky figure in his worn police uniform, he left the police station and made his way rapidly along the waterfront to Dr. Brodie's home.

Angela, the doctor's wife, answered the door in her dressing gown. "Why, Hamish, you're early," she cried.

"I need help," moaned Hamish. "I'm dying."

"Come in. He's in the kitchen."

Dr. Brodie, wrapped in a camel hair dressing gown, looked up as Hamish entered, a piece of toast and marmalade halfway to his lips. "Hamish!" he said. "You look like death."

"You've got to give me something quick," gabbled Hamish, grabbing his arm. "I am in the mortal pain. I haff the toothache."

"You look as if you've got mad cow disease," said Dr. Brodie sourly, jerking his arm away. "Oh, very well, Hamish. Sit yourself down while I get my bag."

Hamish sank down in a chair and clutched his jaw. One of Angela's cats leapt lightly on the table, studied Hamish with curious eyes and then began to drink the milk out of the jug.

Dr. Brodie came back with his bag, opened it, and took out a small torch. "Now, open wide Hamish. Which one is it?"

"It feels like all of them," said Hamish. He opened his mouth and pointed to the lower left of his jaw.

Dr. Brodie shone the torch in his mouth. "Ah, yes, nasty."

"Nasty what?" demanded Hamish.

"You've got an abscess there. The bottom right-hand molar. Ugh! I don't know that a dentist could treat you until it's cleared up. I'll give you a shot of antibiotic. I'll need to go to the surgery. Stay here and Angela'll get you a coffee. I'll need to get dressed."

"Where am I getting this injection?"

"In the backside."

"Then I will be coming with you."

"Why?"

Hamish blushed. "I do not want your wife seeing my bare bum."

Dr. Brodie laughed. "I'm glad there's one woman left in this village you don't want to show your bum to."

When he had gone upstairs to change, Hamish whimpered, "No coffee, Angela. I'm in such awfy pain, I couldnae get it past my lips."

"You're nothing but a big baby, Hamish Macbeth," said Angela, her thin face lighting up with amusement.

"Women!" said Hamish sourly. "All that talk about maternal feelings and womanly sympathy is chust the myth."

"If the abscess is that bad, why did you let it go so far?"

"I felt a few twinges," muttered Hamish, "but, och, I thought I had the cold in the face."

Angela smiled again at him, sat down at the coffee table, grabbed the cat by the scruff of the neck and dragged its face out of the milk jug, poured some in her coffee, and picked up a book, saying before she started to read, "I am sure you do not feel like talking."

Hamish glared at her and nursed his jaw. Dr. Brodie eventually appeared. "Let's get to the surgery, Hamish, and spare your blushes."

They walked silently along the waterfront. The day was cold and still. Smoke from the cottage chimneys rose straight up into the clear air. A heron sailed lazily over the sea loch. The village of Lochdubh in Sutherland—that county which is as far north in mainland Britain as you can go—dreamed in the pale sunlight making one sad constable feel like a noisy riot of pain.

Once in the surgery, Dr. Brodie injected Hamish with a stiff shot of antibiotics, gave him a prescription for antibiotic pills and told him to go home and lie down. Hamish had told him about the appointment with Gilchrist. "You'd best cancel it," said Dr. Brodie, "until that abscess has cleared up. You don't want to go to Gilchrist anyway. He'll pull the tooth and there's no need for that these days. You'd be better off in Inverness. There's been some awfully nasty stories about Gilchrist circling about."

Hamish crept off back to the police station. He had bought a bottle of aspirin from Patel's, the local supermarket on the road there. He took three aspirin, swallowing them down with a stiff glass of whisky. He undressed slowly and climbed back into bed, willing the pain to go away. To take his mind off the pain, he began to think of Gilchrist and all the rumours about the man, and then he suddenly fell asleep.

He awoke two hours later. The pain had almost gone, but he was frightened to get out of bed in case that dreadful pain came roaring back. He clasped his hands behind his head and stared at the ceiling. He missed his dog, Towser, who had died so suddenly. Towser would have lain on the end of the bed and wagged his tail and he, Hamish, would have felt that someone in the whole wide world cared about his suffering. Priscilla Halburton-Smythe, the once love of his life, had gone to London to stay with friends and no other woman had come along to fill the gap left by her going. They had once been unofficially engaged, but he had broken off the relationship because of Priscilla's odd coldness when he had tried to make love to her. He missed her, but he tried to tell himself that missing Priscilla had simply become a habit.

His thoughts then turned to Gilchrist and his Highland curiosity about the dentist was fully roused. Hamish had never met the man. He would phone up and say he could not see him that day and then he would make another appointment. If Gilchrist showed any signs of removing the tooth, he would remove himself from that dentist's chair and go to Inverness. But that way he would be able to see the dentist and form his own opinion. It was all so easy to lose one's reputation in the Highlands of Scotland where one tall tale was embellished and passed around and another added to it.

The phone rang shrilly from the police station office. He got gingerly out of bed and went to answer it. It was from the owner of a hotel fifteen miles away on the Lairg road, complaining he had been burgled the night before.

Hamish promised to be over as soon as he could, dressed again, got into the police Land Rover and drove out to The Scotsman Hotel where the burglary had taken place. He expected to find vandalism, broken windows, the bar a mess, but it transpired that the break-in had been a professional one. The safe in the office had been broken into and the week's takings stolen.

The safe looked heavy and massive and the door undamaged.

"How did they get into that?" he asked, pushing back his peaked cap and scratching his fiery red hair.

The manager, Brian Macbean, nodded to two men, who swung the safe round.

"Oh, my," said Hamish. For the back of the safe had been made of a panel of chipboard which the burglar had simply sawn through.

He took out his notebook. "Can we sit down, Mr. Macbean, and I'll take some notes. Then I'll phone Strathbane and get them to send a forensic team over. How much was in the safe?"

"Two hundred and fifty thousand pounds."

"What on earth were you doing keeping that amount of money on the premises?"

"It's the giant prize for this Saturday night's bingo session. Man, we've got folk coming from every part of the Highlands."

"So someone knew about it, and someone knew about the back of the safe."

Macbean, a squat, burly man with thinning hair, looked morose. "The big bingo night's been in all the local papers, so it has."

"But why cash?" Hamish was puzzled. "A cheque would ha' done."

"That was the attraction. It was all in twenty pound notes. All the press photographers were coming. It would have made the grand picture, some winner with all those notes."

Hamish licked the end of his pencil. "So why the wooden back on the safe?"

"I needed a safe and there was this one over at the auction rooms in Inverness. I thought that would do me fine."

"And probably charged the owners for a real safe."

Macbean looked mulishly at the floor and did not reply.

Hamish patiently took him through exactly when the theft had been discovered and then said, "Who knew the safe had a wooden back?"

"The barman, Johnny King, and one of the waiters, Peter Sampson. They helped me bring it back from Inverness."

"What about your family?"

"Well, of course they knew. My wife, Agnes, and my girl, Darleen."

Hamish racked through his mind for any gossip he might have heard about Macbean's family, but could think of nothing in particular. "I'll need to interview the barman and the waiter," he said, "and then I'll talk to your wife and daughter."

"Whit! Leave my family out of it."

"Don't be daft, Mr. Macbean. They might have seen something or heard something. How old is Darleen?"

"Twenty-two."

"Where is she now?"

"She's over at the dentist in Braikie with her mother."

6

Gilchrist again, thought Hamish, and then realised with a sort of glad wonder that the hellish pain in his tooth had subsided.

"How come a Highland hotel can afford to offer such a huge money prize?"

"We run the bingo nights all year round with small prizes and the profits are put in the bank. I drew the big money out of the bank in the middle of the week."

"I'll just use the phone there," he said, "and call Strathbane, and then I'll take a look around."

Detective Chief Inspector Blair when contacted said he was busy on a drugs job but would send his sidekick, Jimmy Anderson, over with a forensic team.

Hamish examined the hotel office. Apart from the gaping hole in the back of the safe, there was no other sign of a break-in that he could see. "You discovered this in the morning," he said. "What was going on here last night?"

"There was a ceilidh."

"How many people?"

"About a hundred or so. But the office was locked."

Hamish examined the office door. It was wooden with a frosted-glass panel. The lock was a simple Yale one, easily picked.

The barman and the waiter were brought in. Hamish questioned them closely. They hadn't finished their duties until one in the morning and then had gone straight to bed. The barman, Johnny King, was a sinister-looking man in his thirties with his hair worn in a ponytail and his thin face marred by a long scar. Peter Sampson, the waiter, was a small, smooth-faced youth of about twenty.

After he had finished interviewing them, Hamish walked around the public rooms of the hotel. It was typical of the more depressing type of Highland hotel, everything in pine and plastic and with the once gaudy carpets looking as if they badly needed shampooing. Tartan curtains hung at the windows and the walls were ornamented with plastic claymores and plastic shields along with bad murals of depressing historical events like the Battle of Culloden and the Massacre of Glencoe. The artist had not liked Bonnie Prince Charlie, for there he was with a cowardly look on his white face fleeing the Battle of Culloden. And he hadn't liked the Campbells either, witness their savage and gleeful faces as they massacred the Macdonalds of Glencoe.

"What's the polis doing here?" demanded a shrill voice behind him.

He swung round. A small blonde middle-aged woman stood

glaring at him. Her hair was wound around a forest of pink plastic rollers and a cigarette hung from thin lips, painted orange. Beside her stood a tall, sulky girl in micro skirt and black suede thigh boots, fringed suede jacket and purple blouse. Her makeup was dead-white, her lipstick purple and her black hair gelled into spikes.

"Mrs. Macbean?"

"Aye, what's it to you?"

"The safe in the office was broken into last night, Mrs. Macbean," explained Hamish patiently.

"The bingo money! It's gone?"

"All gone," said Hamish.

"Cool," said Darleen. Her eyes were flat and dead. Valium or sheer bovine stupidity, thought Hamish.

"Where is he?" demanded Mrs. Macbean.

"In the office," said Hamish, and then turned away as he heard cars driving up outside.

He went out to meet the contingent from Strathbane.

Detective Jimmy Anderson's foxy features lit up in a grin when he saw Hamish.

"If it isnae Mr. Death hisself," he said cheerfully. "Where's the body? Wi' the great Hamish Macbeth on the scene, there's bound to be a body."

"No body. The safe's been broken into like I told you. I figure someone from the hotel did it."

"Aye, maybe, Hamish. But what makes you think that?"

"I chust have this feeling."

"The seer of Lochdubh," jeered Jimmy. "Man, I could murder a dram. Any chance of them opening up that bar?"

"You shouldnae be thinking o' drinking on duty," said Hamish primly.

"Och, Hamish, it's only on the TV that they say things like that."

"And in police regulations."

"If you paid any attention to police regulations, you would smarten up that horrible uniform. Your trousers are so shiny I can see ma face in them."

"Are we going to investigate this," snapped Hamish, "or are we going to stand here all day trading insults?"

"Where's the body, then?" said Jimmy with a sigh.

"If you mean the safe, it's in the office. Afore you go in, Jimmy, is there any gossip about Macbean?"

"Not that I've heard. Somat Enterprises, a Glasgow company who owns this place, employed him two years ago. The food's rotten and the drinks are suspect, but they come for the bingo and the dancing. You know how it is, Hamish, it's not as if Sutherland is a swinging place. No competition. Oh, well, lead the way."

Macbean was standing outside the office in the entrance hall. Through the open office door, the white-coated forensic team were busy dusting everything for fingerprints.

"Damn," muttered Hamish. "Two of the men turned the safe around. Their fingerprints will be on it."

"I'll tell them," said Jimmy.

"You stupid fool," Mrs. Macbean suddenly shouted in her husband's face. One pink roller shaken loose by her rage fell onto the carpet. "I tellt ye that safe was silly. But you had tae go and dae things on the cheap."

"Shut your face," growled Macbean, "and go and do something to yourself. You look a right fright with them curlers in."

Hamish's tooth gave a sinister twinge. "Wait a bit, Mrs. Macbean," he said, "you went to the dentist in Braikie."

"Aye."

"What's Gilchrist like?"

She looked at him in amazement. "It wisnae me. It was Darleen that had the toothache."

Hamish turned questioningly to Darleen, who was slumped against the wall, studying her long purple fingernails.

"Darleen?"

She suddenly opened her mouth and pointed to the bottom front row of her teeth where there was a gap.

"He pulled your tooth?"

"Too right."

"Couldn't he have saved it?"

"Whit fur?"

"Because teeth can be saved these days."

Darleen stifled a yawn. "No shit, Sherlock."

"Whit the hell are you asking questions about some poxy dentist when you're supposed to be finding out who burgled my safe?" howled Macbean.

"I'm working on something else," said Hamish.

Jimmy Anderson came out of the office. "Okay, I'll take you one at a time. There's no need for you any mair, Hamish. You can get back to your sheep dip papers or whatever exciting things you usually do in Lochdubh."

Hamish went reluctantly. There was an odd smell of villainy

9

about the hotel. "I'll type up my notes for you," he said stiffly to Jimmy.

"I wouldnae bother," said Jimmy cheerfully. "When does that bar open?"

Hamish left. He drove back to Lochdubh but instead of going to the station, he stopped at the Tommel Castle Hotel just outside the village. The hotel was owned by Colonel Halburton-Smythe, Priscilla's father, a landowner who, on Hamish's suggestion, had turned his family home into a hotel when he was in danger of going bankrupt. The hotel had prospered, first through the efforts of Priscilla and then under the efficient management of Mr. Johnson, the manager. He went through to the hotel office where Mr. Johnson was rattling the keys of a computer. Hamish pulled up a chair to the desk and sat down opposite the manager. "Help yourself to coffee, Hamish," said the manager, jerking his head in the direction of a coffee machine in the corner.

Hamish rose and helped himself to a mugful of coffee and sat down again. "That's that," said Mr. Johnson with a sigh. "I miss Priscilla. She's a dab hand at the accounts. What brings you, Hamish, or are you just chasing a free cup of coffee?"

"There's been a burglary over at The Scotsman."

"Druggies from Inverness?"

"No, the safe was robbed. The bingo prize money. Two hundred and fifty thousand pounds."

"Did they blow it?"

"No, Macbean got the safe on the cheap at an auction in Inverness. It had a wooden back."

"I mind that safe. I was at that auction myself. That safe was made by a company nobody had ever heard of. I couldn't believe that wooden back."

"So what's the gossip about Macbean?"

"Sour man with a slag of a wife and a drip of a daughter. Came here about two years ago. Somat Enterprises seem to have given him a free hand. It's run by some Scottish Greek. Got lots of sleazy restaurants and dreary hotels. As far as I can gather, as long as The Scotsman showed a profit, he didn't interfere. Macbean may have been creaming some of the profits, but he'd need to be smarter than I think he is, because Somat has a team of ferocious auditors who regularly check the books. Macbean thought up the bingo night and it's been a big success. Do you know the colonel even had the stupidity to suggest we do the same thing? People come here for the fishing and shooting and the country house life, they don't want a lot of peasants cluttering up the place."

"What about the staff?"

"Don't know. You know what it's like trying to get staff up here, Hamish. No one's anxious to check out references too closely."

"Well it's got nothing to do with me now." Hamish sipped his coffee and winced as the hot liquid washed around his bad tooth. "Jimmy Anderson's taken over. It'll be a long slog—checking out Macbean's past, checking out the staff's past, checking out Macbean's bankbook."

"It's more Blair's line to keep you off a case, Hamish."

"Aye, well, there been talk about Blair's liver being a wee bit damaged and Jimmy Anderson aye goes through a personality change when he sniffs promotion." He winced again.

"Toothache?"

"I've got an abscess. Dr. Brodie gave me a shot of antibiotic. I was going over to see Gilchrist. Oh, I forgot to say I wouldn't be going."

"I wouldn't go near that butcher, Hamish. There was a bit of a scandal. Jock Mackay over at Braikie got a tooth pulled and Gilchrist broke his jaw. Jock had impacted roots and the tooth should have been sawn in half and then taken out a bit at a time. Turned out Gilchrist hadn't even X-rayed him first. Folks told him to sue, but you know what it's like. A lot of them are brought up to think that doctors, lawyers and dentists are little gods. They never seem to think that they're just like the butcher or the baker. You get bad meat from the butcher, you find another butcher, but they'll stick with a bad doctor or a bad dentist until the end of time."

"Can I use your phone? I might go over myself tomorrow, now that I've got the excuse. What does Gilchrist look like?"

"White."

"I didn't think he was African or Indian."

"No, I mean, very white, big white face, big white hands like un-cooked pork sausages, very pale eyes, thick white hair, white eyebrows, white coat like the ones the American dentists wear."

"Age?"

"Fifties, at a guess. Bit of a ladies' man, by all accounts. Use the phone by all means, but only ask for a checkup or that man will have the pliers out and all your teeth out."

Hamish dialled the dentist's number. Maggie Bane answered the phone. He had never met her any more than he had ever met the dentist although he knew her name and had heard of her. Her voice on the phone was sharp and peremptory and he imagined a middle-aged woman with a tight perm, flashing glasses and a thin, bony figure. "This is Mr. Macbeth," he said, appalled to hear his own voice sounding cringing and apologetic. "I won't be over today after all. I couldn't call you earlier because I was on a case."

"We've got enough to do here," snapped Maggie, "without having to cope with people cancelling appointments. I just wish that folk would tell the truth and say they're scared."

"I am not scared," howled Hamish. "Listen here. I haff the abscess in my tooth and the doctor says I will need to wait until the antibiotic works before seeing the dentist."

Maggie's voice was heavy with sarcasm. "Oh, and when is that likely to be?"

Hamish took a deep breath. He was suddenly determined to see this dentist with the unsavoury reputation and this horrible receptionist. "Tomorrow," he said firmly.

"There's a Miss Nessie Currie has cancelled at three. You can have her appointment."

"Thank you." Hamish slammed down the phone.

Nessie Currie and her sister, Jessie, were the village spinsters. It was their fussy, gossipy manner which damned them as spinsters in a country like Scotland where women who had escaped marriage were sometimes considered fortunate, a hangover from the days when marriage meant domestic slavery and a string of children.

He decided to go and call on Nessie.

Nessie and Jessie were working in their small patch of front garden where narrow beds of regimented plants stood to attention bordering a square of lawn. A rowan tree, heavy with scarlet berries, stood beside the gate as it did outside many Highland homes as a charm to keep the fairies, witches, and evil spirits away.

"There's that Hamish Macbeth," said Jessie. "Hamish Macbeth." She had an irritating habit of repeating everything.

Nessie straightened up and pulled off her gardening gloves, the sunlight glinting on her glasses. "We heard there was the burglary over at The Scotsman," she said. "Why aren't you over there?"

"Over there," echoed Jessie, pulling a weed.

"I'm working on it. Why did you cancel your dentist's appointment, Nessie?"

"It is not the criminal offence."

"Criminal offence," echoed the Greek chorus from the flower bed.

"Chust curiosity," said Hamish testily, his Highland accent becoming more pronounced as it always did when he was irritated or upset.

"I don't see it's any business of yours, but the fact is, Mr. Gilchrist has a reputation of being a philanderer and I was going to have the gas, but goodness knows, he might interfere with my person."

"Interfere with my person," said Jessie, sotto voce.

Hamish looked at Nessie's elderly and flat-chested body and reflected that this Gilchrist must indeed have one hell of a reputation.

He touched his cap and walked off. The sun was slanting over the loch and soon the early northern night would begin. He felt suddenly lonely and wished he could speak to Priscilla and immediately after that thought had a sudden sharp longing for a cigarette although he had given up smoking some years before.

"You're looking pretty down in the mouth." The doctor's wife, Angela, stopped in front of him. "Tooth still hurting?"

"No, it's fine at the moment. I was wishing Priscilla was back. We aye talked things over. Then the damnedest thing. I wanted a cigarette."

Angela smiled, her thin face lighting up. "Why is it everything you let go of, Hamish, ends up with your claw marks on it?"

"I haff let go," said Hamish crossly. "I wass chust thinking . . ."

"And I'm thinking you could do with a cup of tea and some scones. Come along, I'm on my way home."

As Hamish walked beside her, he suddenly remembered that Angela's home-baked scones were always as hard as bricks and his diseased tooth gave an anticipatory twinge.

The scones that Angela produced and put on the kitchen table looked light and buttery. "A present from Mrs. Wellington," she said.

Hamish brightened. Mrs. Wellington, the minister's wife, was a good cook.

He had two scones and butter and two cups of tea. But disaster struck when Angela produced a pot of blackberry jam and urged him to try another. Hamish buttered another scone, covered it liberally in jam, and sank his teeth into it. A red-hot pain seemed to shoot up right through the top of his head. He let out a yelp.

"I say, that tooth is hurting," said Angela. "Probably the jam. There's a lot of acid in blackberries. Here." She rummaged in a kitchen drawer and drew out a handful of new toothbrushes and handed him one. "Go to the bathroom and clean your teeth and rinse out your mouth well. Then come back and I'll give you a couple of aspirin."

Hamish grabbed the toothbrush and went into the long narrow bathroom. Two cats slept in the bath and another was curled up on top of the toilet seat. He ripped the wrappings off the toothbrush, brushed his teeth, found a mouthwash in the cabinet and rinsed out his mouth. By the time he returned to the kitchen, the pain was down to a dull ache. He gratefully swallowed two aspirin.

"I thought you would be over at The Scotsman Hotel," said Angela.

The cats had followed Hamish from the bathroom. One began to affectionately sharpen its claws on his trouser leg and he resisted an impulse to knock it across the kitchen. Angela was very fond of her cats and Hamish was fond of Angela.

"Jimmy Anderson is on the case so I'm off it. Blair's liver is playing up so Jimmy has dreams of glory."

Angela cradled her cup of tea between her thin fingers. "I'm surprised you haven't been called to that hotel before."

"Why?"

"I suppose I shouldn't be telling you this, but I heard a rumour that Macbean beats his wife."

"Neffer!"

"I think he does. She had bruised cheeks two months ago as if he'd given her a couple of backhanders."

Hamish leaned back in his chair and clasped his hands behind his head. "Now there's a thing. A battered wife and two hundred and fifty thousand pounds missing from the safe. She could get a long way away from him on that."

"Battered wives don't usually have the guts to do anything to escape. Not unless there's another man."

Hamish thought of the acidulous Mrs. Macbean with her thin, lipsticked mouth and hair in pink rollers and sighed. "No, I don't think it can be anything to do with her. Thanks for the tea and everything, Angela. I'd best get back to the station."

Jimmy Anderson was waiting for him. "Typed up your notes yet on that burglary?"

"You said you didn't want them."

"Well, I would like them now." Jimmy followed Hamish into the police station and through to the police office. "Got any whisky?"

Seeing that Jimmy was restored to something like his normal self, Hamish said, "Aye, there's a bottle in the bottom drawer. I'll get you a glass."

"What about yourself?"

"Not me," said Hamish with a shudder. "I have the tooth-ache."

"Get them all pulled out, Hamish. That's what I did. I got a rare pair of dentures. I even got the dentist to stain them a bit wi' nicotine so they look like the real thing."

He bared an evil-looking set of false teeth.

Hamish got a glass and poured Jimmy a generous measure of whisky.

"So what's happening with the burglary?"

Jimmy looked sour. "Nothing. We'll need to wait for the reports on Macbean and the staff to see if any of them has a criminal background."

"I hear Macbean beats his wife."

"This is the Highlands, man. What else do they do on the long winter nights?"

"Just thought I'd tell you, which is very generous of me, considering you sent me away wi' a flea in my ear. You had a touch of Blairitis."

"You'd best keep your ear to the ground, Hamish, or we'll have that pillock, Blair, poking his nose in."

"I'll see what I can do."

"Maybe you'd best go back there tomorrow."

And Hamish would have definitely gone straight to The Scotsman Hotel in the morning but for one thing. After he had typed out his notes for Jimmy, he found the whole side of his face was burning and throbbing with pain. He decided to go straight to Gilchrist and ask him to pull the tooth. He could make time between appointments. There was just so much pain a man could bear.

He got into the police Land Rover and set out on the narrow one-track road which led to Braikie. The weather was milder, which meant a thin drizzle was misting the windscreen and the cloud was low on the flanks of the Sutherland mountains.

Braikie was one of those small Scottish towns where Calvinism seems to seep out of the very walls of the dark grey houses. There was one main street with a hotel at one end and a grim-looking church at the other. Small shops selling limp dresses and food of the frozen fish fingers variety were dotted here and there. The police station had been closed down, Braikie having some time ago been considered near enough for Hamish Macbeth to patrol. But he hardly ever went there and had no reason to. Braikie might be a dismal place, but he could not remember a crime ever being committed there.

He asked a local where the dentist's surgery was and was told it was next to the church. It was situated above a dress shop where dowdy frocks at outrageous prices were displayed in the window, which was covered in yellow cellophane to protect the precious goods from sunlight, even though the dreary day was becoming blacker by the minute. The entrance to the dentist's surgery was a stone staircase by the side of the shop. He mounted slowly, holding his jaw although the pain had suddenly ceased in that mysterious way that toothache has of disappearing the minute you are heading for the dentist's chair.

He stopped on the landing and cocked his head to one side. It was quiet. No sound seemed to filter from inside.

A frosted-glass door with Gilchrist's name on it faced him. It was the only door on the landing.

With a little sigh, he pushed it open. The waiting room was empty, the receptionist's desk was empty. The silence was absolute. A tank of fish ornamented one corner, but the fish were dead and floating belly up. A table with very old copies of *Scottish Field* was in the centre of the room. Hard upright chairs lined the walls.

His tooth gave another sharp wrench of pain, and stifling a moan, he pushed open the surgery door.

A man was sitting in the dentist's chair, his back to Hamish. "Hullo," said Hamish tentatively. "Where's the dentist?"

Silence.

He strode around the front of the chair.

From the white hair and white coat, he realised he was looking at Mr. Gilchrist.

But his face was not white. It was horribly discoloured and distorted.

Hamish felt for a pulse at the wrist and then at the neck.

Mr. Gilchrist was dead.

DON'T MISS THESE
HAMISH MACBETH MYSTERIES!

"This series is pure bliss."
—*Atlanta Journal & Constitution*

- *DEATH OF A CHARMING MAN*
(0-446-40-338-5, $5.99 USA) ($6.99 CAN)

- *DEATH OF A MACHO MAN*
(0-446-40-340-7, $5.99 USA) ($6.99 CAN)

- *DEATH OF A DENTIST*
(0-446-60-601-4, $6.50 USA) ($8.50 CAN)

AVAILABLE AT A BOOKSTORE NEAR YOU
FROM WARNER BOOKS